What a ch...
place, deep end of the ocean,
Jeth thought.

He opened his eyes and sighed. "Okay. I probably need my head examined, but okay. Wife."

"Husband," Allyn confirmed, then wrapped her hands around his wrists and stood on tiptoe to seal the pact with a kiss.

If he hadn't recognized it previously, that was the exact instant Jeth knew he was lost. And knew he had to walk away from Allyn.

So he kissed her back with feeling, an early goodbye, with all of himself poured into it. With longing and desire, but mostly with need.

"Wow," Allyn murmured, dazed, when he lifted his head. "Wow. That was—that was—" She blinked. "Can we do that again?"

Jeth smoothed back her hair with his thumb, more than a little bemused himself. "Yeah, definitely," he muttered, cherishing her mouth, her being.

And therein lay both salvation and destructive flame.

Dear Reader,

Happy New Year! Silhouette Intimate Moments is starting the year off with a bang—not to mention six great books. Why not begin with the latest of THE PROTECTORS, Beverly Barton's miniseries about men no woman can resist? In *Murdock's Last Stand,* a well-muscled mercenary meets his match in a woman who suddenly has him thinking of forever.

Alicia Scott returns with *Marrying Mike... Again,* an intense reunion story featuring a couple who are both police officers with old hurts to heal before their happy ending. Try Terese Ramin's *A Drive-By Wedding* when you're in the mood for suspense, an undercover agent hero, an irresistible child and a carjacked heroine who ends up glad to go along for the ride. Already known for her compelling storytelling abilities, Eileen Wilks lives up to her reputation with *Midnight Promises,* a marriage-of-convenience story unlike any other you've ever read. Virginia Kantra brings you the next of the irresistible MacNeills in *The Comeback of Con MacNeill,* and Kate Stevenson returns after a long time away, with *Witness... and Wife?*

All six books live up to Intimate Moments' reputation for excitement and passion mixed together in just the right proportions, so I hope you enjoy them all.

Yours,

Leslie J. Wainger
Executive Senior Editor

Please address questions and book requests to:
Silhouette Reader Service
U.S.: 3010 Walden Ave., P.O. Box 1325, Buffalo, NY 14269
Canadian: P.O. Box 609, Fort Erie, Ont. L2A 5X3

A DRIVE-BY WEDDING
TERESE RAMIN

Silhouette®

INTIMATE™ MOMENTS®

Published by Silhouette Books

America's Publisher of Contemporary Romance

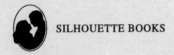 SILHOUETTE BOOKS

ISBN 0-373-07981-8

A DRIVE-BY WEDDING

Copyright © 2000 by Terese daly Ramin

Visit us at www.romance.net

Printed in U.S.A.

Books by Terese Ramin

Silhouette Intimate Moments

Water from the Moon #279
Winter Beach #477
A Certain Slant of Light #634
Five Kids, One Christmas #680
An Unexpected Addition #793
Mary's Child #881
A Drive-By Wedding #981

Silhouette Special Edition

Accompanying Alice #656

TERESE RAMIN

lives in Michigan with her husband, two children, two dogs, two cats and an assortment of strays. When not writing romance novels, she writes chancel dramas, sings alto in the church choir, plays the guitar, yells at her children to pick up their rooms (even though she keeps telling herself that she won't) and responds with silence when they ask her where they should put their rooms after they've picked them up.

A full-fledged believer in dreams, the only thing she's ever wanted to do is write. After years of dreaming without doing anything about it, she finally wrote her first romance novel, *Water from the Moon*, which won a Romance Writers of America Golden Heart Award in 1987 and was published by Silhouette in 1989. Her subsequent books have appeared on the Waldenbooks romance bestseller list. She is also the recipient of a 1991 *Romantic Times Magazine* Reviewer's Choice Award. She hasn't dreamed without acting for a long time.

For all those who are just learning to claim
their power as a woman
and for
All those who are old enough to have claimed theirs.
May you all seek what you find.

To my own best beloved, Bill,
guardian angel to children and little old ladies
everywhere.

And to Ann Leslie Tuttle,
whose patience should be named Legion.

Chapter 1

The sight of the jogger's tush stopped Allyn Meyer's meandering thoughts on a dime, swiveled her attention a hundred eighty degrees.

Whoa, baby! her libido breathed. Never in her life had she seen anything to match it—or at least anything like it that had caught her attention. Perhaps it was the brief black shorts that gave her such a perfect view of where she suddenly and uncharacteristically wanted to place her hands. Or perhaps it was the length of muscular thigh and calf visible beneath, or the narrow waist and the expanse of broad, heavily bronzed, sweaty, shirtless back above, the straight shock of hair above that as black as his shorts, that took her breath and turned her cave woman enough to state without question, *He's mine.*

Or perhaps it was simply that omniproblematical twin thing, that *telepathic*—for want of a better term—connection she and twin sister Becky had always had; that thing that had made Allyn feel it when Becky burned her hand on the frying pan or gave her morning sickness before Becky even knew she was pregnant.

That thing that had caused Becky to experience the sensation of drowning the time Allyn actually had been during a freak mishap with a faulty tank during one of Allyn's research dives. Or that caused them to call each other to share in the good news before the one who was getting the news even knew there was some.

That *thing* that had forced Allyn to build psychological walls that were high, steep and thick enough to prevent her from, er, *feeling* some of the things Becky shared with her husband, to allow her sister privacy.

Or made them choose to take two completely separate paths, then suddenly wind up with the same seven-year itch and the desire for sudden and drastic change.

Anyway, perhaps it was only *that* coupled with Becky's ever unruly hormones, blending with Allyn's, mixing Allyn up and turning her into a lust-starved woman she didn't recognize. Even though her love life had ever only included her husband, it was Becky who'd allowed herself fantasies enough for the two of them—then told her best friend-confidante-sister Allyn about them so that Allyn would be indirectly forced to use her imagination on something besides a life spent researching dolphins, whales or some as yet undiscovered reef fungus or freshwater mollusk.

Whichever, for the first time in her life, Allyn knew without doubt she'd finally spotted a man who majorly kick started impulses she'd never before entertained, and here she was driving on by and never going to meet him ever even once in her life. And all she'd seen of him so far was the rear view.

Lord, she'd led a spinster's life, hadn't she, getting hot and bothered over a guy in running shorts with a tight rear? Maybe Becky was right. Maybe it *was* time Allyn left academics behind for a while and explored the lustier side of the world. At least let herself find out what it was like to flirt a little.

Just a little.

A *very* little.

Smiling derisively at her penchant for equivocation, Allyn pulled ahead of the jogger, slowing for the light that turned yellow then red in front of her. Unable to help herself, she sneaked a peek in her sideview mirror to see what he looked like from this angle. No disappointment there, either. Every inch she could see of him—and the black shorts didn't conceal much—was bronze and sculpted, gleaming with sweat.

Funny how good the sweat looked on him when she'd never particularly cared for the sight of it on herself or anyone else before in her life.

She pursed her lips and narrowed her eyes and wondered exactly what was going on inside her this morning. Lord love us, she hadn't even looked at his face yet, that's how bad this libido thing was. And Allyn believed firmly that what was in a person's face the first time you looked into it said everything about him. A naive viewpoint, perhaps, if her stepfather, Gabriel, a former deep cover FBI agent, hadn't spent as much of the last seven years as possible teaching her what to look for in a person's demeanor that could spell good or ill to a woman on her own. Summed up, Gabriel Book's theory of life for stepdaughters went something like, *Trust everyone, but a little bombproof glass never hurts.*

Allyn grinned wryly and refocused her attention on the man jogging alongside her car. His body still intrigued hers mightily, but now that she got a real look at his face, she could see there was something dark, distinctly dangerous and unmistakably formidable about him. Also intense, a trifle skittish and more than a little wary. Almost as though he wasn't running for pleasure or health, but running from someone or something instead.

The heavy-looking bag and the sweatshirt he shifted from one hand to the other while she watched seemed to confirm rather than deny the impression.

Allyn sighed, disappointed and relieved at once. Definitely not her type, then, regardless of what her body said. She'd get over never meeting him. Her mind was a lot brighter and more self-preserving than her body would ever be. Still...

Firmly Allyn grabbed hold of her wayward hormones and shifted her attention to stuffing a Prairie Home Companion tape into the tape player. Let Garrison Keillor take her mind off of—

The passenger door opened suddenly, the seat was slung forward, and the jogger's duffel bag crossed her vision on its way into the back seat. The car filled with the overpowering scent of salt, musk and man.

"Wha—"

Startled, she looked into the jogger's beautiful but expressionless, and therefore infinitely frightening, face. Lord love us. An uncommon car jacker. She'd broken the cardinal rule of traveling alone by car in the city: bombproof glass doesn't do squat if you leave your doors unlocked.

She pulled her hands off the steering wheel, held them up and open, pacifying. "Here," she said, "take it. I'll get out. I'll leave the keys."

She reached for her door handle, but he shut his door, grabbed her arm and hauled her back with a terse comment, "Uh-uh. Stay here. Drive."

"But—" *Idiot, idiot, idiot,* the terrified half of her mind screamed at her. *What are you, arguing with a madman?* While the calm and collected, FBI-stepdad-trained half of her said, *Stay alert. Do what he says until you can find a way out. You can find a way out.* "But if you have the car, you don't need me. You'll only make things worse for yourself if you take me, too. You can have my purse, my cash—half my bank account's in there—just let me get out—''

The gun hidden by his sweatshirt made a swift, hard impression beneath her ribs. She looked at him. His eyes were flat, his voice low and intense, terrifying. "Drive," he said. "Now."

Allyn swallowed. *Becky,* she thought, *I'm in trouble. Can you hear me?*

Sweet mother of God, she hoped Becky's twin radar was in tune now, the way the two of them had always been tuned to each other's frights in the past—and that her sister would somehow be able to focus in on where Allyn was, then figure a way to convince their overprotective stepfather to respond that didn't involve calling out the National Guard.

Eyes never leaving the car jacker's face, Allyn swallowed again and nodded. "Where?"

Mental note, she advised herself furiously, *detours to visit friends in Baltimore don't pay.*

Jeth "never-call-me-Jethro" Levoie took his first look at the person he'd decided would be his and his burden's salvation and knew without doubt he'd made the biggest mistake of his life.

The woman who'd left the doors of her dusty Saturn unlocked as if in open invitation to him viewed him through eyes filled with a shock and fright that was quickly replaced with an intelligence that bore just the right amount of fear to make her both careful and dangerous. She would do what he told her only as long as it suited her before she figured out how to dump him unconscious on his head in the nearest ditch and go for help. And then she'd do him as much damage as possible.

"Turn right," he said, refusing to swallow, to reveal his own suddenly increased, cotton-mouthed fears. Heck, he was the one with the gun here, after all. What did he have to be dry-mouthed about? "Don't wait for the light. Then floor it. Take the first left. Drive until I tell you to turn. Do it."

Damn, what had he done?

The only thing on Jeth's mind this morning when he'd eased his way out of the row house had been to get the toddler now sleeping in his duffel bag out of the crack house where the boy had been kept for the two weeks since his mother had sold him to her dealers in exchange for a cleared debt and two days' worth of fixin's. And now Jeth had this.

The possibility of stealing a two-year-old and car jacking a civilian hadn't even entered his mind when he'd accepted the assignment to go undercover. The Baltimore prosecutor's office had wanted him to look into allegations of corruption among the Drug Enforcement Agents working a major operation in Baltimore's interior.

For one thing, Jeth didn't do kids, and he'd considered civilian women of *any* age off-limits big-time since the day his youngest sister was killed three years ago by some goons looking for him. He'd tried, in fact, with everything he had to put that particular incident behind him and go forward with the knowledge of innocent blood staining his hands.

He'd used Marcy's death to keep himself sharp and focused, to make sure innocence never tainted his hands again. But today he'd figured that, just for a minute, in these extreme circumstances and for the protection of the toddler for whom he'd assumed responsibility, a civilian woman, an unwary traveler alone, would be his best option for getting away clean—or as clean as would be possible under impossible circumstances.

For better or worse, he'd figured that maybe there would be some way to convince a woman to keep quiet, appeal to her maternal instincts where the child was concerned, but this woman... Hell, by choosing this woman he'd screwed up big-time, he could feel it in his gut.

His gut had rarely ever been wrong.

Damn, he was stuck now. No real good way to get this woman to drop him off so he could car jack a more likely prospect—or even simply steal a car. Besides, he was in too much hurry to waste time trying to find a car to steal. Not to mention that carting a kid about in a duffel bag— even a kid as tiny and undernourished as this one—didn't exactly make the auto-theft option easier or safer to consider anyway. Nope, he was just flingin'-flangin'-flaming stuck.

The Saturn moved through traffic at a rapid pace, but not at a speed or in any other way that would draw law enforcement attention. Jeth blew out a mental breath; there it was, his worst suspicions confirmed. If this woman was a novice in the art of being car jacked, she was a damned smart one.

He eyed her profile, took in the tightness of her jaw, the determined set of the half of her mouth he could see—the length of curly chestnut hair French-braided from the top of her head to the nape of her long neck to keep it out of her way, then left hanging in carefree abandon from there— and something long ignored inside him tightened. If he'd seen her in a bar, a supermarket, the park, anywhere but here, he'd go out of his way to hit on her, and that was a fact.

No, actually, since hitting on her only implied doing some mild flirting that a guy hoped might lead to a night's romp in bed, Jeth was pretty certain he'd go out of his way *not* to hit on her. He'd go out of his way to start a conversation, get to know her and head hip deep and sinking into the quicksand of starting a relationship with her. And if he wound up in over his head, he had the awful sense that he wouldn't even care.

Judas, he was out of his mind. He didn't even know her

name. He was making use of her like some macho, chauvinistic PI in some old dime novel. And he wanted to slide his hand up along her ribs and let it replace where his gun was.

He blinked. Oh, for the love of… He'd snapped. Totally, completely. So far this morning he'd stolen a kid, blown his cover, car jacked a woman he'd never met but now was contemplating how to go about having a relationship with. What came next? Doing his damnedest to coerce her into a convenient marriage so she couldn't testify against him when he was inevitably caught and tried for whatever the DEA could come up with and make stick even marginally because he'd fudged up their case?

Providing, that is, that she was single.

He caught himself checking the ring finger on her left hand and cursed himself silently, roundly. Oh, man, he was tired. Had to be it. He'd never be so stupid otherwise. Too much on guard recently…too little sleep waiting for his chance to rescue the kid from hell…the constant talk of women and sex that went on around him combined with a nonexistent love life… Yeah, it all added up. He was a fool. A worn-out, double-lived, paranoid fool.

But at least he could label himself.

He felt the Saturn slow slightly, hesitating.

"Turn here?" the woman asked, glancing at him.

Jeth forced himself not to note the all-too-evocative huskiness of her voice or the unnerving depths of the one green, one blue eye looking at him, and nodded. "Drive. I'll tell you where to turn next."

God bless the universe, Jeth swore. Where in Satan's hell had he mislaid his mind?

Trying to keep her mind clear and focused, Allyn drove automatically, noting pedestrians and traffic signals, paying only enough attention to where she was to make sure she wasn't passing any of Baltimore's police precinct houses.

Finding a spot with a lot of cops around seemed like a promising way to dump this situation.

Or maybe not. A lot of cops around meant the possibility of a lot more casualties than just her. She'd never particularly thought of herself as either noble or heroic, but the idea of bringing a man desperate enough to car jack her at gunpoint into an arena of even more weaponry suddenly didn't appeal as strongly as she'd supposed it might. She didn't want anyone shot or killed. And she knew, because it was one of the things Gabriel had taught her, that minimizing a situation like this was not only possible, but plausible.

She let her eyes flick carefully toward the rearview mirror where she could glimpse only a small portion of her kidnapper. Her lungs were tight, the muscles in her throat contracted to keep from breathing him in. He still had the gun in her ribs, but a significant portion of her mind was traitorously occupied with the taste the scent of him left on the back of her tongue. Never in her life had she inhaled anything that matched him.

Probably fear, the incorrigible half of her brain said, and snorted. *His and yours.*

The thought, unexpected as it was, caused Allyn's mouth to quirk sideways, made her relax. So she liked the taste of fear—or was it adrenaline—did she? Well, that was something she wouldn't have thought of herself.

Always before she'd considered her life a matter of choosing the safer path: ordered, straight, narrow-paved and without potholes. Now all of a sudden she'd hit a totally unforeseen and rather dangerous chuckhole, and she found it terrifying but interesting.

And downright exciting.

Mentally rolling her eyes at herself, Allyn risked another glance at her abductor. His face was turned mostly away from her while he did something to adjust the bundle in the back seat. There was strain in the set of his shoulders,

obvious strength in the cord of muscles along his arm and
neck when he struggled one-handed with the duffel bag.
She heard the light *whishk* draw of a well-soaped zipper,
felt rather than saw the man beside her strain harder for a
moment before relaxing slightly. His left arm remained
stretched over the seat, apparently to keep his bag propped
upright.

Curious, Allyn stretched her neck slightly to see what
divided his attention. A bag full of ill-gotten cash? Drugs?
Some rare and priceless artifact? Or maybe it was—

A baby.

Her heart caught, slammed upward into her throat and
started to pound. Her foot reflexively pressed the gas pedal,
hands stuttered on the steering wheel, and the car veered
sideways toward a power pole. A *baby*. Oh, holy mother.
Oh, sweet merry Christmas. However unwillingly, she was
aiding and abetting someone whose picture would wind up
on a milk carton alongside somebody else's baby's. She
couldn't let him do this, couldn't let him threaten a child.
She had to do something, she had to—

"Watch it!"

In one swift move the man beside her jerked, dumped
his weapon and grabbed the steering wheel, forced the car
away from the pole, out of the line of oncoming traffic and
into a side street lined with houses, cars and scraggly trees.
Tires squealed as the Saturn swerved back and forth, jock-
eying a none-too-straight path down the street. A lone, early
morning cyclist swiveled hard between two parked cars and
over the curb to avoid them.

Allyn's captor swore and reached for her clam-digger-
clad knee. "Get your damned foot off the freaking gas,"
he ordered, yanking the steering wheel so they skidded into
the empty school parking lot at the end of the street.

"Quit telling me what to do, you baby-stealing bastard,"
Allyn retorted. With a furious twist she wrenched control

of the Saturn back. Nobody who kidnapped kids for a living was getting away with it on *her* watch.

She spun the steering wheel hard, sending the car into a controlled sideways skid over the parking lot gravel, gave the wheel a second tug and stamped on the brakes. Unbalanced by trying to keep the duffel-bagged toddler safely on the rear seat, the man rocked back and forth across the seat, then banged forward into the dashboard before winding up on the floor. Momentarily stunned, he waited a fraction too long to regain control of the situation. Before he could react, Allyn did something she'd done only once before in her life—and that was at her stepfather's insistence when he'd taken her to the shooting range to teach her how to handle them. She picked up her captor's weapon. Then she got out of the car and did something she'd never before done: pointed the gun at a human being and threatened him with it.

"Get out of my car," she told him flatly.

Chapter 2

Jeth viewed her, stunned, trying to decide whether or not she'd actually use the weapon. Hard to tell. He couldn't read her eyes from here, but she certainly held his Browning properly.

Like she knew exactly how much kick to expect from it.

Damn.

Her weight was well balanced, two-handed grip classic and firm. *Nuts,* the functioning half of his brain thought. One of the new breed of women who believed in handling their own affairs—and being responsible for their own safety in all ways. Her mother was probably a member of the women's lib generation. Damned do-it-yourself bra burners had a lot to answer for. Blasted woman probably believed in the turkey-baster school of procreation, too.

Good grief. Jeth shook his head lightly, checking for dizziness and nausea. Where had *that* come from? Must have hit his head harder than it felt like to even bring that thought up at a time like this. Especially when he had greater things to worry about.

Like if anybody from this neighborhood saw her with the gun, witnessed this standoff, they were well and truly cooked.

If the local cops got involved in this so, undoubtedly, would his own chain of command which, at the moment, included the FBI as well as the DEA and a few other agencies he wasn't particularly comfortable with. Because whichever one got hold of him first would not only put his head in a basket, but they'd take the kid from him and put the baby—Sasha, Jeth thought that's what he'd heard the boy called—back smack where Jeth had found him. And that, above all, was not going to happen. Because even if the locals were willing to take Sasha into protective custody, Jeth had seen politics win out too often to be willing to risk Sasha's life anywhere but with him.

A tad arrogant, perhaps, to think that he could protect Sasha better than an entire unit of cops, but it was his experience that the fewer people in on a plan, the fewer places for leaks to pop up. And since he was currently the acting Dutch boy with his finger jammed into the dike, that made him Sasha's best chance for survival.

The way it should have made him Marcy's. He forced the thought aside. Now if only he hadn't gone and screwed things up by choosing the wrong car to hop into.

Focus, babe, he commanded himself. *Don't let it get away from you.* Probably ought to be glad the damned woman hadn't chambered a round before she'd drawn down on him. *Take it slow and easy. Don't spook her. Gotta check the kid.*

He held up his hands, offering appeasement. "Be careful with that thing, okay? I just want to get up and see if the kid's all right."

"He's still in the bag on the back seat," she said, as though he were an idiot to think otherwise. "Get out of the car and spread it across the hood. I'll make sure you haven't done him any permanent damage."

Spread it across the hood? Jeth's eyebrows crooked, and a startled grin trickled through him. He controlled the almost amusement before it reached his face. God almighty Moses, what had he gotten himself into? Sheesh, she probably carried a badge and handcuffs, too. And wouldn't that just be super.

"Who *are* you?" he asked.

"The person with the gun gets to say what happens next," she said coolly. "That's me."

He stared at her, disbelieving.

She shrugged, less a movement than an attitude. "You made the rules. I'm following them." Then, when he still didn't move, she motioned with her chin, not taking her eyes off Jeth. "Go on, back out that side." She slid her thumb up to make sure the safety was off the nine millimeter. "Move," she ordered softly, calmly, in a tone he'd have been foolish to ignore. "I've got a kid to look at."

Oh, yeah, she was dead serious—or he was about to be. His gut was right on about this one—too late to do him any good, true, but right on nonetheless. She was afraid, but not so much that the fear had stopped her from thinking—or acting. Which meant he was deep in it now. Better come up with a way to make this work—for her sake as well as his, and to his and Sasha's advantage, and fast, because if she found a way to take off with the kid but without *him* and the guys he was running from found out and caught up with her... Well, he didn't want to think what that could mean.

His brain was full of the vivid images of what that could mean. Not nice people, these guys he'd rescued Sasha from. Cannibals and headhunters had better manners. So even did the men who'd killed Marcy.

"Look," he said, sliding onto the seat and reaching behind him for the door handle. "I know what this looks like, but it isn't what it seems. Well, it is, but there's a reason for it. A good one."

She looked at him over the top of the car as he rose out of it at the same time she reached inside and flipped the driver's seat forward. "You've got a good reason for car jacking, kidnapping and baby snatching? Don't tell me, let me guess. Ex-wife, ex-girlfriend, current girlfriend doesn't want your child but has full custody and hates you enough not to let you see him. Or she wants your child, has full custody and won't let you see him. Or she has full custody but is abusive and you snatched the baby for his own good. Or you're gay and you didn't find out until after your marriage ended and your ex won't give you access—"

Startled once again, Jeth snorted. "I'm not gay."

He thought he heard her mutter *good* before she said, "Fine, you're straight. Pick one of the other scenarios, then."

"Scenarios?" he asked, incredulous. Who talked like that? "How much TV do you watch?" Only FBI agents and people who watched too many FBI shows on TV, maybe a few corporate executives with delusions of danger talked like that. And he had the distinct feeling she wasn't among either of the latter. Judas, she couldn't be with the bureau, could she?

He could almost feel the grave opening at his feet ready to welcome him.

"How 'bout I pick *E* as in none of the above?" he asked.

"How 'bout you spread your legs, stretch out across the hood of my car facedown and lace your hands behind your head?" she returned.

Oh, yeah, Jeth thought, reluctantly doing as he was told. Deep in it and getting deeper all the time. Much as he hated to do it, he was going to have to tell her the truth.

He only hoped she'd believe him.

The car hood was hot against his chest, stuck to his skin in itchy patches full of sweat. Even minute movement was painful, but move he had to if he wanted to see what she was doing. Carefully he raised his head. She sat in the back seat, Sasha spread limply across her lap, and stared at Jeth through the windshield, coldly furious. Fear circulated through him. Something more was wrong here than the circumstances.

Ripping himself upright, he swung around the Saturn's open driver-side door without thinking about the weapon she'd taken from him. It lay in quick pieces, bullets scattered in the well of the passenger floor, clip tossed empty on the back seat beside her, gun wide-open and clearly harmless, wedged neatly under her foot where he obviously wasn't going to get at it easily even if he wanted to.

He didn't.

"What's wrong?"

He stooped in front of her, automatically reaching to touch Sasha's throat, feel for the pulse. She slapped his hand away and gathered the toddler protectively against her.

"What the hell have you done to him?" she asked.

"Nothing," Jeth assured her—or tried to. Tried to assure himself, too. "He was like this when I took him. It's why I took him."

"He smells bad and he's too small," she said, paying no attention. "What is he, two? He doesn't weigh anything. They sleep hard at this age, but not like this. He's malnourished, he's probably sick and he needs help." She aimed a swift but awkward kick at Jeth that he blocked with a forearm. Damn, she was going to be a handful, and he was stuck with her now. Her eyes were bright; anger and something more painful, more accusing—and, unaccountably, disappointed. It was an odd thing to feel, but he didn't want to disappoint her. "Why aren't you helping him?"

"I am helping him—I did help him. I got him out of hell. I found you. You're going to help me help him." The hair on the back of his neck stood on end: a caution he knew to heed. They weren't far enough away from the house he'd removed Sasha from to stop for any length of time. He felt naked and vulnerable, weaponless thanks to his stupidity and her, and now he had more than a tiny child to protect; he had *her.* A school parking lot in a populated neighborhood was not the place for long explanations—especially not this explanation.

"Look," he said, and she did. Looked him straight in the eye and waited for him to lie convincingly to her. He swallowed. Who needed falsehood when the truth would suffice? "Look," he repeated, "I wish I could let you go, but I can't. I wish I didn't need your help but I do. I wish you'd turned out to be somebody else, some other kind of person—" what was he saying? He didn't know what kind of person she was "—but you know what they say about wishes."

"If wishes were kisses all frogs would be princes," she said. "Or were you thinking of the one where all beggars would ride?"

Animosity was palpable. So was the sudden and out-of-the-blue desire to find out if he could become a prince if she kissed him. He wanted to taste her, that was sure.

The hair on his arms fuzzed to attention. God, he was an idiot. If he kept on letting her make his mind wander, they were dead.

He tightened his jaw. Whatever it took, no kids or strangely fascinating women died on his watch ever again. Especially not because of him. He drew a breath and focused his whole attention on his...captive.

"We have to get out of here," he said. He reached out to stroke Sasha's head. "I promise you I don't mean you or him any harm. I want to get this little guy whatever help he needs, but it has to be far away from here. If we stay here discussing what's right or wrong about what I've done so far this morning, we put him and ourselves at more risk than I can tell you. That's the truth."

She had no reason to believe him, but she studied him seriously nevertheless; held herself perfectly still and assessed him with those strangely colored eyes. It was almost a cop's stare, flat and unyielding, guaranteed to make the guilty look away first. Well, he might be guilty as hell, but he'd be damned if he looked away.

Time passed, a minute, two, before she dropped her chin in the merest fraction of a nod. Then she inclined her head toward the keys still sitting in the ignition.

"You drive," she said.

He took great pains to belt her and the little boy securely into the rear seat before he grabbed the padded duffel bag, pulled a black T-shirt out of it and mopped himself off with it before sliding it on. Then he climbed into the car, repositioned the driver's seat to fit his height and did as Allyn suggested. Gravel spit out from underneath the tires when they pulled out of the parking lot, punctuating the urgency with which he drove.

The sensation of power shifting and balancing uncomfortably between them was almost overwhelming.

Allyn did her best not to look at him, not to watch his face in the mirror. The accidental touches when he'd wrapped the shoulder belt around her had been wholly impersonal but nonetheless a challenge to ignore. She liked the smell of him, the taste of him, the muskiness that lay heavy in her lungs. The very thought scared her to death.

He scared her to death.

Of course, being afraid of him only made sense, but there was no way on earth she planned to let him know it.

Reluctantly, Allyn turned her attention to the child in her arms. She'd held a lot of little ones in her lifetime; she was a fair bit older than most of her cousins, and then there were Becky's kids. All in all, in a family as closely knit as her mother's, it added up to experience. Experience told her that this youngster was not at all in the shape he should be.

He was dressed in a toddler's dirty undershirt and a pair of cotton training pants, underneath which he wore a soggy disposable diaper. His hair was blond, skin white to the point of translucence, threaded with the blue and lavender of veins; the light pulse at his throat was visible. Aside from the occasional twitch of eyelids, the pulse was the only movement she could detect in him. And while outside it was hot, he felt cold and clammy to touch; instinctively she wanted to bundle him tight, to warm him. She twisted as best she could to reach behind her for the blanket she kept on the car's rear window shelf.

"What are you doing?" her captor queried sharply.

"He's cold." She met his gaze in the rearview mirror, noted the color of his eyes for the first time: midnight blue. Concerned, but about as genial as a hawk's. "I'm wrapping him up."

"Good." Then, almost apologetically, "There weren't any blankets where he was. There wasn't much of anything. I'm not even sure he's worn clean clothes in the past couple of weeks. Or had a bath. Or eaten much, or done anything kids do. I couldn't do anything for him where he was. I had to take him."

Again he met her glance in the mirror. Truth and something more were there where she didn't want to see either of them. She dropped her gaze first, stroked the child's hair.

"Do you really mean to help him?" she asked finally, quietly.

"Yes." Succinct, ferocious. A man who'd found himself in an untenable situation he'd no control over and who'd decided to change the circumstances to appease his conscience—even if it meant forcing his ends to justify his means.

And that included abducting Allyn and stealing her car. She glanced at *him* again, considered the simplicity of

his *yes,* the shape the child was in. And for the second time
in her life made an abrupt and rash decision—and never
mind that she'd currently been in the process of regretting
the first quick decision she'd ever made. She decided to
throw caution to the winds for the sake of a child. Doing
so didn't mean rashly trusting the guy driving her car, after
all. It simply involved making sure that the baby got
cleaned up, got help, got home—or got someplace that
would make him a good home. In which case, if they were
going to spend any time together—if she was going to help
him help the toddler—she'd need a name for both of them.

"Okay." For the second time she offered the man in the
front seat a clipped nod. "I won't do this for you, but I'll
help him. Understood?"

Allyn thought she saw him swallow a grin of relief. "Got
it."

"Don't get cocky," she advised him. "Nobody's home
free."

Astounded, he glanced over his shoulder at her. "Don't
get cocky?" he asked. "Who *are* you? Who the hell do
you think planned this expedition? Cocky, my left little toe.
I get cocky, all three of us get killed."

This could involve all three of them getting killed? Allyn
refused to gulp. "As long as we understand each other,"
she said—with a great deal more serenity than she felt. But
heck, he didn't need to know that. "And by the way?"

"What?"

"I don't think you planned this *expedition* at all well. In
fact, I think your planning stinks. The shape this baby is in
stinks. Literally. We need to get him cleaned up and find
out what's wrong with him."

"I saw an opportunity, I grabbed it," he told her—a trifle
huffily, truth be known. "I intend to get Sasha cleaned up
and to a doctor as soon as we're out of the city and I can
find someone who'll accept cash for silence." He paused.
Then, "I suppose you'd have planned things better?"

"Well, I wouldn't offer cash for silence, that's for sure," she said tartly. "Says you've got something to hide. No." She shook her head. "I'd go to someone I trusted and—"

"No." Refusal was flat and unnegotiable. "Last time I did that my baby sister was killed."

Killed? Startled, she looked at the mirror, trying to see his face. His gaze remained resolutely on the road in front of them, telling her everything and nothing. "Oh, so you thought kidnapping a perfect stranger would be safer for both your emotional psyche and the stranger?" Her hold on the baby—Sasha, was that what he'd said?—tightened involuntarily, and for the first time a thin cry erupted from the child. She looked at him; his eyes remained closed, but there was some movement in the thin frame, the flop of an arm, the fisting of a hand. She loosened her grip slightly and cuddled him closer, bundled the blanket more securely around him. "I don't *think* so."

"Neither do I." Denial was savage. "That's why I have the gun and I'm not letting either you or Sasha out of my sight. I need to figure out who to trust who won't either get killed or turn on me, and how to let you go safely."

Silence was abrupt and complete. At the fringes of their concentration on each other and the moment, cracks in the pavement thudded beneath the car's tires; intermittent traffic whooshed and receded. Allyn broke the silence first.

"I'm sorry about your sister," she said.

"Me, too," he agreed tightly. "So," he asked when the moment had passed. "Any other *better* ideas than the ones I've got?"

Sarcasm fairly dripped from the question. But there were things he didn't know about her, either. Like the story behind the beginning of her mother's relationship with her stepfather. She thought of how her mother and Gabriel had pretended to be lovers, pretended to know each other well in order to hide him in plain sight.

About how pretense had become reality.

She shook the thought away. Or rather, she almost shook it away. Something in it didn't want to leave. "We should probably exchange names," she suggested. "Make it look like we know each other. Then maybe you should tell me who's out to kill you—and why, don't leave that out—and therefore by default me and...did you call him Sasha?"

The grin came this time before he could stop it, wry—and a mite sardonic. "Yeah, I did. That's what his mother called him when she sold him to her dealer. I was there. Jeth Levoie. Special Investigator for the Tucson prosecutor's office."

"Tucson, Arizona?"

"Yeah. You want some ID?"

She ignored the irony in favor of keeping her wits from deserting her. Daughters' lives were not supposed to parallel their mothers', they really weren't. But here was hers apparently paralleling the single deciding event that had happened seven years ago in Alice's right down to the finding a man at the side of the road and the you-just-happened-to-be-there-and-I'm-from-out-of-town-and-need-your-help coincidence of it. "Please."

Muttering something about her being a piece of work, Jeth rummaged around in his bag until he found the flat leather case that contained both his picture identification and his badge and tossed it to her. Allyn inspected it carefully, trying not to let her face betray her while her heart thudded hard against her ribs and her breath went short. Unless it was an elaborate fake—and really, since she'd had her nose stuck in her books and lab work for the best parts of the past seven years, how would she know?—he really was Jeth Levoie out of the Tucson prosecutor's office.

She flipped the case into the front seat. "Allyn Meyers," she said. "You're a long way out of your jurisdiction, Jeth Levoie."

"Hopefully not for long," he said grimly. "And anyway—'' he slanted a glance over his shoulder at her, giving her another glimpse of a profile she'd have really enjoyed looking at and meeting, getting to know and perhaps flaunting at Becky under other circumstances ''—what do you know about jurisdictions?''

She made a face. The subject was at least as distasteful to her as being kidnapped by him. Or rather, actually, as often as she'd heard Gabriel fume over the subject of ''cooperative efforts between the jurisdictions,'' it was more disagreeable than being abducted by Jeth Levoie. ''More than enough to fill a thimble, but not much more. Enough to know that Tucson and Baltimore are a long way apart, and I don't just mean geographically. So what are you doing here?''

''Exchange program. Nobody knows me here. Same with the guy they sent to Nogales to work undercover in my place down there. You know anything about the Russian Mafia?''

''No.'' Thank God. Or maybe not, since it appeared she was about to learn more than she ever wanted to about it.

''What about drug cartels?''

Allyn felt herself blanch. ''This is about drug cartels?''

Jeth nodded unhappily. ''Yeah, indirectly. Mostly it's about territory. The Colombians have it, the Russians want it. There's a war on. Sasha's mama stuck him in the middle of it. Her ex is with the Russians. Courts gave her full custody in the divorce, but Daddy wants his heir. Her addiction of choice is Colombian cocaine. Her dealer found out who Sasha's daddy was, sold the information to his source, who instructed him to offer Mama a deal. Sasha in exchange for clearing up the debt from her habit and a few days' worth of highs. She took it. Sasha's a hostage. His daddy's supposed to trade for him, but everything goes kerflooey, and my guys tell me to get Sasha out. Only then I'm told they'll be the ones exchanging Sasha to the highest bidder for information. I tell 'em no way I can live with that, I've seen the shape the kid's in, so they pull me.''

"But you didn't stay pulled," Allyn said.

"No."

Something warm and unexpected fuzzed through Allyn. Maybe the body matched other things she'd wanted to see in him, after all. "Good for you."

He snorted. "If you say so."

"Hey," she told him flatly, "I was brought up by practically the Good Samaritan of all Good Samaritans and her sisters and mother and other relatives. I don't think a whole lot of the way you involved me in this, but I can appreciate the sentiment big time. Accept a compliment when you get one. I bet it doesn't happen often. Now when are we going to stop and take care of Sasha?''

A chuckle, dry and unwilling, spilled from Jeth. "You don't quit, do you?''

"Stubbornness is, like, one of my worst features," Allyn agreed tongue-in-cheek, reverting to the Valley speak practiced in one of her favorite movies. If Sasha was all right, she might actually discover she was enjoying herself—except for Jeth Levoie's assertion of danger waiting in the wings, of course. "Now when are we stopping? I think he's starting to wake up. When he does he's probably not going to be happy to be wet and cold. If he's sick... I don't know if you've ever traveled with a cranky two-year-old before, but I have. It's not pleasant.''

"Was it your two-year-old?" Jeth wasn't sure why it made a difference—except from the standpoint that he didn't want to deprive another child of its mother. But it was also more than that. It was that ringless left hand niggling uncomfortably at the back of his mind.

Whether this was the time and place or not.

"Not mine, no. Single, never married, no kids." Then wickedly, because in her estimation he deserved the dig,

"Just lots of relatives who're expecting me to show up in Kentucky sometime tomorrow or the next day. You?"

He heard the denial with a sort of peculiar relief that fastened in his mind on many fronts: no child awaited her return, and neither did a husband. That made her fair game. Reaction to the part about relatives awaiting her arrival was delayed, made his gut wrench when he heard it. No way could he let her go tomorrow or the next day. The only place he felt certain Sasha would be safe was deep in the Grand Canyon reservation where Jeth had grown up, and where tourists needed to schedule visits well in advance and where there was only one real access open to non-natives. It was a place where those who didn't belong were noticed at once, and where tribal members were friendly but closemouthed and didn't encourage contact between themselves and the outside world. All of which meant that he had over twenty-three hundred miles to travel before he could even *begin* to feel Sasha might be safe, and public transport of any sort was out because it was too damned easy to trace. A car, a family off on a summer vacation, that was the way he'd intended to play this, and paying cash all the way. But if she had family that'd be looking for her...

Nuts. He didn't even have a car seat for Sasha, nor much in the way of clothing for either himself or the baby. Grabbing opportunities when they arose didn't leave a lot of time for the kind of planning traveling cross-country with a toddler required. He needed this blasted woman he'd stuck himself with—a trace of something soft and elusive swirled around his senses, and he felt himself tighten suddenly—in more ways than he cared to admit.

A lot more ways.

He couldn't go with her to meet her family. He knew nothing about her, and they sure as hell wouldn't be expecting their darling *Allyn* to turn up with a strange man and a sick baby in tow. Not unless they hadn't seen her in a while, which he doubted, because that wasn't the way his luck was running today.

But he couldn't exactly just avoid the issue, either, now, could he?

Damn. *You're tired, but no falling apart. Sort it out,* he ordered himself. *Take it one thing at a time. You've bought a few hours, at least, before anybody figures anything out. Stop for food, clothes and a phone book with a list of free clinics. Make the rest of your plans from there.*

He drew a breath. "There any place we can get clothes, food, diapers and a car seat all in one stop?" he asked.

Allyn rocked the beginning-to-whimper Sasha and shook her head. "This is your temporary stomping grounds. I'm just passing through."

"Pig whistles," he muttered.

Allyn swallowed the beginnings of a grin. She didn't think she'd ever heard that particular expression before. "Excuse me?"

"Had to pick a damned out-of-towner. No use whatsoever."

"I didn't ask to be picked, you know."

He grimaced. "True."

She waited a few beats. "Where have you shopped while you've lived here?"

"Corner liquor store, corner grocery store, corner pharmacy."

Allyn cleared her throat, trying hard not to laugh at how disgruntled he sounded. "I see."

"I doubt it," he assured her darkly. Then he sighed, checked the Saturn's side mirrors and switched lanes, zigzagging through the city toward the expressway where he hoped to find an exit labeled Shopping.

Chapter 3

They stopped fourteen miles from Baltimore at a super-store in Ellicott City.

After a fair amount of negotiation over who would go in, Allyn bundled Sasha into the smallest zip-front sweat-shirt she had with her. Then all three of them went into the store.

This was what he'd wanted when he'd started out this morning, wasn't it? Jeth thought. A woman whose mother tiger instincts would come straight to the fore once she took a look at Sasha? He simply hadn't bargained on finding one who was quite so…uniquely qualified to hand him his head and stir up his senses at the same time.

Or quite so enthusiastic about helping him shop.

As Jeth watched, Allyn spent a fair amount of his cash on hand with a certain flair he found both impressive and frightening—as though she'd been trained by a take-no-prisoners master in the art of procurement. Other than for staples, he shopped as infrequently as possible.

But when she headed into the men's department, Jeth had the most disturbing sense that he was doomed.

In the parking lot, she'd ransacked his duffel bag, then her suitcases in search of something to diaper Sasha in. What she found had made her roll her eyes and tsk disgustedly at him.

"What?" he'd asked, feeling a certain impatience and paranoia to be moving—and also feeling suddenly daunted by the fact that she found his wardrobe wanting.

She'd blinked at him. He looked at her eyes and was suddenly more afraid of her than of the people from whom he'd retrieved Sasha. Because what he saw there told him better than anything she'd yet done that she was not some timid flower he'd plucked on a whim; she was the wind that blew the flower.

"These all the clothes you've got with you?"

"Yeah. You got a problem with it?" Oh, good, be belligerent. Show her the tough guy. Intimidate the hell out of her.

Yeah, right. As if. Instead of being either intimidated or impressed, she'd offered him exaggerated patience.

"How far do you plan to travel with me 'n' Sasha?" A two-beat pause, then she did a little fishing. "Or at least since you've already said you don't trust me, I presume you're not planning to let me go until this thing of yours comes to some sort of resolution?"

He bit down on his temper, at once wanting to strangle her and, surprisingly enough, kiss her until she couldn't speak.

He gritted his teeth against the unwanted impulse. Blast, in one way or another this entire trip was going to be hell, he just knew it. "As far as it takes to make sure I can keep him safe. And no, even though you're the most annoying woman I've ever car jacked, I'm not letting you go any time soon."

"You've car jacked other women?" Innocent. Unremittingly interested.

God save him, he was definitely going to kill her. "No." The patience he had to exert in order to say it calmly was galling. "You're my first and my only."

"Oh." Clearly, if cheekily, charmed. "What a nice thing to tell a girl."

Understanding for the first time that the only way to win here was to remain silent, Jeth crossed his arms and stared at her.

She pursed her lips and stared back, giving him a look that stated as clearly as words, You're behaving like a child. Cut it out. You're the one who kidnapped me so I could help you—now don't give me dense. "You *do* have a destination in mind?"

"Yes." The paranoia of his experiences of the past several weeks caused him to glance about, looking for enemies, to not want to tell her more than he had to. He hadn't really intended to tell her anything at all; she was simply to have been a tool. Not to mention that the less she knew, the safer she'd be.

"Jethro," she said patiently, mildly.

"*Jeth,*" he snapped. "I don't care how much my mother liked Max Baer. I'm neither a Beverly Hillbilly nor a Clampett."

Her turn to stare at him somewhat nonplussed but waiting, tapping her fingers on the car door. As though he was the one wasting the time here, not her.

"Fine." He shut his eyes, unwillingly granting her another win. "I'm taking him home."

"Tucson?" she asked.

"Close enough."

"Family on vacation?" she guessed, taking his plan a step further than he'd taken it himself.

Surprised at how easily she made it fall into place, he'd nodded cautiously.

"Okay." She'd pursed her lips and nodded. "Okay. Now we know you'll need stuff, too, and I know how to shop."

And that had been that. They had two shopping carts full of toddler supplies that were certain to deplete his hastily scraped together escape fund, and she was off to buy him clothes, too. When he tried to talk her out of the extra purchases, she canted her head and eyed him with more of that apparently trademark patience.

"We're a family on vacation?" she'd repeated, automatically rearranging the sweatshirt around Sasha while she looked at Jeth.

Just somebody's mom discussing something mildly irritating with somebody's dad.

Jeth's jaw tightened with the unsought observation. No, hell, no. He was playing a role, and she'd done stage work in college maybe, understood theater, too. And yet...

Deliberately he ignored the sensation of rightness that scurried through him with the mom-dad-baby image, instead gladly noting that Sasha seemed to be responding to whatever it was Allyn was doing for him and was more with it than before. Marcy would have liked her. If Marcy could have met her. "That's the idea."

"Well, then," Allyn said, as if that explained everything. When she saw that it didn't, she elaborated, "I have a full two weeks' worth of luggage, Sasha's now outfitted for travel, but you look like you're on the run. How safe will any of us be if people don't see what they expect to see?"

Jeth paled, once again jolted by her seemingly instant insights. "What?"

"How safe—"

"I heard you. Where'd you learn that?"

"It's true, isn't it?"

"What undercover school did you go to, and where's your badge?"

"Don't have one." She smiled, a flash of slightly

crooked teeth in a small mouth bordered by dimples. He found himself suddenly and dangerously captivated by her mouth, fascinated equally by its shape as by what came out of it. "I just listen to my mother and read undercover nonfiction a lot. Makes a break from studying sharks and coral reefs and things like that. Now, what kind of underwear do you like, boxers or briefs?"

At that, and in spite of himself, Jeth nearly lost it. Before Marcy's death and even before he'd arrived in Baltimore his sense of humor had been excellent, but lately it had been a tad…lacking. Obviously such would not be the case for long with Allyn Meyers around—regardless of the circumstances under which he'd forced their meeting.

"Boxers," he managed to say, strangling on laughter. Lord, yes. Marcy would have had a ball with her and so would the rest of his siblings. The thought almost made him sober; the kidnappee with the odd sense of humor didn't offer sobriety a chance to take root.

"Ah," Allyn said, plainly pleased, leading the way to the section of apparel in question. "A man who intends to have children—unless you already have children?"

Laughter wheezed out of him, astonishment edged with painful humor. God, she was killing him, and the worst of it was, he was pretty sure he'd be more than happy to let her.

Especially if she continued to go about it like this.

"No. No children," he said when he could speak. "No wife. No anything." And no intention of ever having either, of getting close enough to anyone who could be taken away from him again.

"Probably a good thing," Allyn said. "I can already see where you might be hell on a relationship of that sort."

He should have been beyond amazement by now, but he wasn't. "Do you always talk to strangers like this?"

"Only those who car jack me," she told him, at the same time she supervised him to make sure he added an adequate number of boxer shorts to her cart. "Then I find it's mandatory not to let them think they've ever got the upper hand. Take them by surprise, that's what my stepfather says, keep them off balance, make them think you're one with them. Makes it so much easier to get away when they won't listen to reason and just take your car without you in it."

With which pronouncement she left Jeth standing openmouthed in the aisle behind her while she sashayed ahead of him to men's jeans.

He had to admit that, bust-him-in-the-chops personality or not, she had one hell of a spectacular sashay.

She floored him only once more during their shopping expedition. She stopped in front of the jewelry counter, looked at the wedding rings, then leaned into him for all the world like an excited wife who'd gone too long without and whispered for his—and the sales clerk's—ears only, "It's been almost three years since we eloped. We can afford them now, can't we, honey?"

Torn between mirth and total disbelief, Jeth could only nod. Even as briefly as he'd known her, he should have realized that if she'd decided to play the part of family on vacation, she'd play it to the hilt, wedding rings and all.

With the two thoughts, *Talk about one-stop shopping,* and *Judas, what have I gotten myself into?*—which seemed to be his mantra of the day—he helped Allyn choose slim silver rings formed into Celtic knots, then on his own chose a small but lovely sapphire engagement ring that surprised genuine delight out of her and fit very neatly on her finger atop her wedding ring.

When she turned, raised herself on tiptoe and planted a shy kiss on his cheek, it was all Jeth could do to maintain his rather shaky equilibrium.

Allyn's obvious giddiness over the unexpected addition of the engagement ring not only dumbfounded Jeth—who wanted to ask her about it then and there, but managed to refrain—but seemed to tickle the salesclerk, who mouthed, genuinely pleased for them, "Nice," at Jeth over Allyn's head, then offered them both congratulations and best wishes, and told them the rings would be waiting for them at the service desk when they were through shopping.

In the checkout line it appeared to be all Allyn could do to wait to get her hands on the rings once again—especially the sapphire—and Jeth could only watch her animated face and hope that maybe this trip he'd inadvertently arranged for them wouldn't be complete hell after all.

When the cashier rang up nearly a thousand dollars' worth of merchandise, he paid without any reluctance whatever.

Allyn couldn't believe he'd thought of adding in the sapphire on his own.

More than that, she couldn't believe she'd kissed him over a darned ring. For God's sake, the man had stolen her, scared her, made her angry and ruined her vacation plans barely a couple of hours ago, and she'd kissed him?

His cheek was warm and bristly beneath her lips, with a slightly salty aftertaste—the result of his jog, she guessed. She'd liked the feel of it.

She'd also liked the feel of him when she'd leaned into him, stretched against him to kiss his cheek. That visceral recognition she'd experienced when she'd first seen him running at the side of the road was there in the flesh, enticing, hot.

And more than a little electrifying. And she knew all this because of one small, oval-cut sapphire circlet that now perched snugly on the third finger of her left hand.

She couldn't help it. For reasons she could neither fathom nor have expected, Allyn saw Jeth differently than she had earlier. Perhaps that was normal. They'd spent a little time together. They'd shared an argument or two. They shared a single goal in the life of a lost child. But none of that really accounted for this.

When she'd paused at rings and considered the silver ones, she'd done so because silver wasn't as expensive as gold, the idea of having matching rings had a practical side, she'd always loved playacting, and this little car jacking of Jeth's was turning into her idea of theater of the finest kind. Also, her mother's stories of how she had met Gabriel and forged a life with him had taught Allyn that sometimes desperate people did scary things for the right reasons. And although Allyn found herself having difficulty imagining Jeth's alleged pursuing dangers as reality, she was having a grand time with everything else.

Of course, if Jeth had turned out to be a really badly dangerous guy...well, she was up hell's creek. But at the moment she was going to fully enjoy the first ring any man—or even any boy—had ever chosen and given her. She'd cross hell's creek when she came to it.

Now if only Sasha was all right.

She'd wanted to find a doctor for him first, but had settled for the shopping spree instead because, as she'd suggested to Jeth, if Sasha was cleaned up and they looked like a normal family on vacation, then they could visit any pediatrician and be found unremarkable in the extreme.

Unless, as Jeth pointed out darkly, the little boy was suffering from some extreme illness, or drugging, or abuse other than malnutrition that neither of them could see.

Which made it Allyn's turn to point out that Jeth reminded her of her aunt Edith, the family disaster-monger. With Jeth's black hair and looks and her brown hair and obvious Irish ancestry, it was quite apparent Sasha hadn't actually been born to either of them. In which case he had to be adopted, recently and directly out of Russia.

Which meant, in Jeth's estimation, that any doctor they saw in a small town in Maryland was sure to remember them clearly.

Unless, Allyn argued, they only told the story if they had to.

Since Jeth was equally as concerned about Sasha as she was, he conceded the round—reluctantly. Then he elicited a promise from her that if it began to look like they were going to have to tell a story, *she* would follow *his* lead, just in case he came up with something a whole lot less memorable on the spur of the moment. Because he, after all, was the one who'd come up with the rest of this...whatever this was on the spur of the moment and look how well it had worked so far.

His self-congratulatory tone made Allyn snort inelegantly, but keep her peace when he eyed her a dark admonishment of *yeah, yeah, get over it and don't remind me.*

After a quick stop to pick up traveling grocery staples, they started searching for a doctor. Since it was Sunday, a doctor was difficult to find.

"Why don't we ask someone?" Allyn said finally.

"Ask?" Jeth countered, teasing, continuing to drive. "For directions?"

"Cut the guy comedy," Allyn told him firmly. "You don't know where you're going, and it's for the good of the baby. Besides, we have to stop somewhere anyway so I can wash Sasha up and change his clothes so he looks like somebody cares about him."

The moment the words were out, she wanted to take them back; Jeth looked unaccountably stung. "I care," he muttered.

"I didn't mean you," she told him truthfully. "Or at least not since you let me buy all that stuff for him—and you."

Ah, there it was, Jeth reflected ruefully. One of the benefits of shopping with a woman like there was no tomorrow: guys didn't do it unless they cared.

Allyn returned full swing to her original conversational path. "Not only could Sasha use a bath, but a little soap and water wouldn't hurt you, either. Fear and jogging don't mix very well in a small car. Which means if we stop, everybody gets clean, you and I get some breakfast and coffee, you ask for directions…"

"Or you can ask for directions."

"I don't have any problem asking for directions," Allyn said. "You're the one who's afraid I'll tell someone you kidnapped the baby and me at gunpoint and they'll call the police and it'll all be over."

"You won't tell anyone anything," Jeth said flatly. "You've decided you don't mind being in this situation because it's exciting and not your ordinary life, whatever that is, and you don't believe anything could really happen to any of us, that this is some great fluke of an adventure that'll work out just fine for all of us. I just hope you're right."

Allyn swallowed and stared at him. It was okay for her to take him by surprise, but not for him to have figured her out so easily. Heck, she couldn't even usually figure herself out that easily. If she'd thought about it, the sense of familiarity between them, the idea of feeling comfortable with him after so short a time and under such circumstances would have scared her a lot more than the gun he'd pressed against her ribs earlier.

"Say you're right," she said carefully. "Then what?"

Something in the way she asked made him smile. "Then we stop at a fast food place for a quick cleanup and some breakfast and you ask for directions."

Allyn viewed him suspiciously. "Does that mean you've decided to trust me or that you're keeping your ego intact?"

Jeth merely grinned at her and drove.

After changing, breakfasting and asking for directions, they found what they were looking for in a twenty-four-hour ambulatory emergency care center.

Though still pale and groggy, Sasha looked like a different child, one who had someone looking after him.

Even half out of it as he was, he clung to Allyn's neck and sobbed when the nurse and physician on duty tried to look at him, so neither thought to question her maternity; it was clear to whom Sasha belonged. While Jeth stood in the background, out of the way, Allyn rubbed the youngster's back and held him gently so the doctor could look in his ears, at his throat and nose and probe his neck, abdomen and listen to his breathing.

"How long has he been like this?" the doctor asked, motioning for Allyn to hold Sasha up so he could use the stethoscope against the whimpering child's back.

"A couple of days," Jeth said, before Allyn could think of a response. "We're on vacation, and he came down with a fever. We stopped at a clinic in Maine. Even though they gave him some medication and us a prescription for him, he's been like this ever since. We're on our way home, but we've still got a ways to go, and he's not improving."

The doctor nodded. "Probably a combination of a high fever, some dehydration and something in the other prescription he was allergic to. Do you have it with you?"

"No," Allyn said quickly, "I'm sorry, I didn't think of it."

The doctor made a sound of disapproval. "Hard to prescribe something new for him if I don't know what he's already got in his system."

"He hasn't had any medication since yesterday morning," Jeth said positively. The look he turned on Allyn said, *I know this for a fact, I watched him.* "Does that help?"

"Should. Anything he had is probably pretty much out of his system by now." He probed Sasha's ribs and stomach. "Has he been eating?"

Jeth shook his head. "Not much. Hard to get anything into him."

Allyn looked at her make-believe husband with approval.

For a guy who didn't seem to know anything about kids, he spun a pretty good story.

"We've tried Popsicles, ice cream, anything we can think of," she said, "He just shoves it away."

"Well," the doctor said, "we should be able to take care of that. The nurse will give him a little something that should perk up his appetite, but you've got to get fluids into him or your next stop will be a hospital to get him IVs. You folks have insurance?"

Again Jeth shook his head regretfully. "Not yet. Headed into a new job. Old insurance cut out, new one hasn't picked up yet."

The doctor nodded, wound his stethoscope and put it in his pocket. "I'll give you some samples of the medication I want you to give your son for the next few days. Don't worry, I think he'll be fine, but have him checked by your own physician when you get him home."

"Thank you, Doctor," Allyn said gratefully.

"No sweat. Go ahead and get him dressed. The nurse will be right in with his shot."

Jeth and Allyn waited until he left before giving vent to sighs of relief.

"He'll be okay," she said, hugging Sasha.

Watching her, Jeth understood for the first time that morning how fortunate he'd been. Somehow, some way, and pushing aside all Allyn's stubborn oppositeness, he'd been guided to car jack the right person to help him help Sasha. "He might not have been if we hadn't stopped."

She looked at Jeth, a simple glance with eloquent thoughts behind it. "But we did." Impulsively she held out her newly beringed hand to him; he hesitated, but when she didn't drop it, allowed himself to cover her hand with his. "Thank you," she said.

Inside Jeth's chest, something tightened and made it hard to breathe. What kind of woman thanked the man who'd car jacked her—even if he had done so for real, if unthought out, reasons?

"I—" He paused, uncomfortable. "After the morning I've given you, I don't know what to say to that."

She laughed, the sound warm and rich, wholesome and unbelievably intimate within the confines of the examining room. For the second time that day she reached up and planted a kiss in the vicinity of his chin. "Say you're welcome," she advised. "It's all the response you've got."

Her mouth hovered dangerously, easily close to his. Sliding his arm around her waist, hauling her into him suddenly seemed the most natural thing in the world to do. "You're welcome," he whispered—and dragged himself from the brink of sure disaster only at the sound of the examining room door sliding into the wall and the nurse stepping into the room.

"Sorry," the nurse said, clearly amused.

"Not necessary," Jeth said quickly. He stepped to the door. "How 'bout I go settle up out front while you finish in here?"

He didn't wait for Allyn's response before he left.

"Big baby," Allyn said affectionately for the nurse's benefit as well as to cover her own confusion. Gee, holy crikey. She'd kissed him again. She'd practically invited him to kiss her. What on earth was going on inside her today? "Can't stand the sight of needles near his son."

The nurse grinned. "It's always the strongest-looking dads who go weak when their kids get sick."

"Weak is not quite the way I'd describe him," Allyn managed to mutter before her attention was switched irrevocably to Sasha, who started to scream at the sight of the needle.

It wasn't the first time Allyn discovered exactly how strong short humans could be—especially short humans who were only half-awake. She'd been so fortunate as to help Becky take her toddlers to the pediatrician on more

than one occasion. She hadn't been crazy about the results
then, but this was the first time she'd ever really felt the
child's fear on a personal level. Nails on a blackboard
didn't begin to describe a toddler's shrieks on the willies-
down-the-spine scale.

Maybe it helped if you weren't their primary caretaker.

Still, she survived, and so did Sasha. As a matter of fact,
although he was still sobbing, sniffling and clinging to Allyn for dear life, by the time they left he was also awake
enough to accept a red sucker from Jeth who'd managed
to find a basketful at the admitting desk. Jeth had a purple
sucker tucked into the corner of his mouth. The one he
offered Allyn was green. She crooked an incredulous brow
at him.

"I don't *believe* you," she said. "You're supposed to be
on the run from everybody in the world, but you stop for
a sucker?"

He pulled the lollipop out of his mouth and shrugged.
"Got a sweet tooth, what can I say?" He waggled the
candy at Sasha. "Whaddya think, huh, kiddo? Good, huh?"

Sasha buried his face in Allyn's neck and drooled red
into the fabric of her shirt. She rolled her eyes at Jeth and
gave him an exaggerated, "Thank you sooo much."

Jeth grinned and swept her a bow. "My pleasure," he
drawled, and it really was. Because for all that Sasha clung
to her, it was Jeth who'd found the youngster something
he'd eat.

Chapter 4

They didn't discuss the almost-for-real kiss that hadn't taken place in the examining room. They looked at each other when they thought it was safe to do so and wondered what if, but they didn't talk about it. The possibilities were far too idiotic even to contemplate.

Instead they exchanged minor information about themselves, worried over Sasha, praised him when he accepted not only a couple of animal crackers but also some water after he finished the sucker—or rather, sort of finished it. Allyn allowed him only to lick it until she heard the first slight crunch before relieving him of it—much to his fury—so he wouldn't choke on any big chunks of hard candy. By the time he'd opened his mouth on extended protest, however, she'd popped several animal crackers into his hand and he had to stop yelling in order to see what she'd given him. When he found it edible, blessed silence reigned briefly once more.

They'd gotten only six miles farther down the Pike when Jeth spotted what he thought was a tail.

He glanced over his shoulder at Allyn, sitting in the rear seat beside Sasha, holding a straw in a bottle of Pedialyte while the little boy greedily drank.

"I think we've got company," he told her grimly.

She let her head snap around to look out the window before she could stop herself. "Which car?"

"Black Mercedes on our left, three cars back."

Rational thought returned, prompted by the fact that she didn't believe anyone knew he hadn't just gotten on a bus and left town that way. "How do you know it's tailing us, Jeth?" His name slipped easily off her tongue, as though she'd known him a lot longer than one interminable morning and most of an afternoon. "How would they know my car? How would they even know you're with me? A lot of people take the Pike."

"I don't know, Allyn." The first time he'd actually used her name, Jeth realized. It felt strangely…right…rolling around in his mouth. Allyn. Lynnie. Lyn. *Al-lyn.* The whole thing and all its diminutives settled in his head and flowed without thought to his lips. "Call it paranoia. I've got a feeling. It's been with us awhile. I think it was with us when we left the grocery store, and again after the emergency center. My belly's crawlin' on this one."

"If you're right?"

"Keep driving. See if they maintain distance. Only stop in populated areas for gas. Try and lose 'em."

Allyn moistened her mouth. She'd been working with him as much as possible to this point for Sasha's sake, but she really couldn't fathom how anyone might possibly have found Jeth in her car so quickly—especially since they'd had no connection before this morning. She swallowed. What if he was just plain crazy—paranoid, as he had suggested? What if him taking, having Sasha was everything she'd first thought and she'd simply gobbled up the lines of a chemically imbalanced, albeit somewhat believable and charming hotty because he'd managed to play into her own secret, though probably momentary, fantasy of living Becky's normal family life? She really couldn't let him jeopardize any of them on some sort of paranoid, out-of-control whim.

"I'm not crazy," he said quietly, reading her mind. "And I'm not out of control. Someone from the neighborhood could have seen you draw down on me in that school yard this morning. They could have called the police. Reports go out. Other agencies pick 'em up. Word gets around. Coincidences happen. I'm not taking any chances—with you or Sasha."

Guiltily she glanced up, met his gaze in the mirror. The midnight eyes were steady and unwavering. She looked at Sasha.

"I'm sorry," she said, equally softly, "but I don't know you, and I can't accept at face value that you might be right. I read a lot, but I don't live like this. The most exciting thing I've done recently is go down in a shark cage with a research team to do some filming. I just held the fish to feed the sharks—"

Startled, Jeth looked over his shoulder at her and nearly swerved into a car in the next lane. Good grief, no wonder she'd taken to this business with him so easily. Far as he was concerned, anyone who swam with sharks willingly— even protected by a steel cage—was crazier than he'd ever considered being.

"—but that's nothing like this."

"Nothing like—" Flabbergasted as he was, words failed him. "Geez-oh-pete, woman, you swim with sharks? What the hell do you *do?*"

She grimaced. "Marine biologist. Doctor. Graduated this past Tuesday. Sharks are only one of the species I've worked with." She made a face and shrugged self-deprecatingly. "I've studied a lot of underwater things up close and personal. Sharks are pretty predictable compared to this—to you."

"Thanks," he said dryly. "I think."

"You're welcome," she responded, equally wry. "I think."

They were silent for a moment. Then:

"So," Allyn said, poking Jeth verbally a smidge. "Are you going to try to force their cover or something? Speed up or slow down or get off 70 or something and see what they do?"

Jeth cleared something akin to laughter from his throat. "You that anxious to know?"

"Aren't you?" she countered. "I mean, don't you think it's better the devil you know?"

"Not always. Sometimes it's better to let things ride. Especially when you don't have more of a plan." He should know. If he'd let things ride three years ago... No, he would not think it. He would *not*.

"But not this time," Allyn suggested.

Jeth glanced at her in the mirror, read the need to know, to believe in her eyes and lost any desire to laugh. Without another word he switched on his blinker, dropped back and moved into the right-hand lane as though he was about to take the next turnoff. While Allyn watched as unobtrusively as she could, the Mercedes dropped back three cars and gradually did the same.

"It could just be coincidence," she said, but she didn't sound sure.

"It's not coincidence, Lynnie."

She eyed him sharply. "Why'd you call me that? It's a child's name. No one calls me that except my mother and sister."

Use of the diminutive surprised him, too, but he didn't apologize for it. "It fit the moment," he said. "It's the kind of nickname a man uses for his wife when she's scared."

"I'm not your wife, and I'm not scared."

"In a pig's eye you're not," he told her flatly. "Hell,

I'm scared, too. I'd rather it just be chance that Mercedes is following us, but I can't treat the situation that way. Scared is better than foolish."

"I'll remember that."

"You'd better." He cast another look her way. "And just so we're clear—if this masquerade is going to work, I'll call you anything that fits the moment. Got it?"

Allyn's mouth flattened, jaw tightened. "Long as it's reciprocal, Jethro," she agreed.

Silence fell between them, thickened and grew unhealthily stuffy. The only sound other than the rush of the road under the tires were the noises Sasha made jabbering and playing with some of his new toys in his car seat, and Allyn reading softly to him until he started to get squirmy and unhappy. Then she put the book down and talked to him, asking if he was cold, hot, wet, hungry, et cetera. He stared at her without comprehension.

She sighed and felt his legs and arms before she hiked up Sasha's shirt and tucked the tip of her finger down the front of his diaper. Sure enough, just as she'd suspected. Couldn't rehydrate a kid with as many fluids as Sasha had guzzled without eventually finding him soaked.

"He needs his diaper changed," she said without preamble. "We have to stop."

Jeth swore under his breath. "You can't change him there?"

Allyn glared at the back of his head until he turtled his neck into his shoulders against the weight of her glower.

"All right, fine." Not happy. Not cordial. "Apparently not." Decidedly grumpy. "We need gas, anyway. Let me lose the tail and we'll stop."

"Sooner would be better." No, she didn't know better than to poke a bad-tempered alligator with a stick when it was close enough to bite.

"Not at all would be best," he snapped.

She was concerned for Sasha's comfort as well as for

the little boy's safety—not to mention her own and Jeth's. But that didn't mean the good-looking, clean-shaven, libido-startling jughead in the front seat wasn't starting to rile her temper—heck, her misbegotten Brannigan obstinance—in a major way. "Then drop me off, and *you* float away when Sasha's diaper overflows."

"And risk losing you to them?" Jeth wasn't exactly feeling casual about their situation at the moment. "Uh-uh, babe, not a chance."

"You could always leave the gun with me." The retort was instant, deliberate and provoking.

Jeth snorted. Stubborn, single-minded, sweet-smelling woman. If she didn't quit playing havoc with both his brain and his body pretty darn quick, he was going to have to jam on the brakes, turn around, reach back and shake her. "Oh, sure. That'd work."

"You never know," Allyn retorted. "It might—Hey!" Jeth slammed on the brakes and veered hard onto the shoulder of the highway, causing Allyn to jerk forward into her seat belt and grab for Sasha's baby seat. "Geez, Jeth, what are you doing?"

Jeth shoved the transmission into reverse, sent them squealing and whiplashing backward down the side of the road. "Shutting you up and losing that damned tail." Swearing, he watched the Mercedes blow past them in traffic, its driver swiveling angrily in his seat, taken unaware by his maneuver. "Judas, they spotted us. It's the Colombians. I recognize the driver. We've got to get out of here, switch vehicles, find a safer route. These guys are not out to take hostages—except maybe Sasha. And even that's only a maybe."

"A maybe?" Panic was an unwelcome and instant companion, changing the circumstances. Allyn felt her stomach clench, her lungs squeeze, her heart pound. "A *maybe?*" Her voice rose and squeaked, and she hated it. "What does that mean? What the hell have you gotten him into? You think they'll kill him if they catch us? How does that make it better for him to be here than where he was before? What is the matter with you? Do you ever think before you act?''

"What's the matter with me?" It was difficult to carry on a knock-down, drag-out while he was driving backward and east down the edge of the westbound I-70, but Jeth managed. Hell, he might not get another chance to give her a piece of his mind if he didn't do it now. "You, you're the matter with me. You're not who you were supposed to be. You were supposed to be June Cleaver, but look at you. I'm running this show, damn it, but you gotta step in, take my gun and tell me we've got to stop for baby supplies, stop for groceries, find a damned doctor and I take one freaking look at you and my brain takes a hike. You've got hair made for touching, eyes like I've never seen, a mouth I'd really like to make shut up, and you're freaking ornery enough to punch all my buttons. So this, this is your fault, not mine.''

"My fault?" Somewhere underneath Allyn's outrage a part of her recognized exactly what he'd said and tucked it away in a drawer labeled *Oh, my God, now what?* for later perusal. The rest of her told him what she thought of him. "You pigheaded, chauvinistic, macho hunk of beef. *My* fault? You car jack me, but the three of us being followed by a group of drug dealers you gelded is my fault? I don't think so." Fuming, furious. "God, I should have known a guy as pretty as you would have to also be a giant pinhead. I'd really like to see you try to shut me up, I really would.'' Unfortunately, her body really *did* want to see him make her shut up.

By kissing her.

Which was just about as pinheaded a desire as they came, under the circumstances. But apparently her body liked the threat of danger a lot more than her head did. And if she hadn't realized it when he'd stuck his gun in her ribs, she knew it for certain now: Jeth Levoie was as dangerous to her as they came—and in a lot more ways than one.

And this whole line of thought was just a bit more revealing than she wanted it to be—especially while they were in the middle of a big-screenlike chase scene. Or getaway scene. Every instinct Allyn possessed told her to do whatever it took to make this stop.

Trouble was, how?

She'd spent the past several years learning how to think fast under conditions that most people would consider abnormal—including, once or twice, in potentially life-threatening instances—but even Gabriel's admonitions and training aside, none of her underwater experiences compared to this.

She'd thought quickly enough in the school yard, but that had been as much luck as it had been fury. That had been before she'd understood Jeth Levoie at all, before she'd known about Sasha. Now she didn't have the steering wheel beneath her hands, she had a cranky baby disturbing her ability to think and an infuriatingly dangerous man who liked purple lollipops making his subtle way under her skin. Her normally more-than-able mind was a blank.

Fortunately, she didn't have to come up with a way to get them out of trouble; Jeth already had one.

He waited until he saw the Mercedes U-turn into the eastbound lanes and gather speed, then took advantage of a grouping of westbound eighteen-wheelers, let a couple of them get ahead of him, a couple to the side and a couple behind with barely enough room for the Saturn to squeeze into the pocket between them before he jerked the transmission into drive and skidded onto the highway. Allyn covered Sasha's eyes and shut her own so neither of them would see the mega car squash she was certain was inevitable. When, after a reasonable length of time, no crunch sound occurred, she opened one eye, then the other, then took her hand away from Sasha's face.

And flat-handed Jeth upside the back of his head with her ring hand.

"Don't ever do that again," she said hoarsely. If her voice had been steady she'd have made more of an impression, she was sure.

Without looking, he grabbed her hand before she could withdraw it and imprisoned her wrist. Arizona lightning couldn't move more quickly, and Allyn knew it at once.

Lightning couldn't crackle and burn with more electric intensity where it hit, either.

"Don't ever distract me while I'm saving your butt," he returned grimly. "You'll get all three of us killed. I won't have that."

"*You* won't—" Allyn stared at him breathless, speechless. Too aware of his fingers around her wrist, of how immediately the tension had changed, the threat had grown, of the taste he left on the back of her tongue.

Too aware of him, period.

She would not let him get to her under these or any circumstances, she would *not*.

"If it wasn't for you—" The accusation was petty, and she knew it, but that didn't stop her from making it. From wanting to verbally beat his culpability into him.

From wanting to escape her own.

"—we wouldn't be here—"

He squeezed her wrist hard, once, and released it. "Give it a rest, Lyn. I don't apologize for the choices I make anymore. I can't. We're here. Make the best of it."

Startled, she looked at him. Not because the fire in his touch lingered, though it did. Not because his fingers had left a visible imprint on her wrist, though that was true, too. She looked because the passion in his refusal to apologize for who he was and what he did equaled her own.

And because, unlike men she knew in her field whose passion for their work left little room for a three-dimensional life outside it, there was a lot more to Jeth than whatever he was doing at the moment.

She'd recognized that before—sort of—in the way he'd put Sasha's comfort and welfare first, before himself, in his willingness to try to make her feel easier despite putting her in an unthinkable predicament, but this was the first time she'd known it. Understood it way down deep where it played havoc with the nerves that butterflied about her stomach, and in whatever emotion squeezed heart and lungs inside her chest.

Recklessness and petty accusations whooshed silently out of her, made her subside into her seat where she sat quiet and wary, watching Jeth while absently rocking Sasha's car seat trying to hush the little boy.

In his own place, Jeth found himself trying not to scrub the distracting feel of Allyn out of his hand. The harsh imprint he'd made of her wrist in his palm lingered in the nerves beneath his skin; the tips of his fingers thrummed to the beat of her pulse. He could feel where her wrist bones had molded the ball of his thumb, the pads of his calluses.

With some new desperation, he concentrated on driving, on getting them as far away from the Colombians as possible. He shouldn't have touched her, not like that. He should have known touching her would result in him getting burned. In fact he wouldn't be surprised to find blisters seared along his palm. And if by some chance he didn't have third-degree burns there, it would be sheer luck only, not because the fire wasn't hot enough.

He glanced at her in the rearview mirror and saw his own wariness written on her face, in the green and blue eyes fastened on him. Something akin to comprehension passed between them before Jeth's jaw clenched and they both blinked away from the connection.

In the middle of a smooth ride down southbound I-75 somewhere in Ohio on the way to Kentucky, Rebecca Meyers Catton suddenly shot forward hard into her seat belt. When she recovered her equilibrium, she rubbed her bruised collarbone and eyed her husband, Michael, in outraged indignation, then clipped him a good one upside the back of his head with her ring hand. Michael eyed her in shocked disbelief.

"What was that for?"

Quickly Becky turned to check on the welfare of the three children, ages two, four and six, carefully belted into the rear seat of their Lumina van, before rounding on him furiously. "You could have killed me or the kids, stepping on the brakes like that at this speed. There's nothing in front of us. What's the matter with you?"

"The matter with me? What the—" Ever mindful of little pitchers out to collect language of all sorts, Michael swallowed the expletive. "What do you mean, what's the matter with me? What's the matter with you? You're going to cause an accident swatting me like that. Never should have given you a platinum wedding ring. You're going to knock me out with that thing yet."

"I'm going to cause an accident? *I'm* going to…" Anger throttled Becky's ability to speak. "You're the one who stepped on the brakes."

Clarity dawned on Michael. "I didn't step on the brakes, Beck. Ask Andy. Did you guys jerk like Daddy hit the brakes, Andy?"

Becky's oldest child shook his blond head at his mother. "Uh-uh, but Momma jerked really hard up there, I saw her. Maybe you only hit them in the front seat."

Michael chuckled. "I don't think that's possible, An, but thanks." He glanced at Becky. "No brakes," he said, carefully neutral. "UFO, you think?"

Becky rolled her eyes, gave him a look of withering scorn. "Yeah, right. UFO." She tsked her tongue against the back of her teeth, then bit the inside of her cheek thoughtfully. "You know, that's the second really weird thing that's happened today."

"Oh?"

"Yeah." She nodded. "This morning I all of a sudden felt like I was being whipped around until I got dizzy, then it was like I had a gun in my hand. It was weird. I kept wondering if I could pull the trigger if I had to on a weapon that wasn't there." She bit down on sudden concern for her sanity. "I've never held a gun in my life, Mike, not even when you and Gabriel wanted to teach me, so what is going on?"

They eyed each other, and light dawned almost simultaneously.

"Allyn." Michael said it first. He'd known his wife's twin sister as long as he'd known Becky, after all. And although he'd never understood it, he knew about and accepted Becky's and Allyn's extra connection with each other, had witnessed the results of it on more than one occasion. This time, though, he didn't particularly care for the effect the extrasensory tie seemed to be having on his wife. She'd gone pale, appeared nauseous and terrified. "Beck?"

"She's in trouble," Becky said, horrified. "We've got to do something."

Michael hoped she was wrong. "Are you sure this isn't just something like when she gets morning sickness when you're pregnant?"

"She's not pregnant," Becky told him. "She's never even…" She paused, aware of avid ears in the back seat, embarrassed to even think she'd know when Allyn lost— or that Allyn had probably known when she— She shuddered. Talk about your inconvenient abilities, and thank God she'd realized this one in time to put a lock on it before Allyn did…you know. "It's nothing like that," she said lamely. "I'd know."

There were some knowledges better left unpursued, and

Michael had the distinct impression this was one of them. "You have any idea where she is?"

Becky shook her head. "It doesn't work like that. But she was supposed to be leaving from that friend of hers in Baltimore this morning. She told me she got a Triptik Route Map from Triple A, and I don't think she planned any more detours."

"She still driving that Saturn?"

"Far as I know."

"Then Gabriel can probably get the license number and put out a description, have the staties along the way keep an eye out, pull her over and make sure everything's co-pacetic."

Becky looked at her husband, viewing him for the first time in several weeks the way she used to before the seven-year itch had come along. "You think he could do that just because I feel weird?"

Michael smiled slightly and squeezed her hand. "I think he'd do that if you didn't feel weird. Give him an excuse to be overprotective, he'll take it." He picked up the cell phone between their seats. "Call him."

Wordless, Becky stared at her husband a minute, then caught his hand and brushed a kiss across the back of his knuckles. Took the phone and speed dialed her stepfather.

Jeth gave them twenty minutes amid the protection of the big rigs before ducking off the interstate into a truck stop.

The thing about two-year-olds was that when they were sick, they were very, very sick, but when they decided they were well… Well! Keeping them down to insure their recovery was, to say the least, a joke. On you.

While Allyn took Sasha inside and changed his diaper and generally learned a little more about him—like the fact that he could not only walk, but run fast if a trifle drunk-enly—Jeth emptied and rid them of her Saturn and found them a Dodge Ram as a replacement. He toyed briefly with the idea of finding some way to change their appearances, but decided against it when he couldn't find hair dye he was sure wouldn't do harm to Sasha's tender scalp. He also couldn't find wigs or anything else that he thought would be the least convincing to disguise himself or Allyn. Such was the problem of keeping a low profile on the fly between small towns and truck stops. That was why when she and Sasha met him in the restaurant portion of the truck stop, he handed her a bag with her license plate and paperwork inside, shook his head at her consternation and said, "Don't ask."

He had the keys to the Dodge with him, so despite a world of misgivings, she didn't.

It was also not like misgivings were exactly new to her where he was concerned. In fact, if she'd had to name the primary emotions she felt about Jeth Levoie, they would be misgiving, uneasiness and disquiet—among other shadings of the term.

She would also have to say that, for the first time in months, due to him—not thanks to him—she felt alive.

The van was far more comfortable for family travel than Allyn's coupe. There was room to stretch out, spread out, feed and change and play with Sasha while they were moving—although Allyn was adamant about regular stops to give the little boy a break, and Jeth reluctantly obliged.

It was at her insistence, too, that they stopped for the night at about dinnertime just inside the Pennsylvania border after shifting their direction from the straight south-westerly route that Jeth had originally planned to one that was more convoluted, varied and, as Allyn put it, "more vacationlike." Feeling slightly henpecked by this time, Jeth nonetheless did as she requested, recognizing the wisdom in the move for Sasha's sake—even if he wasn't entirely convinced of its safety. He felt better when he was able to find a two-story motel with parking at the back—hidden from the road.

They ate at a nearby diner that listed macaroni and cheese on the children's menu. Sasha viewed the dish with wide-eyed, cocked-head suspicion even after Allyn took a bite of his meal and smacked her lips to show him how good it was. He dug in with imprecise gusto, however, when Jeth stuck his fingers in the dish and showed the tyke how much fun it was to squish the macaroni in his hand and eat it that way.

Allyn stifled a grin and offered her ''husband'' a look of rolled-eye disgust when he gave her a triumphant—and all too appealing—smirk that said, ''Ha! I got him to eat when you couldn't.''

She didn't bother to stifle the wicked chuckle that exploded when Jeth needed two napkins to clean the cheesey guck off his hands—and Sasha immediately reached for Jeth's T-shirt to copy him.

It was easy to establish a comfort zone, a rapport that meant paying attention to Sasha while they largely ignored each other, their present situation and the fact that they would soon spend the night in a single motel room—albeit with two beds.

Daytime, babies and chase scenes were quite one thing. Twilight, stardust and closed rooms, especially one where a child slept, were quite another. Twilight meant intimacy, a proximity that was unavailable on the road with a seat and other concerns between them, and a sleeping Sasha meant silence, quiet voices, whispers, leaning near to each other to hear....

They looked at each other across the Formica restaurant table, and awareness was a spooky sizzle raising goose bumps on the skin, a tumbling wave of an image without substance, a discomforting sensation in the small of the back that sent furtive fingers of heat furling forward through the belly.

Desire, the sensation murmured. *Anticipate, delay, deny. Give in.*

To what? Allyn wondered wildly. To the lust she'd experienced at the first sight she'd had of him on the road this morning? They'd shared a day. She didn't know him. This wasn't like her.

She wanted the moment anyway, whoever he turned out to be.

The knowledge made her blush and duck her head, hiding her face behind the activities-of-the-day-loosened curtain of her hair. Of course, she reasoned guiltily, she flushed easily when it came to any kind of thoughts of human sexuality. This had nothing to do with him.

Yeah, right.

For himself, Jeth regarded her with both amusement and curiosity, an in-spite-of-himself desire to take his thumb and smudge away the embarrassment staining her cheeks and throat.

Cruder thoughts, more primitive cravings followed full tilt on the heels of that simple want, turned his baser instincts on full volume, made them impossible to ignore. He'd been rebuffing them with only varying degrees of success all day, but now...

When he looked across the table at her his pulse quickened, senses roared, wildness muttered with the breath in his lungs, *Want, need, take, consume.*

Leave alone.

He had to—for the sake of his sanity as much as for her welfare.

He didn't do one-night stands, didn't fling himself wildly into a moment without first considering the consequences—and he'd had all day to consider the ramifications of bedding Allyn Meyers. When he wasn't seriously tossing thought to the wind in order to live on the wing and a prayer that was keeping them alive, that is.

No, bedding Allyn would be a mistake he wasn't prepared to make. They were going to know each other a few days, that was all. She was a convenience to his cause. He was using her as a cover to help protect Sasha. He couldn't allow himself to make her a convenience to his bed, as well—even if she was willing. One of them was sure to regret the momentary liaison later, and he had the uneasy feeling that the one to do so would be him.

She had a face that could bother a man's dreams, a body built specifically for cradling a man's and a spirit it could take him three lifetimes and a half to understand. If he found a way to sleep with her, as his body demanded, there would be no going back. He would be involved, she would be involved. He knew it as certainly as he didn't know what he was doing here. Despite the rules he'd laid down for himself, he already knew there would be no easy way to let her go.

Damn, the things a man discovered about himself when the timing was shot to hell.

The moment broke when Sasha gabbled at them, reaching for his milk glass.

"He's darling," a grandmotherly woman at the next table said. "How old is he?"

"What?" Still distracted, Allyn looked at her, tried to focus on the question while she brought Sasha's straw to his mouth. "Oh, he's two. Almost."

"Aw," the woman cooed, wiggling her fingers at Sasha. "They're so sweet at that age."

"More like holy terrors," her companion, a slightly younger woman who looked like she knew whereof she spoke, corrected her. "What's his name?"

"Adam," Jeth told her, not missing a beat. "After my father." He signaled for the check, touched Allyn's hand. "We should probably get going if we want to get to Dad's tonight."

Allyn nodded but let Sasha finish his drink before beginning to clean up the little boy.

"Aw, there's the face." The older woman chucked Sasha's chin. "I'll bet you're not a holy terror, are you, Adam."

Suspicious of overly familiar strangers who cooed, as only a toddler can be, Sasha pulled away from the woman and looked down his nose at her. When she reached to tweak his nose he swung toward Allyn, arms wide. Hiding elation over this show of trust, Allyn dampened a napkin and finished wiping the cheese off his hands, then picked him up and cuddled him.

"It's all right, baby," she crooned. She looked at the disappointed woman. "I'm sorry, he's a little shy around people he doesn't know."

"And well he should be," the younger woman said firmly. "Never know who's out there looking for cute little blond babies these days. Make sure you teach him to *stay* shy of strangers, too."

"Oh, we will." Allyn jiggled Sasha's tummy until he giggled and bounced on the seat beside her. "We wouldn't want to lose you, would we, babe?" She smiled at the women, glanced at Jeth, who'd returned from the cash register to lay a suitable tip on the table. "Ready, love?"

He nodded and took Sasha from her, set the tyke astride his shoulders. "Saddle up, cowboy, let's go," he agreed, then jog-trotted Sasha to the front of the diner and ducked him neatly out the door.

Allyn shook her head and rolled her eyes, gathered her purse and the diaper bag to follow them. "Men," she said affectionately. "Little boys all."

"And women are the packhorses," the younger woman agreed with feeling.

The older woman simply looked after Jeth and Sasha, turned to Allyn and smiled. "You've got two beautiful boys there, hon. I hope you always enjoy them as much as you do now."

Touched, Allyn swallowed both half-wish and outright lie and nodded. "I'm sure I will," she said. "Thank you."

Then she beat feet after Jeth before anyone else had time to say something she might think too much—or too wistfully—about later.

Chapter 5

Evening crept in on its proverbial cat's feet, settled in long shadows across the parking lot that Jeth kept an eye on through a minute opening in the motel room drapes. No longer putting on a show for the benefit of diner patrons or other onlookers, he found himself both exhausted and restless, and the day's strain showed.

Allyn's scent in the half-lit room tortured him; he wanted nothing more than to dump her on her back and lose himself in her body, relieve the tension, rid his muscles of the tightness engendered by a day spent driving in the healthiest way he could think of. But to love her—even to merely have sex with her—that way lay madness.

Torture or madness. Hell of a choice.

Instead of allowing himself to select either, he roved between the door and the window with his retrieved and loaded Browning settled where he was used to carrying it: the shoulder holster under his left arm.

The silence was as loaded as his weapon, and equally

awkward to carry. But awkward or not, simultaneously carrying a gun and silence were things he knew how to do.

While he wandered, Allyn played with Sasha on the floor between the beds, dividing her attention—the way a real wife might—between the men, big and small, who occupied her life.

Sasha seemed to have no concept of shapes or colors the way Allyn's experience told her he should. His language development also seemed to have been arrested by his life to date. It wasn't until he described her correctly if inaccurately as *mama* and Jeth as *papa* that Allyn began to figure out Sasha's language development might not be impaired, but merely that he wasn't speaking English. Perplexed, she turned to Jeth.

"I think our son speaks Russian instead of English," she told him matter-of-factly.

Jeth stopped pacing, looked at her. The word "son" and the instant images it conjured did nothing to allay the accompanying tumult of emotions—mostly ones he didn't want to feel. If he hadn't been able to look after his little sister, what made anybody think he'd ever be able to look after a son of his own? "What?"

"Sasha doesn't speak English," Allyn repeated—and forgave herself immediately for enjoying the consternation that crossed Jeth's face. Some days one took one's amusement where one found it, if one was wise.

Jeth started to swear and stopped himself, but not before Sasha rolled to his feet and gleefully announced the entire word for him.

Choking, but trying not to encourage Sasha to repeat his pronouncement by showing the laughter, Allyn covered her mouth and looked at the dumbfounded Jeth.

"No, maybe I was wrong," she said, as the toddler launched into an entire stream of unprintable words he could say in English. Shaking with merriment, she caught

Sasha and covered his mouth with her hand. "No, no, love, we don't say that. *Nyet.*"

"*Nyet,*" Sasha agreed joyfully and, just like any normal two-year-old, flung his arms around Allyn's neck, bussed her on the cheek and went right on with what he was saying anyway.

Convulsed with laughter, Allyn wrapped her arms around the tyke and buried her face in his shirt while she once again attempted to shush him. Jeth viewed her with disgust.

"Great," he said. "Just great. Apparently he speaks *some* English."

"Uh-huh." It was all Allyn could do to trust herself to reply.

He gave her male macho pseudo-helpless sarcasm. "You're the one who knows all about kids, what do you suggest we do?"

"Don't use the words and don't encourage him," Allyn managed to say before breaking the latter rule herself by going off into more gales of stifled laughter when Sasha broke loose and marched over to Jeth, called him *Papa,* and launched into a serious repeat of his blue lecture for his benefactor's benefit.

"You're not helping," Jeth told her severely.

"Hey." She offered no apology. "I'm not the one who gave him the opening."

"You're the one who's laughing at him."

"I'm laughing at you," she corrected. "There's a difference."

"Like he knows that." Jeth picked up Sasha, sat on the bed and pressed two fingers gently across the toddler's lips. "No," he said firmly. "Bad. Sasha say good things."

"Sasha," the little boy concurred. "Papa bad."

Taken aback, Jeth stared at him. "Who's papa?"

Seeming to understand a world more English than he appeared to speak, Sasha patted Jeth's chest. "Papa," he said slowly, for all the world as though he were the translator identifying an object for a student. "Papa bad."

Allyn pulled a pillow over her head to muffle the explosion of mirth she couldn't hold back. Jeth was completely out of his depth. He knew it, she knew it, but there was no way he planned to lose track of a conversation with a two-year-old.

"That's not what I said," Jeth corrected him. "I said Sasha not say bad things."

Eyebrows screwed up in a miniature copy of adult confusion, Sasha regarded Jeth. "Papa ucky t'ings?" he asked.

Unable to contain herself, Allyn roared.

"Thanks a lot," Jeth told her darkly. "I wish to hockey sticks I'd never car jacked you."

"Hockey sticks?" she asked, full of innocence—and mischief. "As in H. E. Double?"

He glared at her.

She struggled for a semblance of sobriety. "Oh, dear, and just when I was starting to have such a really good time at your expense."

"That's the problem." Sasha squirmed to get out of his lap, and Jeth set him on the floor. "This entire day has been your good time at my expense. Most self-respecting kidnap victims would offer their abductors a little more deference, treat the situation with the reverence it deserves."

Allyn waggled a book at Sasha. "Most self-respecting abductors don't eat purple lollipops or let their victims talk them into buying a carload of baby stuff or wedding rings."

"And you would know that because?"

She ignored the question. "Besides, I don't remember having any fun at all when you committed the actual crime *or* during that mad chase sequence." She captured Sasha when he reached for the book, tickled him until he giggled. "You were, however, awfully cute when we went shopping." She stripped Sasha of his clothing, fitted him into his new pajamas, careless of the effect her pronouncement had on Jeth—or of the effect it would have on her later when she had a chance to realize what she'd said. "Leads me to believe you've got possibilities beyond your chosen profession."

It was a quirk of thought, an aberration, Jeth assured himself, that made him suddenly want to know just what possibilities she believed he had.

"What possibilities?" he asked before he could stop himself. It had never occurred to him to consider other ways to live his life than the one that had led to Marcy's death. "What else am I if not that?"

Startled, Allyn looked at him, flushed under the intensity of his gaze. "I don't know. Just…possibilities. I work with a lot of men. Banter is how I handle their idiocies where women are concerned. It was something to say."

"Liar," Jeth accused softly.

He rounded the outside bed, caged her in the narrow path between it and the inside bed. She tried to take Sasha and duck around him, but now that he'd begun the question he had no intention of letting her answer slide. It had been a long day, and wise or not, he needed human contact, wanted to know her, what made her tick, made her help him without any reason whatever.

Except Sasha, that is. And even there, now that he thought of it, Jeth realized he'd actually left Allyn alone with the boy often enough today—trusted her implicitly for reasons he wasn't sure he comprehended—so that if she'd chosen to take off with Sasha at any of several points, she might easily have done so. And since Allyn was both bright enough and stubborn enough to have found a way out of this mess for both herself and Sasha if she'd wanted to, Jeth suddenly understood that something had to have kept her with *him*, made her choose to help *him* as well as Sasha. He wanted to know what and why.

Had to know.

He caught Allyn's arm, hefted Sasha away from her and sat him on the inside bed with the word book they'd purchased. Walked across the room to the chest of drawers with Allyn in tow, sat on it so they were nearly at eye level and drew her to stand between his thighs.

Physically it was an exquisitely painful, torturously dangerous position for him. Her hip merely brushed his denim-covered crotch, but that was all it took to tease him alive. For better or worse, however, he knew instinctively that the way to get truth from Allyn Meyers was through the intimate use of a moment.

However hard on him it might also prove.

He winced at the unintentional mental pun, but he didn't back away from it. Once begun was, as the old rhyme went, half done, after all.

Allyn looked almost into his eyes, looked away. He was much too close like this, much too tempting, brought her past week and early-this-morning druthers too easily within reach.

She could imagine—well, almost imagine—what it would be like to *be* with him, lie down with him, take him into both her body and her life. The very thought, the mere idea was beyond silly, outside of fantastic, ludicrous beyond belief, but still she entertained it. The semblance of what she'd recently begun to envy in her sister's life lay inside this room: adorably near in Sasha jabbering away on the bed; devastatingly, kissably close in Jeth, whose touch sent heat tingling through every nerve and pore, torching the brain cells that had once been so wise about trying to keep Becky out of trouble.

That had never, until today, been made dim-witted by the sight of a man's mouth.

Of their own volition, her eyes fastened on Jeth's lips, tried to discern what it was about that wry, late-day-beard-surrounded line that fascinated her hormones so much. Simple proximity, perhaps, as her grandmother often said. Her mind taking an unknown, unwelcome situation and turning it into something pleasant, pleasurable that she could deal with. That's what, Julia Brannigan often proclaimed, had happened to Allyn's mother, Alice, when Gabriel Book had come to town.

Of course, Julia always hastily added, Alice and Gabriel had proved the exception that made the rule. Which was why, Allyn understood suddenly and with trepidation, she'd *thought* about calling Gabriel to help her out of this situation, but hadn't actually done so. Her stepfather would, she knew, blow reality through this adventure like a force-five tornado, destroying a fantasy Allyn had never entertained before now.

Nor wanted to.

Trying to sort it all out, make sense of the suddenly insensible, Allyn breathed. Air tangled in her lungs, left her natural ability to inhale and exhale as muddled as her thoughts.

Aware of the abrupt shift in her breathing, the pulse beneath his fingertips, the temperature and color of her skin, Jeth wedged her closer, more tightly between his legs. Lifted his hand to her face and raised her chin so she was forced to see him, not simply parts of him.

Used two fingers to brush the hair out of her eyes and was instantly lost to what he saw there: vulnerability, availability, need.

"No," he heard himself say raggedly, distantly. "This is stupid, it's not what you really want, I won't let it happen," but even as he said it, his body recognized the lie for what it was; he cupped her face in his hands and dragged her in.

She came willingly, bracing her hands on his chest and leaning into him. Her breath caught against his lips.

"What do you want from me?" he asked.

"Nothing," she whispered. "Everything."

Her mouth pressed his, hesitant lips slightly parted, light as a moth's caress on his.

When she ducked her chin and drifted away from the half-kiss, he scooped up a handful of her hair and hauled her back, bumped his mouth against hers again and again, seducing her lips until they no longer parted company with his, merely unsealed enough to share his breath, his life, feed his passion.

Realize her own for the first time.

Thought did not exist. Neither did the motel room, the events of the day, any druthers outside of this dark instant, this heady seduction that deepened with every movement of his mouth against hers.

He was wrong, she knew it in every nerve, every cell, every fiber. She did want this, want him. Craved this sensation of time out of mind that only he could give. When he slid his tongue over the sharp edges of her teeth, she opened for him eagerly, moaned low in her throat, slid restless fingers across his chest, encouraging the mating play, the prelude.

Lifted her arms to slide them around his neck, wordlessly offering him access to parts of her she'd never let a man touch, begging Jeth alone to teach her what she'd chosen to ignore in favor of twenty years of nonstop education.

Jeth felt the tide shift, the world begin to slide out from underneath him, draw him into a vortex that threatened not to let him go; he couldn't give in. He drew a harsh breath, pulled himself together and pushed the gift away. Allyn made a small sound of denial and tried to pull him back. Only Sasha tugging at his leg prevented Jeth from returning to her embrace.

Even though he'd been the one to pull away, Allyn was the one to recover first. A little unsteadily, she backed away from Jeth and reached to pick Sasha up.

''What's up, squirt?'' she asked hoarsely. Lord, had that

really been her kissing Jeth like there was no tomorrow and no consequences to consider?

Like she was the neediest, most sex-starved woman on the face of the earth?

Sasha bobbled his head back and forth and told her something absolutely fascinating and completely unintelligible that sounded—phonetically spelled—a lot like *Cheetat, cheee-tat!* She nodded as though she understood.

"Is that so? You think maybe we should brush your teeth and get you ready for bed, then go read some more about it?"

Nodding, Sasha pointed to the book on the bed, named it *knee-ga* or something similar and tried to use his legs and knees as he might on a horse to turn Allyn in the direction he wanted to go. She held firm.

"Nuh-uh, bud. Teeth first, then book." She glanced at Jeth, blushed at the look of disbelief and desire he sent her in return and glanced away. "I'll get him ready for bed then read to him for a bit."

She didn't ask, "Okay?" but the question seemed somehow implied—useful victim to genial car jacker. Jeth's jaw clenched, unclenched; he gave her a clipped nod.

"Good." He stalked to the door. "I'm taking a walk. Lock up and put the chain on behind me. Don't let anyone in but me."

"I won't."

He put his hand on the doorknob, hesitated. Eyed Allyn up and down. Grimaced and worked his jaw. "That shouldn't have happened," he told her flatly.

Something wilted inside her. Maybe for reasons she couldn't remember at the moment it shouldn't have happened, but he didn't have to sound so disgusted that it had.

"No," she agreed. "I'm sorry, it's my fault. I shouldn't have attacked you like that. You must think—but that's the first time I ever—" Her mouth twisted with self-contempt, she straightened and eyed Jeth squarely. "I've never thought of myself as a dolphin, no matter what you must think right now.''

Jeth eyed her quizzically and, it must be admitted, with more than a little poker-faced resolve. He would not make this worse by laughing, no matter what odd thing she said to provoke him. ''A dolphin?'' he asked with effort.

''A dolphin, a dolphin,'' Allyn repeated exasperated. ''A deep-sea mammal, bottle-nosed, natural enemy of sharks, incredible skin, more intelligent than humans, promiscuous as minks. I really don't have a libido like theirs, I promise. It won't happen again.''

''A libido like—'' Astonished, Jeth stared at her for a full two seconds, torn between wry laughter and the desire to shake Allyn Meyers—and her mistaken view of why he'd pulled away from her—silly. Three long strides brought him to catch her chin in his palm so he could haul her into a swift, fierce kiss. ''It's not your libido I'm worried about,'' he told her dryly. ''It's mine. It's been a long time since I've felt—'' He paused, shook his head. ''No, back that up. Make it, I've never felt anything like *that*. And I can't, Allyn. I can't. Not now. Not here. Not with you. Not ever.''

''Not with me?'' She couldn't believe her ears. The very idea that she'd managed to throw herself into the arms of a man who would kiss her like that only to have him tell her practically in the next breath *not with you,* well, it made her blood boil. ''What are you talking about, not with me? If you felt and I felt, and you want and I... Well.'' She shook her head. ''I mean, I can understand the not here and now part, but you realize you make no sense with the rest of it. Because I have never, ever done anything like that before in my life, so you just stick that in your shorts and think about it while you're walking, buster!''

For the approximate space of two shakes of a lamb's tail Jeth simply gaped at her dumbstruck. Then laughter bubbled to the surface, left him doubled over, snorting and gasping for breath. My God, she was a handful and a half. Stick that kiss in his shorts and think about it? He doubted he'd think of anything else, imagine anything else, fantasize about anything else for the better part of what was left of his life other than stripping her naked and letting her have her way with him until they were both too exhausted and too sated to move. And the way he felt right now, he was pretty sure he wouldn't want to leave any bed she was in sooner than Christmas, and that'd be to get a snack to bring back to bed with him.

He leaned against the wall weak with mirth. Stick it in his shorts and think about it. Yeah, right. Sheesh.

Allyn grabbed the front of his T-shirt, rattled him physically the best she could with a toddler in her other arm. "Don't you dare laugh at me."

Jeth laughed harder. "I can't help it. Do you realize how funny you are or how painful your suggestion is?"

Allyn stuck her nose in the air and gave him miffed. "I know where there's a cold shower, and you can just get in it and shrivel."

Amusement and astonishment threatened to drop him to his knees. Judas, what avenging angel had wished her on him this morning? What devil incarnate made her do this to him now? He tried to hide fresh sputters of laughter, failed. If she kept on like this, he'd never survive. But he'd sure as hell go enjoying himself. And he hadn't been able to say that about himself for a good three years.

Allyn ignored him in favor of completing her thought. "In fact, you can take Sasha right in with you and bathe him, too." She eyed the tyke with some maternal worry. "Just don't douse him in cold water, okay? I don't want him sick again."

Sobering only enough to marvel anew, Jeth stared at her. How did she do that, he wondered. Go from vamp to mother without so much as a finger snap between the phases?

Talent, he decided. Plain old awesome woman talent.

"Okay, Jeth? Please? Come on." Allyn prodded him out of his reverie by poking him in the chest.

He blinked at her. "What?"

"Don't take a walk, just take a shower—with or without Sasha," she pleaded, "I mean because he's already ready for bed except for his teeth even if I didn't bathe him, but it must be safer for all of us if you stay indoors, isn't it? Don't go out there just because I'm an idiot who got you to kiss me. It—really, it won't happen again. I'll stay on my side of the room, you stay on yours, we'll be fine. I just, well, I'd never forgive myself if something happened to you—" she bit her lip, backed up into hopefully less personal territory "—that is, if anything happened to *Sasha* or you, so—"

Amazement turned to astonishment turned to wonder, to awe and back again. Even his thoughts failed to form adequately around the thing he wanted most to know. All he knew was that as of this moment, if from none of the moments before, he was lost. Now might not be the time or place, but someday, when this was over and things—her emotions—had a chance to settle, he would find her, knock properly on her door, wherever it was, and then they'd see.

And his rules about civilians be damned.

For now, he did the only thing he could: lifted Sasha out of her arms, set him on the floor and drew Allyn into a kiss that was as long and promise-filled but unerotic as he could make it—a difficult feat at the moment. Then he took Sasha's hand, led him into the bathroom and shut the door behind them.

Chapter 6

By the time Jeth and Sasha came out of the bathroom, Allyn was curled up on the outside edge of the inside bed asleep, a gate of pillows beside her along the inside edge of the bed.

Jeth's lips curled and twitched at the sight. Clearly she'd decided where Sasha would spend the night: with her. He looked at the little boy.

"I think you've got yourself a mama for as long as you need her," he said. Lord, he wished he could be the one to crawl in beside Allyn. Wished he could wrap himself around her and will away everything but the instant she wakened in his arms and turned to him. Opened to him.

Loved him.

Loved him? He gave himself a mental shake, staggered half a step back from the thought. Yeah, her kiss had lengthened his stride and practically polished his zipper from the inside, but holy hell, *loved* him? Where had that come from?

Sasha bounced in his arms, providing sudden and necessary distraction. "Mama," he agreed and gestured impatiently at the book on the bed beside Allyn. *"Chee-tat."*

Chuckling, Jeth tousled Sasha's hair, marveling at the resilience of babies. "Anyone ever tell you you've got a one-track mind, kiddo?"

Sasha wriggled, trying to get down. "Mama *chee-tat*," he insisted loudly.

Jeth put a finger to his lips. "Shh. Mama sleeping," he whispered, and stepped over to pick up the book, careful not to let his wistful fingers graze Allyn. "How about Papa *chee-tat?*"

He wasn't sure he'd gotten Sasha's accents on the word exactly right, but it didn't seem to matter. Sasha nodded enthusiastically, dug his heels into Jeth's torso, spurring his human horse forward.

"Chee-tat," he urged in his two-year-old version of Jeth's whisper. The effort hardly came close, was, in fact, louder than Sasha's normal tones. "Papapapapapapapapapa!"

Stifling laughter, Jeth covered the toddler's mouth lightly with a hand, urging silence exactly as Allyn had only a short time before. This time, however, the youngster stiffened without warning, his eyes went wide with terror, and he began to struggle in earnest to get away from Jeth. Instantly Jeth withdrew his hand, dropped into the armchair where he'd planned to read to Sasha and hugged the little boy close, instinctively pressing Sasha into his shoulder and gently rubbing the toddler's back.

As inexplicable and frightening as the sudden terror rose tears; Sasha clung to Jeth's shirt and sobbed.

"Shh," Jeth pleaded, wishing he knew what he'd done wrong. Wanting to kill whoever had terrified Sasha by doing it first—whoever had continued to do it. "It's all right, Sasha, I promise. It's all right. Ah, please, babe, I don't know what I did, but I won't do it again, I promise, just hush, please? It's okay, I promise, nobody's ever going to hurt you again, I won't let them. Shh. It's okay, it's okay.''

"Jeth?" Yawning but aware, Allyn rolled over to see the man and the baby on the other side of the room. Reflex brought her upright at the sight of Sasha's way-more-than-I-hurt-myself tears. "What happened? What's wrong?"

Feeling helpless but still attempting to soothe his charge, Jeth shook his head. "I don't know. He was getting loud. I didn't want him to wake you so I covered his mouth." He looked at her, distress evident. "This happened."

"Somebody scared him doing that before." She was on her feet and across the room in a wink. "Somebody hurt him." She dropped to her knees in front of Jeth, ran a gentle finger down Sasha's cheek, cupped the back of his head in her hand. "Here," she said, "Let me have him."

At a loss for what else to do, Jeth peeled Sasha reluctantly away, turned the little boy so he could see Allyn reaching for him. One peek was all it took; Sasha released Jeth and flung himself into Allyn's arms, wrapped his own around her neck and hung on for dear life.

"Oh, sweetheart." The sound choked involuntarily out of her, a strangled, mother-toned croon. She sat on her heels and hoisted Sasha into her lap, rocked him. "There, there, darlin'. It's all right, I'm here." She glanced at Jeth, whose anxious fingers continued to stroke Sasha's hair. "We're here," she corrected herself. "We're here, we'll take care of you. We won't let anything bad happen to you ever again." Assurance was fierce and absolute, inviolable. "I promise."

She was talking to Sasha, but it was Jeth who believed her. Nothing would happen to this child that she could prevent. And the very thought of her so willingly and brashly taking on the people who threatened Sasha quite simply and suddenly scared Jeth to death. Dear God, what had he done?

Oh, not much. Stolen a child, car jacked a woman and

created for himself an instant family, instant wife—and gotten all the unexpected but attendant emotions that went with creating the real thing: a woman he wanted to sleep with, a wife and child he'd protect to the death.

What he'd intended should be used only in the line of duty, then be disposable, had in the space of a day become vital to him. Something about her was becoming vital to him.

A quiet lament filtered through this revelation: Allyn singing one of the Childe Ballads, the Skye Boat Song, while she rocked Sasha.

The words themselves—particularly when you thought about them—were hardly comforting, but the tone, the music were. Allyn's voice was an untrained but pleasant alto, and Jeth felt himself relax even as Sasha was soothed and quieted.

Allyn finished the song. "I can't see," she whispered. "It feels like he's asleep. Is he?"

Jeth nodded. "Looks like it from here."

"Good." She sighed with relief, then looked Jeth square in the eye. "You realize I'm going to find whoever hurt him and show them the hooked end of a fishing pike, don't you?" The statement was informational, the question rhetorical and matter-of-fact.

Jeth controlled the sudden rise of bile in his throat with effort. "No." The single word was soft but emphatic. "You won't."

"Yes," Allyn said, still matter-of-fact, still disquietingly serene. "As soon as I'm sure he's absolutely safe, I will." When Jeth would have argued, she shushed him with a meaning glance at Sasha and an offered hand. "Now help me up so I can get him to bed."

"Fine." Jeth grabbed her hand in one of his and spotted Sasha with the other while he helped her to her feet. "But you're not. Uh-uh." He shook his head and put a finger to her lips when she would have argued with him. "Don't wake the baby."

She glared daggers at him but held her tongue and turned on her heel to carry Sasha to the bed and lay him down. The moment she withdrew her hands from underneath him, the toddler sat up, rubbed sleepy eyes and made a single, reproachful—if bleary-voiced—demand.

"*Chee-tat,*" he said, "Mama *chee-tat.*"

Just like that laughter returned, quiet, intimate, shared.

Jeth picked up the book from where he'd dropped it and handed it to her. "Here, Mama," he said, chuckling. "*Chee-tat.*"

Grinning, Allyn accepted the offer she'd no intention of refusing and crawled onto the inside of the bed beside Sasha, rearranged the pillows behind her. Instantly Sasha climbed into her lap. She glanced at Jeth, saw the look of longing he sent the space beside them. Found herself as unable to resist the man as she was the child she held. She patted the bed.

"Come on." She motioned her head at Jeth. "Help me get the words right."

Jeth snorted something probably unprintable under his breath but willingly stretched out beside them. The word book had no actual story to read, but there were plenty of pictures with accompanying descriptions, and Jeth and Allyn took turns reading the words while Sasha pointed out the pictures. In very short order, he began to watch first Allyn's mouth, then Jeth's when either pronounced something; a short while later he was attempting to pronounce the words after them. At every attempted word Allyn clapped and exclaimed her praise. Jeth chuckled, overwhelmed at the sight of them.

Before he yawned and nodded off into heavy sleep, Sasha had *bear, truck, car, dog, cat, house* and a few other simple words down pat, Allyn wore a smile of total delight and motherly pride, and Jeth had an ache in his heart the size of Arizona. When Allyn leaned over and brushed a good-night kiss across Sasha's brow, Jeth thought his heart might burst. When she reached over, squeezed his hand and whispered, ''Thank you,'' before sliding contentedly down beside Sasha and closing her eyes without even suggesting that Jeth leave the bed, he was sure of it.

Swallowing the lump in his throat, Jeth eased himself off the bed and reached for the blanket to cover Sasha and Allyn. Without opening her eyes she smiled sleepily at him and snuggled more comfortably around their charge. Suddenly unable to bring himself to do otherwise, Jeth unholstered his weapon and removed the clip, stripped off his shoulder holster and T-shirt and stretched out on his back beside Sasha. Allyn drew light fingers of welcome down his shoulder. He squeezed her hand and tucked that heat-inducing thing firmly beneath the sheet away from him. Then he got control of his pulse, listened to her breathing and, just when he was sure it wouldn't come, lost himself in sleep.

He woke to the sound of throttled giggling and the intermittent pressure of something that weighed not quite twenty pounds straddling him, then jouncing up and down on his chest. He opened his eyes to find Sasha's baby blues regarding his chest with disapproval.

''Ucky!'' the toddler announced decisively, and yanked at the fine smattering of hair near Jeth's nipples, trying to pull it out.

Jeth yelped and brushed Sasha's fingers away. ''Ow. Thanks a lot, twerp. Remind me to pay you the same compliment when you're my age.''

Beside them Allyn buried her head under her pillow and howled.

Jeth dragged the pillow away from her face and viewed her darkly. ''You got him to do this. This is revenge, isn't it.''

Grinning, Allyn rolled onto her side and jacked herself up on an elbow. Loosened bits of hair fell across her face, making her look tousled and inviting. Jeth thought he'd never seen anything quite so beautiful.

Nor anyone he'd wanted to touch quite so badly.

"Hey," she said cheerfully, "you're the one who kidnapped me so we'd look like a family. Well, this is the sort of thing little boys do with their fathers. Besides, it serves you right for coming to bed without a shirt on."

For the first time since he was nineteen he flushed deeply enough for it to show. "I was hot."

"Ah." Her eyes were bright with amusement.

Jeth wanted them bright with something else.

Without giving himself time to think, he bounced Sasha twice more and hefted him onto the floor. Rolled, and before Allyn knew what was happening, tipped her onto her back and pinned her beneath him. Her eyes widened, nostrils flared. The tip of her tongue flicked nervously between her teeth.

But she didn't pull away.

"Jeth, what are you—I thought you said—" She swallowed. Again her tongue curled around her teeth, slipped out to moisten her lips. Jeth bent his head and nipped it.

"Don't tease me with that thing, Allyn, I mean it."

Exactly as he'd known it would, the command left her unable to do anything else. Again that tantalizing bit of pink poked out of her mouth, withdrew, clearly begging for him to follow. On a groan of relief, he dipped his head and plunged his tongue deep into her mouth.

The tang was intense, warm and spicy, sweet and sour at once. She tasted of morning, of daydreams, of fantasy— of a night spent sleeping in the same bed with him and him wanting her, *wanting*…without allowing either of them to touch.

He drank her flavor into himself and craved more of it, more of her.

She gasped, struggled for an instant to fit herself more comfortably to him, then slid her palms along the sides of his face and opened for him, drew him into her. He deepened the kiss, and she trembled, following him, leading him; treaded heavily down the path with him to more.

She took her hands away from his face, dropped them to his shoulders, dragged them lower; breath rasped harshly in his lungs. Her fingertips on his chest seemed alive with sparks; everywhere she trailed them his skin became as something separate from him, sentient and vital on its own yet wholly part of him. It jumped and shuddered, heated and began to slicken with sweat. His ears roared with the crash of his heartbeat, with the tremble of Allyn's breath pumping life into his lungs. Even if he'd wanted to, he wouldn't have been able to think.

He slipped a thigh between hers, pressed against her and rubbed gently.

"Jeth." His name was half whimper, half moan, imploring. "Jeth, please."

He rode the call of his fingers, like autonomous entities that urged him to haul her T-shirt up her belly so they could introduce themselves to her satin textures, the muscles that tightened and undulated to his stroking, brought her arching into him.

His hand crept higher, shaping her ribs, easing upward to palm the curve of her breast. She felt so good, so good, and he wanted, needed....

"Jeth, please."

The plea was different this time, broken, almost frantic. Her fist wrapped his wrist, held his hand still.

"Jeth, wait, please stop." She struggled to disentangle herself, roll from underneath him. "Stop. Please. Sasha...we can't. I can't. I *can't*."

It took him a moment to come back from that drugged place, the euphoria of the instant, to hear her and understand. The second her *no* registered, he consigned himself to the devil for what he'd done, hoisted himself on his hands and let her go.

Reluctantly.

He swung away from her, dropped his feet over the side of the bed, sat up and dug the heels of his palms into his eyes, silently cursing himself for his reluctance. Judas, he was a cad, he was an ass, he was in more unrelieved sexual pain than he'd experienced in his life, he was—

"Jeth."

Allyn touched his back with tentative fingers, and he jerked, grabbed her hand and held it away from his skin. "Criminy, woman, what are you trying to do, kill me? You said no, now back off. I'm not made of steel."

"No." Flustered. "I mean I'm glad." A tad befuddled. "I mean I'm sorry. I mean I didn't mean... Oh, geez, Jeth I don't know what I mean."

Confused, she pulled her hand back, rubbed her wrist where his fingers had cut into it. Great. Something else to condemn himself for.

He slumped, hooked a knee onto the bed and angled toward her. Sighed at the swollen-mouthed, mussed-hair-and-clothing beauty of her, then steeled himself against a new flare of need. Reached out and tucked the loose hair hanging in front of her face behind her ear, took the wrist she gripped and chafed it to take away the stinging marks left by his fingers.

"You said no, you meant no," he told her gently. "That's all you have to mean. No explanations other than that."

She swallowed; her mouth worked. She looked into his eyes, blushed at whatever she saw there, glanced at Sasha, happily oblivious, playing on the floor with his toys. No man had ever looked at her the way Jeth looked at her. No man had ever been allowed to look at her that way.

Nor to be so physically close.

She shook her head, let the loose hair fall across her face

once more. How could she explain it so he'd understand that even though she'd only known him a day it wasn't him she rebuffed, but herself?

"I know what *no* means," she said, troubled. "I've said it before, but always at the beginning. Always before anything…happened. Before there was ever a kiss, even." She peeked, ducked away. "I mean, I guess you could say I have a kind of reputation. Not exactly ice queen, but prude, maybe. I mean, you know what it's like to get involved with the guys you work with and especially in a graduate program where they'll just figure a woman sleeps her way into the—the…*positions* she wants no matter how qualified she is."

His fingers stilled on her wrist, his mouth tightened. "Allyn, I mean it. You don't—"

She fluttered the hand he didn't hold, brushed him to silence. "Maybe. But it doesn't really matter. Explanations or not, I'm still a virgin, and no matter how much I just wanted to give that up to you, I can't, I just can't. Not in the daytime. Not with a two-year-old in the room." She looked earnestly at him. "But I really did want to. *Do* want to. And I've never wanted to with anyone else before, so maybe some other time… I mean if you're not totally turned off, or—or…anything. If—if we have time?"

Jeth gaped at her, speechless. She'd stunned him how many times in the past twenty-four hours and still he was floored by an admission she didn't have to make? When God made Allyn Meyers He'd taken *unique* to its maximum, then thrown away the mold, Jeth was sure of it.

And she wanted him.

Her eyes flicked nervously over his face, skittered away; she hunched into her shoulders, uncertain. "I wish you'd say something," she told him. "My twin sister doesn't even know I'm still, um, er, unsullied, so to speak. I mean, knowing Becky, she's probably guessed, but it's just not… Well, it's not… It's just…geez, Jeth, just say anything, will you? Tell me where we're going. Let me know you're still in the same room with me?''

"Still in the same room with you?" he repeated incredulously. He dropped her hand, huffed out a soundless *whooo,* and shook his head. "Oh, I'm definitely still in the same room with you." He pinched his arm. "Yep. Me. Right here in front of you. I'm just not sure I heard you right, that's all. And if I did, what planet are you from and…''

Allyn's face crumpled. Somehow she'd managed to do the blithering-idiot thing her mother's family was so talented at and made herself look ridiculous in front of a guy she really thought she liked. Maybe even more than liked.

Liked. Yeah, right, as though Jeth were some teenage boy and she was a sophomore with a crush. She'd been out of high school how long?

Okay, so in future she'd remember: she was a woman, he was a man. Women were from Venus and men were from Mars. Earth was like the person stuck in the middle, wondering how to explain them to each other.

She swung away from Jeth, determined to get things back on an even footing. "Look, it was stupid— I shouldn't have said— I'll take Sasha and get him dressed and we can—''

Before she could move, his arm snaked out and wrapped around her waist, and he hauled her across the bed and into his lap. Strong fingers tunneled into her hair, wrapped the back of her head and pulled her into a kiss that sizzled and scorched and curled her toes.

"Shut up," he muttered against her lips. "Don't go sensitive on me. It's not you. But since it's happened, I'm going to tell you this once. Every time you open your mouth, you say something that drives me crazy. I want you. I have rules against getting involved with civilians, but that didn't stop me this morning. I'm glad you stopped me. I'm glad you told me. Let me tell you, you deserve better than me. You deserve more.''

Allyn smiled and nuzzled his mouth, nipped his lower lip and dragged her teeth across it, self-confidence somewhat restored. ''Not if all I want is a guy with a great body to show me the ropes,'' she whispered blithely.

Then, before Jeth could stop her, she bounced out of his lap, scooped Sasha off the floor and headed for the bathroom, leaving Jeth staring after her shaking with disbelieving laughter and wondering how on earth she always seemed to regain her equilibrium at exactly the moment he was losing his.

Chapter 7

For the better part of several days, they drove a circuitous route through Pennsylvania Dutch country, then down into western Maryland and West Virginia and back north. They alternated between side roads and expressways, tourist traps and truck shops—anything that might allow them to elude trackers or, barring that, to keep a paranoid eye out for anyone following them. Jeth wanted to be sure that when they finally cut and ran for the southwest, anyone following them would be too confused to automatically do likewise.

She said little about it, but Jeth knew it bothered Allyn to realize how late she was to her family reunion and how worried her family must be about her. It bothered Jeth, too, especially knowing that Allyn's family must be searching for her by this time. But he couldn't bring himself to break the silence he'd assured her they must maintain in order to keep Sasha hidden. If, as he suspected, Sasha's captors had figured out who Allyn was, it would be a simple matter for them to find her—and subsequently Jeth and Sasha—by listening in on the receiving end of phone calls she placed.

Jeth didn't like the risk of being captured as her kidnapper, but it was one he had to take. The alternative was unthinkable.

The constant travel was hard on Sasha, who got more and more restless as his strength and color improved. Allyn hated seeing him cranky, but the fact that he was verbal, demanding and full of beans because he felt good was a source of both maternal satisfaction and maternal exasperation. Keeping him occupied was a full-time job.

Getting Jeth to stop at regular intervals so Sasha could get out and blow off steam was another.

Since the morning of their *almost,* he'd gone back and forth between seeming wholly relaxed with her and distinctly uncomfortable. There was a tension between them that Allyn found disturbing and exciting. One moment he touched her, offered her a hand up, placed one in the small of her back to guide her, dropped a kiss on her mouth, and the act was as natural, familiar and profound as breathing. The next moment she'd catch him watching her from as far away as possible, eyes hooded, face brooding, wary. At those moments she wanted to say something exasperated to him, punch him verbally in the chops—anything that would relieve the situation and tell him exactly how ridiculous were his concerns.

Whatever they might be.

And whether she believed herself or not.

Something inherent in her woman's intuition told her this was prelude, temptation—denial of an event as inevitable as time, as plain as history. If they didn't do something about this thing between them—talk about it, relieve it somehow—it would only build to explosive levels. And unless you set them carefully and purposefully, explosions, as Allyn had reason to know, usually happened when you least expected and could least afford them.

Diffusing the situation somehow seemed the wisest course, but since she'd only ever been good at avoiding man-woman-love-sex complications, she didn't know how to dissolve the one before her now.

Nor was she sure she wanted to. Ease it, yes; dispel it, no.

So she bided her time, knowing the squall before the storm would break sooner or later and determined to be ready for it.

Or as ready as she could be when she wasn't sure where the life jackets were kept.

Toward evening of what was the fourth full day of travel, when she saw Jeth staring into the middle distance and had to call his name three times before he heard, Allyn put her foot down.

"That's it," she announced when he finally gave her his attention, "I've had it. This will *not* do. You sit up on guard all night, either afraid I'll jump your bones, you'll jump mine or that some entity we haven't seen behind us since you picked up the van will sneak up and surprise us in or out of flagrante delicto. Then you drive all day because you won't—or don't—trust me behind the wheel. Blast it, Jeth, you're exhausted, Sasha's crabbin' up a storm because he's been cooped up in his seat too long—" she winced at a particularly piercing bellow from the seat behind Jeth "—I mean, in case you can't hear him—and if I don't get a bathroom soon, I won't be responsible for the consequences, and I don't care how embarrassing that sounds, we're pretending to be married, for crying out loud, and body functions are part of the package like companionable silences, but we've been *married* less than a week and you're blessed poor company when you're falling asleep at the wheel or avoiding me altogether—"

Jeth viewed her blankly, shuttled his attention to the road as though mechanized, blinked at her. She was ranting, and she knew it and didn't care. One thing the women in her family did extremely well was point out to their menfolk what was best for them and make sure the menfolk either listened or had their heads examined.

It didn't even occur to her that she'd consigned Jeth to the role of hers.

"—and I didn't sign on for this, I really didn't. I could practically kill for the use of the same bathroom for even two days in a row, I want a real meal that's not sandwiches and carrot sticks and sliced apples because they're easy, I want to call my family so we don't have even more problems than we've already got, and if you don't stop for a while and get some sleep you'll be no good to Sasha or me if the people you're running from do find us, not to mention that I will bonk you on the head and leave you for the buzzards if you don't let me at least drive for you because, you thick-skulled, bean-brained idiot, you dragged me into this and we're in it together now and I'll be jiggered if I let you screw things up for Sasha because you're tired."

She was practically shouting—if violently contained, whip-tongued, low-voiced scolding could be called shouting, that is. But she had Jeth's full and undivided attention, and that's what mattered.

Except that his lips twitched.

"Did you just call me a bean-brained idiot?" he asked, trying hard not to laugh.

It was a losing battle.

"I'm going to call you more than that if you don't pull this vehicle into the nearest rest area PDQ," Allyn said grimly, "because you're going to want to be well rested for the conversation I intend to have with you."

"Oh, no." He cringed; he couldn't help it. Laughter sputtered out of him no matter how severely he tried to marshal it. "There's more?"

"Trust me," Allyn suggested far too sweetly. "There's lots more."

Jeth tightened his jaw and cleared his throat in an attempt to stifle both the mirth and the groan that warred to escape him. For a woman who professed to know nothing about the workings of male-female relationships, she was sure driving him crazy. "You couldn't maybe give me a hint, let me prepare myself for your next, ah, outburst before it hits?"

She set her mouth in a prim line and folded her hands in her lap. "If I tell you what it is, you'll only cause an accident because you won't be able to handle it." She tapped her doorframe, a schoolmarm at the blackboard emphasizing the sums her students were to copy for homework. "Now, come on, it's getting dark. I don't know why we all of a sudden can't stop anymore. It's not like you've been in a big hurry to get where we're going—"

"That was before I knew how badly I wanted to share your bed," Jeth muttered under his breath. And therein lay not only a whole host of dangers, but the abrupt urge to run flat out for the only place he knew both Allyn and Sasha would be safe, if he forgot himself and gave in to the need to be with her the way he had the feeling she wanted him to be.

The way he was beginning to need to be wanted.

She rattled on without having heard him. "—And it's not like we're actually getting anywhere or doing anything constructive, so why don't we just pull into that rest area right there—" she pointed to the sign preceding the offramp "—and stretch and eat and hit the rest rooms and put this child to bed and get some sleep and then come up with a plan that doesn't leave us wandering the earth like the Israelites for forty years."

Jeth bit back a grin. "If we wander for forty years Sasha'll be old enough and big enough to take care of himself and we won't have to do it for him anymore," he pointed out—somewhat to his discredit.

Disgusted, Allyn stuck her nose in the air, looked out the passenger window and gave him huffy.

Last word achieved, and therefore the present skirmish

won, Jeth didn't bother to halt the grin this time. Might as well enjoy the victory—however marginal—while he could. He doubted if his all-too-willing hostage allowed many people to get the verbal better of her often.

Still, he did as Allyn requested and pulled into the rest area—mostly, he assured himself, because the risk really was minimal at the moment, Sasha was still howling in the back seat, and until she'd decided on a new tack, Allyn had been even more ticked off at him, Jeth, than she'd been the morning he'd kidnapped her. And though he couldn't decide exactly what, that meant something to him. Demonstrated something intangible but solid, offered wary insight—however reluctant he might be to define it.

There'd been a new note mixed in among the thunder she leveled at him. She was exasperated, irritated and downright infuriated, but she was truly no longer afraid of him; she was concerned for him. Every word she spoke and the ones she didn't told him how much things had changed since that first morning.

Showed him they were in this together even as she'd told him the same.

He hadn't been in anything together with anyone in a very long time. He wasn't sure he'd be very good at it now.

However, that, at the moment, was entirely beside the point Allyn made. Which point being that he was fagged beyond belief, he hadn't—as she'd said—noted anyone following them since they'd traded the Saturn for the van, he'd started this odyssey in order to get Sasha away from things that were bad for him, and constant driving was apparently not all that good for the little boy, either.

He also wanted—more than anything he'd thought possible in so short a time—to please Allyn.

Needed to please her.

In a great many more ways than one—and which other ways, he ruthlessly informed himself, he would not entertain at the moment. Because no matter what he and his body might want from her, feel for her, she was still a civilian and off-limits.

No matter how tempted he was, nor how easily temptation came to mind.

Not to mention that, truth be told, for the first time in longer than he planned to try to remember, he was downright curious about what anyone might have to talk to him about that might provoke him enough to cause an accident.

He glanced at the altogether baffling, too fascinating woman in the bucket seat beside him. If he let himself, he could take one hand off the steering wheel, reach over and touch her, be pretty darn certain that the hand bearing the rings he'd bought would reach back, that her fingers would twine with his. That she would squeeze his hand and let him know they were both alive and really here and part of this thing.

Together.

He didn't want to know why he was certain of this, only knew that he was, and that certainty was reason enough to make him risk granting her almost anything she requested, if it was within his power.

Almost anything.

He blinked at the lights coming on around the rest stop's travel center, pulled into a parking space under the trees in back, turned off the engine and puffed out a breath. Lord, he was tired.

Allyn unbuckled and slipped between the seats to Sasha. "I'll get him taken care of," she said. "Then we'll walk around a bit. Why don't you wash up and stretch out in the back of the van. We'll be right back."

Suddenly too leaden to move, he nodded and watched her go, holding on to Sasha's hand, letting him go when he protested, turning once to grin at Jeth. His gut wrenched at the sight of that half-smile, full of the devil and the siren's lure at the same time. Wisps of her hair blew from her face as if reaching for him, beckoning. Then she was chasing after Sasha, catching him to zoom him through the air like an airplane. His baby shrieks this time were of laughter, excitement—security. Young as he was, *he* knew beyond a shadow of a doubt that Mama Allyn would not drop him. Trusted that the Allyn Mama would keep him safe, hold him, love him no matter what.

Something stung abruptly behind his eyes; he blinked it away, pinched it back as though trying to hold off a sneeze. Marcy had trusted him as implicitly once. She really hadn't been so much older than Sasha when she'd died. When it happened, three years ago, she'd been ten, the youngest of his five siblings. He was fourth oldest, one of her heroes. She'd trusted someone who'd told her he was Jeth's friend, that Jeth was waiting for them. It had been Jeth's job that brought the grief to his family. His carelessness.

His silence in maintaining a cover no matter what the cost, because that was the job.

It didn't matter that he hadn't known about Marcy until it was too late. It mattered that because he'd been younger and more careless, had considered himself invincible and therefore untouchable, that it hadn't occurred to him to believe what could happen if his cover was blown. He'd thought no one but himself could be hurt if anything went wrong. Neglected to remember there was a reason for sending unattached young guys into the fray; guys with ties had too much to lose.

One undercover, one mistake and the cost…the *cost*.

Sasha, a part of him half hoped, would be payback for Marcy, redemption for him—in his eyes, if in no one else's. He doubted he'd ever forgive himself for what happened to Marcy, but to be redeemed…maybe that would be enough.

Almost enough.

Or at least better than where he still dwelled much of the time.

Ah, hell. He slid upright in his seat, pushed himself out

the van's door. He'd promised himself not to think about the past while the present required his attention. His great-grandfather used to tell him that the past was all well and good as a place from which to learn lessons one didn't want to repeat, but it was no fit place to live. You couldn't change what had happened, you could only change what would. Philosophy to live by.

He missed Grumpy.

He missed the past.

Allyn appeared with Sasha, swinging through the travel center doors and into the warm June air. Jeth's pulse picked up speed and energy at the sight of her; his belly warmed. He smiled at his "wife." There were certain things about the present that looked pretty damned good to him, too.

Sasha barreled up to him, squealing, arms outstretched, ready for Jeth to lift him and whirl him around. Laughing and out of breath, Allyn caught up to them at the same moment Jeth finished Sasha's spin and set the little boy into the crook of his arm.

"You're getting too fast for me, squirt," she told Sasha, poking him gently in the ribs.

He giggled and jiggled away from her, tucking his head into Jeth's neck and screaming happily into his makeshift father's ear. Jeth grimaced and jerked his head sideways, trying to get as far from Sasha's merry screech as he could without getting away from the child. Allyn leaned into them both and laughed at Jeth, provoked Sasha some more. Jeth found his reflection in her one green, one blue eye, wondered if the image would drag him in to drown.

And thought he would sink readily if drowning meant being held in Allyn's eyes the way he was held now.

He sucked air and tried to remember he was a man on a mission that didn't include drowning in this woman's eyes. Expelled a breath and dismissed the effort as futile.

Oh, yeah. The present was very damned good.

Very.

Simply because he wanted to, because it was the natural thing to do, he stooped and placed a lingering kiss on Allyn's mouth. She lifted a hand to the back of his neck, steadied herself against Sasha with the other and melted into Jeth, meeting his mouth move for move, touching her tongue briefly to his lips, inviting his to trace hers.

Planting a promise within the invitation that left Jeth shaken, stirred and downright uncomfortably hard.

"You did that on purpose," he murmured, drawing back.

"Did what?" she returned, with what might have been genuine puzzlement.

Jeth wasn't sure he was convinced, but convinced or not, he could play. He nuzzled her hair aside and placed his lips against her ear. "My pants are tight," he told her. "You make 'em that way. Trust me when I tell you I'm not comfortable."

She pulled away, brows beetled into a visual *huh?* "What?"

Jeth lifted a significant brow in return, canted his head slightly in the direction of his waistband.

It took her a minute to catch his drift. When she did, she blushed crimson. "Oh." She backed up two steps. "I'm sorry. I didn't mean—I mean, I was going to… Oh, blast." She gave him a look of pure feminine *you are toast,* and drew herself up, stepped forward and hoisted Sasha out of his arms. "It's your own darn fault if you're uncomfortable," she informed him primly. "You're so blessed good at this playacting or whatever this stuff between us is that I forget who we are and get drawn into it and it's not make-believe. If you'd stop thinking about it, hardness would stop happening. Not to mention that I was going to talk to you about this sex stuff later, but maybe you ought to just go in there—" she waggled her fingers in the general direction of the brick building that housed the restrooms "—and deal with yourself and we'll talk about it when you get back."

Jeth choked. He couldn't help it. She was absolutely unbelievable. Embarrassed scarlet one instant, high on her dignity and determined to make him insane the next.

"Deal with myself?" he asked, incredulous. "*Deal* with myself?"

"Absolutely," Allyn said firmly. "Deal. Cold water, chaste thoughts, whatever it is you do to handle it. Just go." She waved him away. "Go, go, go. Sasha and I will be eating yogurt and catching June bugs and fireflies somewhere over there. I'll get him tired out, and then you and I will chat."

She started away, but Jeth snorted, caught her hand and hauled her back.

"Oh, we'll chat, all right, little girl, but you may not like where the conversation goes."

Allyn's eyes sparkled at the challenge. "Little girl?" She nodded. "I see. You think you're going to get the upper hand in this discussion by going all macho stud and intimidating me into remembering you'd be the first beforehand. Well, let me point out that I've just finished seven years' study of biology, anatomy, reproduction and a lot of other things relating to life and I probably know more about some things than you'll ever know even if I do turn red when the subject comes up with you, so two can play that game."

Jeth bent and nipped her lower lip, kissed her roughly. "Two playing that game is when it's the most fun," he muttered softly. "Remember that."

Then he left her staring openmouthed after him for a change, turned on his heel and strode off to wash up.

Jeth fell asleep in the back of the van atop Allyn's sleeping bag and the folded-down seats before they had a chance to discuss anything.

Allyn brushed a lock of imaginary hair out of his face, ran the back of one finger lightly over the shock of short-cropped hair over his ear and sighed. She'd rather looked forward to the discussion they might have—on any subject at all. Looked forward, perhaps, to provoking him into kissing her again.

And again.

But at least talking wrapped in the closeness of the deepening twilight would have been good.

She moved forward between the seats, repositioned Sasha, sleeping soundly strapped into his car seat so he couldn't slide out, and used a blanket to prop him so his head was not angled too uncomfortably on his neck. Brushed his baby fine blond hair from his peaceful face. Funny how different and yet the same it felt to want to smooth both Jeth's and Sasha's faces. Strange how basic the urge in both instances, and yet how additionally, achingly complicated in Jeth's. As though she already realized how, like any maternal creature, she would eventually be forced to release Sasha to make his own way in the world regardless of how badly she wanted to protect him always, but releasing Jeth was a different matter altogether.

As though letting go of Sasha would only break off a little piece of her heart, whereas letting go of Jeth would break that sturdy thing irrevocably in two.

Crazy, perhaps, to sense those things—especially about Jeth—after four days of barely knowing him at all.

"When it happens, you'll know, just like that." In her mind's ear her mother's voice whispered, fingers snapped. *"Brannigan women are like that about their men. But it doesn't mean knowing will be easy, Lyn, because he might be too pigheaded to realize anything, so be careful not to tell him too soon...."*

Allyn sank into the driver's seat and stared into the half light at the back of the van where Jeth slept. *Tell him what, Ma?* she wondered. *I don't really know anything except that there's something about him, something I want, something....* She shook her head at the mental image of her mother. *There's something I want from him, maybe with him, but that's all I even know myself.*

Her mother smiled the gentle mother's smile Allyn knew so well and caressed the cheek of Allyn's shadow self. *Wait, my darling. You'll know. You already know. Just wait...*

For what? Allyn wondered. For what?

Frustrated, she broke off the mental conversation. Her mother was a wonderful person but not terribly helpful when it came to things she said Allyn would have to experience for herself in order to fully understand them.

Rolling her eyes and blowing a silent raspberry at herself, Allyn switched her attention away from introspection. Too much of a good thing, and all that rot, had a tendency to leave a woman casting about in her druthers for a place to beach. And merely beaching her life on some man's shore was not precisely what she had in mind when she considered having a family of her own.

Determinedly she cupped hands around her eyes to block intrusive light, peered between them through the open window into the parking lot, intent on making up stories about someone else's life rather than wishing on her own.

The night was thick with shadows cast by trees and floodlights. Toying idly with the keys Jeth had left in one of the front cup holders, she mulled over the plan she had pondered off and on all day.

Like most good plans, it was simple and direct—and probably wouldn't rank high on Jeth's list of approved options for them. It would, however, circumvent a problem they were bound to come across shortly if Allyn didn't show up to meet her family. And the fact of the matter was, her mother and her mother's sisters being the strongly independent and unconventional people they were, there *was* precedence for what Allyn was thinking. And it would be good for Sasha, who needed time to play, and it would stand Becky on her ear—

Headlights swept the van and halted impolitely to loiter on the windshield, startling her from reverie. She squinted against the glare, wishing the inconsiderate turkey behind the whiteness would turn it off.

Hoping whoever would take a hint, she flashed the van's headlights at the other vehicle. The headlights arced slightly to the side so they were no longer directly in her eyes, but remained on; a spotlight swept the van and surrounding area. Sudden fear curdled in Allyn's stomach. Someone was checking them out.

She canted a quick glance at Jeth and Sasha, decided against giving in to paranoia and waking Jeth. Probably nothing to worry about. Police, or maybe the big rig weight enforcement people or whatever they were called making a routine patrol through the rest stop to make sure everything was in order.

If that's who it is, why are they checking you out? the voice of her brain's devil's advocate wondered.

"Shut up," she mouthed at it. "Just shut up."

Naturally it didn't.

Behind the glaring light a figure alighted from the vehicle, approached the van. Hyperalert, but torn as to possible actions, Allyn retrieved the keys from the cup holder, slid the ignition key as silently as possible into the switch. Maybe whoever wasn't really approaching the van, at all. Maybe he, she or it was merely interested in something out of view behind the van. Better, in that case, if she didn't speak first, raise suspicion where there was none. Better she should act the role of yawning wife and mother whose family was simply getting a little rest before proceeding with their journey.

Best, maybe, if she were herself and bold, if she rolled up the windows and set out on a preemptive strike, stepped out of the van as if on her way to the restroom and met the possible intruder halfway, kept whoever away from the van, away from Sasha, away from Jeth.

Yeah. She drew a deep breath, twisted the keys in the ignition and rolled up the front windows. That's what she would do. Lock up the van and distract the would-be interlopers away from her family.

Just like the idiotic killdeers that built nests smack in the middle of Becky's back lawn then ran tumbling and dragging a wing whenever someone mowed, trying to draw off the tractor to keep it away from the nest.

Sucking up instinct rather than courage, Allyn eased the door open, stepped out and directly into the light. She shaded her eyes and squinted at the figure silhouetted by the glare. "Can I help you...officer, is it?"

The silhouette stepped forward, became a more solid gray shape in what appeared to be a uniform. "Pennsylvania State Troopers, ma'am. Got a report there was a disturbance back in here. Wonder if you'd heard or seen anything."

Allyn shook her head. "No, I'm sorry. We've been here for a while, but I haven't noticed anything."

The trooper nodded. "Thank you, sorry to bother you, ma'am, but we've got to check these reports out. Probably a crank call. We get them sometimes. We'll take a swing through the rest of the park, just in case. You have a good night now."

"You, too," Allyn said, and waited for the trooper to return to his vehicle, turn off the spotlight and back away before, heart pounding with relief, she turned and got into the van. Then she waited for her knees to stop shaking and the state police car to finish its circuit of the lot and leave. Switched on the engine, put it in gear and maneuvered them out of the rest area and onto the highway where she picked up the road that would take them to Ohio, where she intended to pick up good old familiar I-75 and head south toward Kentucky.

Chapter 8

When Jeth woke, it was to the feel of sunshine burning his face and heat sticking his shirt to his back.

The van was in motion.

He rocked blearily erect, bracing a hand against the rear window when the speeding vehicle bumped over a pothole, blinked trying to bring memory and surroundings into focus.

Both escaped him momentarily.

Panic settled in for an instant. He wasn't supposed to forget things so important. For him to lose time and place could mean lives. His, Sasha's...

Allyn's.

With the thought of her came a flood of fire through his blood, an elusive taste on the back of his tongue, a distinct and painful tension in his loins. He grunted and shifted to ease the discomfort, looked forward to find its source. Found Allyn in the driver's seat, Sasha still sacked out in his car seat, and memory returned—or at least the part of it that didn't need him to remember where they were now or how they'd gotten here.

He doubted there was any memory of that "how" to restore. Especially when Allyn glanced over her shoulder and saw him, smiled a little too brightly at him and began to chatter.

"Hey, how are you, good morning. I've got coffee. Did you sleep well?"

Jeth eased his way past the sleeping Sasha, sank into the passenger seat and cut right to the chase. "Where are we?" he asked darkly. "And why are you driving? I told you I didn't want anyone who drives the way you did in Balto driving this van. Too much chance of catching a cop's eye. Not to mention that I know where we're going and you don't."

Allyn sank him and his high horse with a glance. "I would if you weren't so secretive about everything 'for my own good,'" she responded tartly. "And we already caught a cop's eye last night, and I do know where we're going. We're getting you out of close encounters of the sort you never imagined when you car jacked me, and we're almost there, so shut up, drink your coffee and follow my lead."

"Touchy this morning, are we?" Jeth asked dryly. Then her comment about last night sank in. "What do you mean, we caught a cop's eye? Where was I?"

"Asleep."

"You didn't wake me?"

She looked at him.

His mouth twisted wryly. "Yeah, okay, that was a duh. So, tell me."

Allyn shrugged. "Not much to tell. Pennsylvania trooper responded to a call saying there was a disturbance in our neck of that car park, wondered if we'd noticed anything. I said no, he left, end of story."

"Allyn," Jeth said quietly, just her name, but it was an order all the same. A question.

A demand.

He traced the tip of one finger up her arm and softened demand to request. "Trust me," he suggested gently. "Tell me."

She loosed a huff of humorless laughter. "The way you trust me?" She shook her head, showed him the goose bumps, the fizzle of sensation the tip of his finger had raised on her arm. "I know you well enough to want to sleep with you," she said, "I don't know you well enough to trust you."

Jeth flinched. The truth stung the way truth has a habit of doing. He wanted her badly, more with each passing hour, but he'd forgotten how little they knew of each other. How little he'd told her despite her vested interest in the outcome. But it wasn't because he didn't trust her; it was because he needed to protect her more than trusting her allowed for.

He swallowed, withdrew his hand. "It's not that I don't trust you—" he began.

"That's good to know," Allyn said with asperity. "Because *I* trust me, and so can you."

Jeth regarded her, rankled. "Do you ever stop?"

"Not until I know what I'm doing."

The grin arrived before he could catch it. "Does that mean you don't know what you're doing right now?"

She leveled him a glance, returned her attention to the road. "I've been more sure of what I'm doing at other times in my life, yes."

"That's hardly comforting under the circumstances."

"You don't know what the circumstances are."

Jeth snorted. "Since I created them, I'm fairly certain I know exactly what they are."

"Yes, well, hmm." Allyn grimaced. "That was then. This is now."

Aggravation warred with amusement. "Come on, Lynnie, spit it out. What is it I need to know?"

"First that you don't get to call me Lynnie. Second that, um, that cop last night? Well, um…" She hesitated, made a face, plunged on. "It'd be my guess there wasn't any disturbance call at the car park and that he found exactly what he was looking for."

Jeth straightened, on guard. "What do you mean?"

Allyn stuck her tongue in her cheek, moistened her mouth. "I think.…" Another pause. "No, I'm pretty sure that when I pulled out on the highway he followed us for a way."

"How long a way?"

"Oh, um…" The shrug was in her face. "Not too far. A few miles, maybe."

Jeth relaxed.

Too soon.

"Then I think an unmarked picked us up and followed us to the Pennsylvania-Ohio border, where another car pulled out of one of those emergency-vehicle-only thingies and has been on us ever since."

The expletive was sharp and succinct. "Judas Priest, woman." Jeth viewed her, horrified. "What the hell do you mean? We're being followed, and you didn't wake me? How the hell would you know?"

"I'm not stupid?" Allyn suggested, irritated. "I've watched you for the last couple of days and have some idea what I'm looking for? The same gray car's been with us all night and it never gets closer to us, but if I speed up it does, too, so it's pretty much always the exact same distance away?"

"Tell me again about the cop," Jeth said grimly.

Allyn hunched her shoulders. "He had a spotlight. He put it on the van. I got out and gave him a good look at me. He went away. Only not too far, apparently."

"What else?"

"Nothing."

A fudge if ever Jeth had heard one. "But you decided

we had to get out of there, that you had to drive all night and bring us where for why?''

Allyn looked at him. "It was the only practical thing to do," she assured him in a rush. "We couldn't keep wandering aimlessly. We needed a direction. I think that cop has something to do with my family looking for me. I thought of a direction."

"Oh, geez." Jeth groaned. "Tell me you didn't."

Allyn braked and turned off the highway onto a side road that ran between two fenced and hilly bluegrass pastures. Aimed the van at an open weathered gate with a sign that read Welcome to Camp Cloverdale.

"What? And lie?" she asked, all astonished innocence.

Jeth made a sound somewhere between disbelief and mock despair. "Yes, lie to me." What ironic demon had wished her on him four days ago and who was it who was being kidnapped now?

"That would be wrong." She was positive, self-righteous—and full of the devil. He was hip deep in the manure she shoveled and sinking fast. "It would set a bad example for Sasha."

Jeth glanced at their charge, sent Allyn a scathing look. "He's asleep."

"There's always subliminal suggestion," Allyn pointed out—and ducked, laughing, when Jeth feigned a move in her direction. "Uh-uh, not while I'm driving." She pointed at a long, low-slung building with a sign on it that proclaimed it was the home of the camp office, dining hall, recreation room and store. "Why don't you wake Sasha and tell him we're here."

Here was the family camp she'd told Jeth she had been headed for the morning he'd so unceremoniously interrupted her plans.

Allyn parked the van outside the office, whisked her purse from between the seats, collected Sasha, winked at

Jeth and hurried inside. He might be tempted to hot-wire the van and make his escape if she left Sasha behind, but she was fairly certain he wouldn't go anywhere without the baby.

She didn't want him going anywhere without her.

She was also pretty darn sure he was about ready to wring her neck, which made it a good thing that the first people she ran into inside the building were her half-sister, Rachel, and several of her younger cousins. Rachel spotted her first.

"Allyn!" she shrieked, and flung herself across the room to nearly knock her big sister off her feet, hugging her around the waist. "You got here! We were worried. Daddy sent out the highway patrol an' called the feds an' made an APB an' everything else he could think of even though Mama said she was sure you were fine and would turn up even—eventu'lly, an' Becky said you were in trouble, then she changed her mind an' said you were having the time of your life." She looked at Allyn. "What does that mean, 'having the time of your life'? And were you? And whose little boy do you have and where did you get him from 'n' what's his name?"

Laughing, Allyn hugged her sister with her free arm while in her other arm Sasha played strange but curious, hiding his face in her neck but at the same time peeking out to see what interesting things were going on. "Well, his name's Sasha, and I guess he's mine since I sort of married his father a couple days ago."

"You got married?" asked her six-year-old cousin Libby, her aunt Helen's only child and, like her Army colonel mother, a born interrogator and meddler to her core. "Who to? Why didn't you invite us? I don't think your mother will like that. What are you doing getting married? I thought you were going to work with dolphins and whales and do something almost as interesting as my mom. Where did you get married at? When? Where is he? Does he know anything useful about karate that my mom won't teach me yet? Is that your wedding ring? Can I hold Sasha? He doesn't look like you.''

"No, he doesn't, does he," Allyn agreed dryly. "And you'll have to ask Sasha if you can hold him. He just woke up and—"

"I know, I know," Libby said, disgusted. "He doesn't know us. Come on, Rach, let's see if we can get him to come to us." She held out her hands. "Come on, Sasha," she wheedled.

"Come here, baby," Rachel crooned, opening her arms and offering Sasha the bright orange woven plastic lanyard she'd just finished. "Come meet Aunt Rachel. I'll show you all your new cousins an' stuff."

"I'll give you a vanilla wafer," Libby offered, digging a somewhat the worse for wear cookie out of her shorts pocket and upping the ante.

"I'll take him, Allyn." The oldest of Allyn's cousins, sixteen-year-old Ryan, reached out and tucked his hands under Sasha's arms, hefted the toddler away from Allyn. Sasha whimpered and scrabbled wildly at his temporary mother for a moment, but Ryan and his fourteen-year-old sister, Kate, were old hands at charming new cousins. While Ryan bounced Sasha, Kate plucked the vanilla wafer out of Libby's hand and gave it to him.

By the time Jeth entered the huge hall, Sasha was standing on one of the long tables surrounded by kids of all sizes, plying him with this, that and the other thing. By the time he reached Allyn to ask her what the devil was going on, the group of youngsters had disappeared outside, with Sasha in the midst of them visibly enjoying himself.

"My little sister and some of my cousins," Allyn offered by way of explanation before Jeth could ask.

Furious, he towed her away from the office where she'd confirmed her reservation and made arrangements to add Jeth and Sasha to it. Sitting in the van beside her and suspecting she'd brought them here was one thing, seeing what she meant by family and the numbers of children involved was quite another.

Marcy.

His sister's name echoed hollowly through him, constant reminder, omnipresent threat of the havoc this part of his life could wreak on children.

"You think we were followed, but you let Sasha go off with a bunch of your cousins?" The question was bitten out, ground to dust, thrown in her face. "You think that's safe for any of them?"

Allyn wrenched her arm away from him. There was something in his face, pain, memory, a thought he refused to share that bore later investigation. But right now was right now, time to get their stories straight.

Put him in his place while she made him understand hers.

Her eyes flashed. "I think he's safer with them than he was in your duffel bag. With them he's just another kid in the group. With you and me standing over him all the time he stands out. Where did you go to safe-house school, anyway?"

"I took classes at the FBI training center at Quantico, what about you?"

"My stepfather taught classes at the FBI training center at Quantico."

It took a second for the pronouncement to sink in, but when it did, it sank hard.

"Your stepfather—what?" He stared at her, aghast. "Your stepfather's a fed, and you didn't tell me?"

"Was a fed," Allyn corrected with a sweetness Jeth didn't buy for an instant. "You didn't ask."

"Judas, Allyn." He jammed his hands through what there was of his hair, rubbed his mouth, walked away, came back. "Once a fed, always a fed. He's got contacts. If he went to them to find you… Hell, Allyn, there are feds in on this. The feds are one of the groups who think Sasha makes a good pawn." He swung away from her. "Geez-oh-damn. I've got to get him out of here."

Allyn touched his arm, made him look at her. "No," she said quietly, "you don't."

She traced his face with a palm, drew his attention, softened his anger, stilled his instinctive urge to fight or flight to protect the young.

"Trust me, Jeth. I know you're worried about him. I am, too. That's why we had to come here. My family needs to see I'm okay. Otherwise you could be in real trouble, and Sasha will wind up back where you got him from just because Gabriel doesn't know the situation. If he knows, maybe he can help."

He knew better, but she leaned into him, pleading.

"Trust me. My family goes off and gets married for life at the drop of a hat. We know who's right for us in a heartbeat, so me meeting and marrying you a few days after graduation...truth or lie, my great-grandmother pocketed the Blarney Stone, no big deal. We can keep that cover and only tell Gabriel as much of the truth as you want. But he needs to see me in order to call off the dogs. Do you understand?"

Jeth shut his eyes against her earnestness, her naiveté. Her stepfather might have the pull to call off the dogs, but that didn't mean all the dogs would stray from the scent—nor that they'd believe anything the ex-fed told them. He, Sasha and yes, even Allyn—maybe especially Allyn, the more her safety came to mean to him personally and depending upon whether or not her stepfather had once been high enough in the bureau that someone might think she'd make a fine hostage to exchange for Sasha—were still in danger, a danger to those around them.

She was undoubtedly also right, though, too. She had family—lots of it, judging from the number of cousins who'd surrounded Sasha and the few things she'd mentioned while they drove. She was not a person whose absence would go unremarked or unmissed. He wasn't sure he believed they'd be as willing to accept him as she was, but she'd gone miles for him already, believed him—in him—when she had no reason to. The least he could do was offer her the same.

God, what a choice: rock, hard place, deep end of the ocean.

He opened his eyes, sighed. "Okay." Cupped her face in his hands, his lips twisted with doubt and capitulation. "I probably need my head examined, but okay. Wife."

"Husband," Allyn confirmed, and wrapped her hands around his wrists, stood on tiptoe to seal the pact with a kiss.

If he hadn't recognized it previously, that was the exact instant Jeth knew he was lost. Knew where any hope for his present, his future lay.

Knew he had to walk away from Allyn before he ran the risk of losing her.

So he kissed her with feeling, in early goodbye, with all of himself poured into it.

With longing and desire, but mostly with need. Need to keep her safe. Need to see her home. Need to have her home.

With him.

"Wow," Allyn murmured, dazed and drug-eyed when he lifted his head. "Wow. That was—that was—" She blinked, losing her train of thought. Lost to any world but his. "Can we do that again?"

Jeth smoothed her hair with his thumb, more than a little bemused. "Yeah," he muttered, and ran his hands down her back to pull her closer. "Yeah, definitely," he said, smiling when she came to him, sank into him, reached for him. Forgetting where they were, neglecting everything but this moment and Allyn, he bent to her.

Cherished her mouth, her being, even as she unreservedly offered herself to him.

Even if he would have, he couldn't help but take everything she tendered, give back all there was available of himself in return. Because he understood with sudden despair there was no other way to be with her.

And therein lay both salvation and destructive flame.

Somewhere outside the cocoon they wrapped around themselves, someone cleared his throat.

Twice.

Reluctantly Jeth came back to the world and started to set Allyn away. Allyn, not only disinclined to give him up but stubborn to remain where she was, as well, turned to face the intruders while drawing Jeth's arms about her shoulders and under her chin. He hesitated not at all, merely hugged her close, smiled into the hair hiding her right ear and blew seductive, pulse-bubbling warmth along her neck. She closed her eyes and pressed against him, let herself savor the heat that curled and slithered down her spine, spread indecent fingers through her belly and headed south.

"Mmm," she breathed for his ears alone—and just loudly enough for anyone who might be listening to overhear, "That's nice. Save some of that for later, would you?"

He ran his mouth along the side of her neck, found a vulnerable spot over her pulse and nipped it. "My pleasure," he muttered, "Just as soon as we can find a room and get rid of this audience."

He didn't need to see Allyn's flush when he said *audience*. He felt the heat rise in her neck and face. Felt her stiffen briefly in his arms when she remembered the crowd of onlookers—the family resemblance was remarkable and unmistakable, Jeth decided—then force herself to relax. Her jaw squared, chin rose determinedly; she settled herself more firmly into Jeth's arms.

He stifled a grin in her hair. God, she was something, wasn't she?

"Hi, Mum," she said and rubbed her ring hand blatantly

over Jeth's arm, showing off the jewelry. "This is Jeth Levoie." She gave the introduction, the view of her rings a healthy beat to sink in before she finished her announcement with a gleeful grin and a grand flourish worthy of a circus ringmaster—which, when Jeth thought about it later, was exactly what the ensuing pandemonium could have used. "My husband."

A flurry of women descended upon Allyn on the instant, pried her away from Jeth and immediately flocked around him.

Neither a murder of crows nor an unkindness of ravens had anything on a curiosity of Brannigan women—as Allyn, a Brannigan by gene pool if not surname, later informed Jeth the mobbing of the aunts, like the clustering of the aforementioned birds, was referred to by her and her sister.

They poked him and prodded him, sized him up, down and sideways and squeezed his biceps. When Jeth impassively but ironically offered to let them look at his teeth, too, the one Allyn referred to as "Oh, my God, not Aunt Twink" took him up on the offer—until her husband reached into the clique and rescued Jeth by dragging the feebly protesting Twink forcibly away and suggesting that Jeth never make an offer to a Brannigan that he wasn't ready to have at least one of them accept.

Before Jeth had a chance to file that advice under Keep Handy, the women were bearing Allyn away, and he was left to face the men alone.

Or rather make that the stepdad.

The ex-fed and sometime Quantico instructor.

Who appeared to be in amazingly good shape for a man who had to be in his middle forties.

And who also appeared to have decided he didn't like Jeth much.

While the men who'd married Allyn's aunts and her sister shook hands and introduced themselves, the man Jeth recognized by reputation as Gabriel Book stood back and observed. When he shook hands with Jeth it was not out of politeness; it was challenge, pure and simple. An unspoken, "Are you as good as you think you are, boy?" A wordless, "What makes you think you deserve to marry my daughter?"

A nonverbal warning that stated, clear as glass, "I don't know who you think you've fooled, but I've got your number. If you hurt her I will dial it, bet on it."

The grin Jeth fed Allyn's stepfather was wide and ferocious, accepted the challenge and informed the ex-fed, "You'll try," even as he squeezed Gabriel's hand hard, returning what he was given. It was a definite bunch of macho-posturing hooey, but hey, they were hard-nosed macho guys; it was what they did.

"Oh, dear," Allyn's mother, Alice, sighed, spotting the exchange—or lack thereof. "For such an incredible man, Gabriel really is a turkey sometimes."

"I don't see Jeth behaving better," Allyn observed.

"He's yummy," Becky said. "Where did you find him?"

"Hey, drool over your own guy." Allyn covered her sister's eyes and turned Becky so she was no longer salivating over Jeth, but appreciating the blond, blue-eyed, none-too-shabby six-foot-two-inch hunk she'd married two days after their high school graduation. "And I didn't find him, he found me. Car jacked me, actually—well sort of," she amended quickly, mindful of the truth. "Not exactly. Maybe heart-jacked me is a better phrase. Him and Sasha." She turned to her mother. "Have you met Sasha? He's with Rachel and Libby and the rest of the kids. Isn't he beautiful? And such a sweetheart. He calls me Mama already."

Alice nodded. "That's how we knew you were here." She glanced at Jeth, back at her daughter. "He wasn't at your graduation. You've never mentioned him before. How long have you known him?"

Allyn hesitated. Now that it came down to it, lying to her mother was more difficult than she'd imagined it would be. She'd never actually done it to Alice's face before. Shaded the truth, hedged, yes, but she'd never told her mother an outright lie. Something to do with wanting to be different from Becky, who'd spent a goodly portion of her high school career sneaking around with Michael and lying to their mother about it.

Standing in Jeth's arms, the lies came naturally—mostly because, she realized in a panicked flash, when she was with Jeth, the lies didn't exactly feel like *lies*. But here, in front of her mother, her sister, her aunts, deception felt like cowardice, like a path she wasn't sure how to take. She blurted the truth because, in the end, it was easiest.

"We met Sunday morning. In Baltimore on my way out of town. I helped him and Sasha out of a jam. We spent the day together, and—I don't know." She shrugged helplessly, gave the waiting women a sheepish grin. "Something was right. We bought the rings and got married Sunday afternoon. Then we got rid of the Saturn and picked up Jeth's van, spent a couple of days in Pennsylvania Dutch country and came here."

There, she thought, trying to convince herself she'd done well. One tiny piece of perjury amid the absolute truth.

"Instant wife, instant family?" her mother asked gently, understanding more than Allyn would have expected about her daughter's latest druthers.

"Add water and stir," Allyn concurred, distracted, unintentionally telling and altogether greedy eyes focused once more on Jeth.

He turned his head and caught her staring, locked gazes with her. His smile was slow and frank, an invitation to touch, to play.

To learn.

Allyn swallowed the impact of that proposition, breathed hard once in and out, tore her attention away. He didn't mean it, she reminded herself. Yes, they were attracted to each other, but this was an act, a skit they performed in front of a live audience. Nothing more.

Nothing more.

"What about your life, your career, Lynnie? You just got your doctorate. Where are you going? Where will you live? What about you?"

Allyn's attention returned to earth with a crash amid her mother's currently unanswerable questions. "I don't know yet, Ma," she said truthfully. "We're still working that part out. But look at him, Mum. Look at him. You always said I'd know. Well, I do, Ma. I *know*."

And frightening as it was to admit, that was truth, too. She did know. Her body knew.

Her heart knew and pounded with the weight of the knowledge.

And that was the worst thing of all. Because except for the part where she and Jeth weren't really married, whatever else Allyn projected about him was true.

She didn't need to act to look at him softly, to play blushing newlywed games with him. To pretend anything at all.

She gave her mother a beseeching look. "I'm sorry you weren't there, but—"

Alice snorted and waved a dismissive hand at her. "Weddings in this family are a good deal more trouble than they're worth. Becky eloped with Michael after going with him for four years, I eloped with Gabriel after knowing him six weeks, you eloped with Jeth the day you met him. That's not the point. What I care about is your happiness. That's all. It's sudden. It's not like you—well, that is, except when you decided to become a marine biologist in the first place. That was pretty unexpected, especially since no one even knew you were interested in the subject in the first place, but—"

"What she's trying to say," Becky interrupted, grinning,

"is that you have her blessing with reservations if you want it, but since you probably don't want the reservations, you might not want the blessing—"

"Oh, heck," her aunt Helen cut in, shushing Becky, "your mother's a worrywart. You're married. If you made a mistake, you'll find out in due course and you'll handle it. In the meantime enjoy the ride—"

"—and that body of his," Aunt Twink interrupted.

"And don't let anybody monger disasters upon you just because you moved too fast without a thought for tomorrow," Aunt Edith admonished.

"Or let women with holes in their heads advise you of anything," Aunt Grace, who was a mere three years older than her niece and the youngest of her aunts, said darkly. "Because they don't know anything of any particular use to you at the moment—"

"—even though we are older and supposedly wiser," Aunt Meg added.

"Definitely wiser," Aunt Sam, who hated her given name Samantha, informed Meg firmly.

"And even though we love you to bits," her grandmother, Julia Block Brannigan, finished.

All of which dizzying advice cum backhanded chiding made Allyn feel oh-so-much better about the entire lying part of the situation. In fact, the whole ridiculous sequence of statements exonerated her conscience entirely. Heck, in a crowd like this, a little truth-hedging of this sort was like storytelling of the finest kind, only real. The great-grandmother who'd left Ireland with the Blarney Stone up her sleeve and spent the rest of her life lying about her age would be proud of Allyn.

So, fortified with this knowledge, Allyn forgot about her conscience entirely and settled in to answering all the questions thrown at her about Jeth and Sasha, whether she knew the answers or not. After a bit the men rejoined them to add their kibitzing to the mix, then the children returned with an exhausted but giggling Sasha, who seemed to have enjoyed meeting the cousins.

By the time Allyn and Jeth finally reached the cabin set aside for them near the rest of the family's cabins, Becky had decided Sasha would spend the night with her since Allyn and Jeth were still on their honeymoon; Helen had gone ahead and found sheets and pillowcases and made up the bed; Twink, Grace, Edith, Sam and Meg had rounded up candles, roses, an ice bucket, some fresh strawberries and a bottle of champagne; and Alice and Grandma Julia had arranged for an intimate dinner for two to be delivered to Allyn and Jeth at seven.

Then they packed up Sasha, his diapers, his favorite book and toys and some clothes and whisked him away, leaving Allyn breathless and quite alone to spend the day with Jeth.

Chapter 9

Dumped, as it were, ceremoniously at the foot of the marriage bed as though by some mountain clan custom, trapped behind draped windows and a locked door while the chortling Brannigan revelers sang an impromptu chorus of "Good night, Irene" mostly in altos and sopranos—and no, it didn't matter that it was only late morning—Jeth and Allyn could do little but stare at each other, gawping and nonplussed.

"Good God," Jeth said profoundly. "You thought it'd be good to bring Sasha into this?"

Allyn sent him a weak grin. "They mean well?" she asked. "Or at least," she amended, and the grin went wide with mischief, "as well as they can when they weren't taught reverence is a virtue."

"I can believe that," Jeth muttered. Then, "Are they always like this?"

"Yeah." She shrugged. "Pretty much ever since I've known them, anyway. And my grandmother says they only get worse with age. And since one of my great-grandmothers is a hundred and something and still going strong, and the other is ninety-five or -six and still jetting all over the world, I believe her. She thinks irreverence keeps them healthy.''

''Ah,'' Jeth said. What else could he say?

He turned to survey the room. The drapes were plaid, sturdy and dark but not overwhelming. There was a set of bunk beds on one wall, a double bed and a crib; a mismatched but utilitarian table and chairs sat atop a large braided rug near the windows. Two twin-size futons doubled as chairs in front of a fireplace, and a rough armoire arrangement acted as closet and chest of drawers. At the back of the cabin a door opened into a three-quarter bath of dubious vintage.

The shower was a luxury, Allyn told him, as most of the camp's visitors made use of the modern showers off the main hall. There were modern restroom facilities up there, too, although many of the cabins had toilets. Some of the more isolated cabins made use of outhouses and outdoor showers and—

In short, Allyn blathered. She knew she was blathering, but self-consciousness had a habit of bringing that out in her. And she was, to say the least, self-conscious. It was one thing to spout invitations in front of people where nothing could happen to the man who lit one's fire, quite another to find oneself tucked into a darkened room with him by one's family, wondering how to get out of the awkward situation and still keep her dignity intact.

''We need to talk about sex,'' she blurted out of nowhere—and buried her face in her hands, scarlet to the roots of her hair.

Well, that simplified that. Obviously there was no way she was going to keep her dignity intact.

A strangled sound reached her ears. She peeked between her fingers to see Jeth struggling not to laugh.

"Do we," he said mildly. Not a question, more a statement of curiosity.

"No." She waffled. "Yes." She glared at him. "Quit laughing at me."

His lips twitched. "But you're funny."

"I don't want to be funny, I want to handle this—you—"

He choked on amusement, and her glower increased with the redness of her throat.

"That's not what I meant, and you know it. I meant deal with this *thing* that keeps happening between us, because I mean it's really started to get to me, and they're off somewhere expecting.... God knows what they're expecting, they're just lunatics, and you're no help because I look at you and my brain rattles even though I'm a more than reasonably intelligent woman—at least according to my academic records—and then we both say no sex, then one of us winds up kissing the other and everything inside me melts and I really want to understand why, and they think we're on our honeymoon and they're giving us time alone to...well, you know, be together, and I want and I don't want and it just seems really awkward to have your mother and her sisters and *their* mother kind of setting you up and saying have at it especially when it's all a lie and—"

"Allyn." A gentle command.

"—I'm really confused right now, but I'm not other times and that just makes no sense because even though I've never done it I know what goes where and why and really, it's just nature, isn't it? But then they come along and I want to make love with you, Jeth, but it's so embarrassing knowing they're lying in wait with their nudge-nudge, wink-wink, say-no-more-say-no-more and their whoo-hoo and their so-what-do-you-think and I just—"

"Allyn." Still gentle but more insistent this time; he stepped close, and she ducked away. He turned her face toward him with a finger under her chin, bent his head and kissed her. "Shut up and let me love you."

Shouldn't, shouldn't, shouldn't, sang the wise man inside his head.

Jeth wasn't in the mood for either wisdom or *shouldn't.* He was in the mood to hold Allyn Meyers close and relieve her embarrassment, her curiosity, her obvious need.

To give her himself—what there was of him to give— before he left her safely with her family and slipped away with Sasha without telling her goodbye.

He laved her mouth open with his tongue, made a foray between her lips. Whispered against them, "I want to love you, Allyn. Love me. Let me."

"Okay," she agreed readily, blurrily, dissolving against him. "If you're sure. If you want to. If it's not too much bother."

He buried his face in her neck on a laugh that was mostly a groan. Slid his hands down her waist and over her rump to bring her tight against the painful stiffness hidden behind his zipper.

"I want," he assured her. "Judas, do I. And it's definitely no bother, trust me."

"Oh," she said breathless. She moved her belly against him. "Oh. That feels—is that what it feels like? Like your jeans are too tight?"

Jeth shut his eyes and grimaced with pleasure and with strain. "My jeans *are* too tight. And the more you do that the tighter and more uncomfortable they're getting."

"Oh." She put space between them. "I'm sorry. I didn't mean—I mean, should I—should we—should one of us…loosen them?"

Jeth grinned. "That'd help, yeah, and we'll get to it eventually. We've got the whole day, remember? No rush." He pressed himself into the hollow of her thighs once more, bent his head and nuzzled the skin beneath her ear. "This is one of those things where anticipation is part of the plea-sure—even when it's, um, cramped anticipation.''

"That's what, um— Oh!" She gasped and liquefied against him when his teeth grazed a particularly sensitive spot, rested her hands on his biceps to steady herself. "That's what the novels say, but, um— Oh, geez, Jeth!" She arched into him, tilted her head to grant him better access to her neck and throat. "What are you doing? That feels—that feels—I can't believe how that feels. I can feel that everywhere, *every*—" She moaned when he pulled her hips against him and rubbed. "—everywhere, even in my breasts, and my stomach feels weird, is it supposed to feel weird? Are my breasts supposed to ache? Oh, please, Jeth, please. Touch me. *Do* something."

He smiled against her throat, amused, delighted, awed by her willingness to tell him what she felt. "Like this?"

He traced his hands lightly up her sides, let his thumbs graze the outside of her breasts, up and around to her col-larbone; outlined the V neck of her camisole to the upper edges of her breasts; ran his thumbs back up and over her collarbone, shaping, teasing…seducing. His tongue and mouth followed everywhere his fingers led, tasted….

Heat.

He locked an arm around her waist when she inhaled sharply and arched against him when his tongue dipped behind her camisole and into the valley between her breasts. Her moans were becoming whimpers of encour-agement, her movements ineptly designed to bring him into greater contact with her breasts, her skin. She tried to slip away from him to get rid of her top. He locked his hands with hers and refused to let her.

"Slow down, Allyn. There's no hurry. Trust me."

"I do. I can't…ooh…" Breath sobbed out of her. "It's too hot for clothes, Jeth, please, I want it off, I need it off."

"Wait," he ordered gently. "We'll get there, I promise. Just let me make this good for you, Lynnie. Let me…."

She rose against him, pulled his head to her chest, offering herself to him. "It's good already, Jeth. I don't know if I can stand it getting much better."

"Trust me," he whispered, picked her up and carried her to the double bed, settled her on it and came down beside her. "It's going to get a lot better, and you'll be able to stand it."

"Okay," she agreed breathlessly. "I'll try." She undulated to fit herself more tightly to him, stretched to give him greater access for the explorations that were making her skin tingle, her body wet, the secret place between her thighs ache. "Is this the time we should exchange medical histories?" she gasped. "I mean it's not like we had blood tests before the non-wedding or anything."

"I'm clean," Jeth murmured, smoothing the sweat off her chest with his lips. "I get tested every six months. I haven't been active in over a year."

"Bully for you," Allyn mumbled—a little churlishly. She had, after all, saved herself for *him*—whoever he might have been.

Jeth laughed and raised his head, looked at her, eyes gleaming. "What, you know me four days and you're jealous?"

"Well…" She considered him for a minute. "Yeah. If I could wait, so could you."

He grinned, showing no repentance. "You are the most contrary woman I have ever known. I had a weak moment or two. I had no idea you'd be coming along. Sue me."

"Maybe later," she sighed, laced her fingers behind his neck and pulled him into the most mind-numbing kiss he'd ever received. Pushed him away when he was sure he was drowning. Ran her hands restlessly over his chest and made another pronouncement. "I got stuck on a needle when we were cleaning a beach 'bout eight months ago. Two tests, both clean for everything."

"Good." He was nearly beyond caring.

She was just getting started. "Do you have any condoms with you?"

He nuzzled her neck, her throat, slipped to her belly and nibbled his way beneath her camisole to graze her skin. "What?"

"Condoms." The muscles of her stomach contracted, her hands gripped the bedspread, pushed her up to meet his mouth. "Do you have some?"

"Not with me," he murmured—then, realizing what he'd said, he yanked himself away from her and sat up with an oath. "No. Damn. I don't. Judas. How stupid can I be? I can't protect you."

Allyn followed him up, slid her hands under his T-shirt and up his back. "You don't have to protect me."

"Yeah," he said flatly, pulling her arms around his waist and twisting to look her in the eye. "I do."

"No," she told him firmly. "You don't." She kissed him silent when he would have protested again. "I can protect myself. My mother got pregnant with Becky and me when she was in high school, Becky thought she was pregnant before she graduated high school. I couldn't make my mother smarten up because I didn't exist at the time— not to mention I wouldn't be here now if she had—and Becky wouldn't use the condoms I went to the school infirmary and got for her. I've never used any, but that doesn't mean I don't go prepared."

Jeth's grin was slow, reluctant and appreciative. He relaxed slightly in her embrace, rubbed the side of his head against her cheek. "A Girl Scout?"

She kissed his ear. "Uh-uh. Eyewitness to possible disaster."

He chuckled, twisted and pushed her onto the bed with a deep, concentrated kiss. "Where are they?"

"Huh?" Her turn to be foggy and vague, to reach out and try to drag him back. "Oh, um, in the van. In one of he small end pockets of my big duffel bag. With my extra underwear.''

"Panty raid." Jeth leered at her. "Never been on one of those.''

Allyn rolled her eyes. "Don't get carried away. It's just practical cotton stuff, nothing exciting.''

"Anything you wear is plenty exciting,'' Jeth muttered under his breath.

"What?''

"Nothing." He leaned down and kissed her senseless once more. "Save my place. I'll be right back.''

He left at speed, winking at her as he went.

When he was gone, Allyn sat up and loosened her hair, pulled off her clothes and sat on the edge of the bed, trying to decide how to be her most provocative. Her skin felt moist and tingly, puckered and goose-bumped with self-consciousness. She wrapped her arms about herself and drew up her knees. It wasn't as easy to be naked and waiting as she'd thought—or she wasn't as brave as she'd hoped, nor as ready to take this step as she'd imagined. Biting her lips, she pulled her camisole and underwear on. Yawned and decided against the underwear. Crawled under the sheets and decided against the camisole, but jerked it on before she even got it off.

Wondered distractedly if the way women were shown seducing men in film and on television really worked. Decided to practice.

Legs akimbo, she tried draping herself seductively across the bed with the sheets positioned just so. She realized she had no idea what seductive looked like when she was doing it because she'd never had any use for the deliberately provocative look nor ever once figured out what it was men supposedly found so almighty sexy about the pouty lips and flicking tongue things women on TV and in the movies did to lure and tease them. Then she tried to determine what it

was Jeth found sexy about her, wondered if there was an
way she could build on that.

Decided she was overthinking the situation the way she'
sometimes overthought her exams, so she shut her eyes an
tried to let herself float in that place where nothing existe
but the moment, the feeling, the act.

She'd read love scenes, experienced the gut-deep wrenc
the words pulled out of her, but she wasn't sure she be
lieved reality could be shaded like words, that making lov
with the proper man could be quite so...intense that som
women fainted or felt transported to an altered state.

That making love with the right man would change you
life and your outlook, make you part of each other no ma
ter how far apart you later became, how much distance s
between you.

It made Allyn consider her choices. Made her wonder i
she was making the right one. Or if she was only fallin
under the spell of the moment—the intense and immediat
desire for a family of her own that had so unceremoniousl
been fulfilled....

The enforced closeness of the past several days wit
Jeth...

The hostage syndrome that Gabriel occasionally talke
about where she, the hostage, fell in love with her capto
because he'd brought her to depend upon him, made he
part of his plans and his life.

Made her trust him for her well-being.

In some odd way trusted her for his.

Suddenly miserable with indecision, Allyn looked to
ward the door through which Jeth would soon return, the
buried her face in her pillow. She couldn't think. She didn'
want to think.

She wanted to go on pretending to be Sasha's mothe
and Jeth's wife.

She wanted to be both.

But she wanted to be sure she wanted to be both for th

right reasons and not simply because Jeth inflamed her body, knocked her heart senseless and had kept her in close contact with him—albeit partially by her own choice—for four days.

Oh, hellfire and salvation. She just wanted to *be*.

Marine biologist, mother, wife...

Exhausted from a long night's drive, an interminable morning's grilling by her family and way too much Jeth to think and dream about, Allyn couldn't help herself. She fell asleep.

Jeth would have sworn he hadn't been gone that long.

Bemused and more than a little frustrated, Jeth stared at Allyn's one exposed long leg and bare hip, the hiked-up and tight-stretched camisole that left almost nothing to his imagination.

His groin tautened at even the suggestion of imagination. He stifled a groan and crushed the box of condoms in his fist. Without her underwear and shorts, and not quite modestly covered by her shirt and the sheet, she presented the most delectable picture of innocence and titillation he'd ever seen; he wanted to immerse himself in the portrait, to lose himself in her, avail himself of her secrets—discover what made her tick at the same time that he discovered what would make her gasp and scream and faint with pleasure.

In short, he wanted a lot; more, he knew, than he was ready to admit, more than could possibly be good for either Allyn or him—although he had a feeling getting involved with Allyn would be a lot better for him than it could ever be for her. Where he was darkness, she was light; her presence could heat the world in which he dwelled; her absence...

He didn't want to consider what her absence might mean. It'd be so much easier to leave her if he didn't know.

Judas. His mouth twisted with self-deprecating laughter.

How had he gotten from autonomy to here? To feel that *now* might stretch into forever in a blink, in a caress he knew without doubt she would return.

Laughter faded. Of their own volition his fingers stretched out, hovered above her hip. He pulled them back. No, he couldn't. He shouldn't. Her slumber gave him an unexpected out, a moment to think clearly, to let sanity reign. He should take it.

He let his gaze rove her body again, take in more than the exposed skin, the surface offer of sexual relief. This was Allyn; she believed in him without reason, helped him because she chose to, offered herself to him the way she had to no other man. Knowing that, he didn't want to be sane. He wanted to be crazy and worry about the consequences later.

But of course there was that niggling *but...*

But his shorts were already three sizes too small from the mere taste of her mouth on his tongue. But if he got into bed with her now, it would be days, weeks, months before he'd want to get out again. He didn't have that kind of time. Sasha didn't have that kind of time. And because she was important enough to him for Sasha's enemies to use her against him—Allyn didn't have that kind of time either.

Hell, it was too complicated. Go, stay... The answers were vague and full of negatives from all angles. Take her with him, leave her behind. Either way was fraught with dangers—for her, for him and most especially for Sasha.

His original intent had simply been to get them all to Tucson where he'd once been certain his home office could help him sort out Sasha's safety, would make sure the toddler was not returned to the men who would do him irreparable harm. Unfortunately, Jeth was no longer certain he could trust his home office any further than he trusted the guys with whom he'd worked in Baltimore. There were simply too many things that didn't add up about this whole assignment—now that he was no longer too bent on self-destruction and self-loathing to realize it. Hell, if it hadn't been for Marcy....

Awareness almost breached the fringes of consciousness before fading. There was something about this that seemed almost familiar, too *similar* to what had happened three years ago, but damned if he could place it. Too focused on the moment instead of on the things that made it up. That's what his father would tell him. And damned if his father didn't have the gall to be right more often than not.

He looked at Allyn and his body reacted, his emotions sputtered alive. He knew without doubt that he was missing something obvious about this whole thing, something he should see.

Something he *had* to see—besides Allyn.

Judas, what had he done? What could he do?

He could walk away from Allyn's bed, that was one thing. Because every instinct he possessed warned him that if he didn't leave Allyn the hell alone, he'd be too distracted by loving and wanting to love her again and again to protect anyone, especially her and Sasha. And that kind of derangement was something he could absolutely not allow. Because more than anything on this earth he wanted his make-believe family to survive.

He didn't think he'd be able to forgive himself if they didn't.

The unexpected image of a box of gelatin labeled Instant Family floated through his mind with the directions, "Add water and stir." In spite of himself, he grinned. He doubted Allyn could have been reconstituted from a package of anything that only required the addition of water; someone had gone well overboard on the spice with her—which was just fine with a guy who'd grown up thinking of jabañeros as a mild pepper.

He looked at her sleeping figure—her loosened and unruly hair, her naked hip and flank, the ripe curve of her breast—with longing. So much there to save a man, so much heart to redeem him. What could a man do when a woman who affected him the way Allyn did told him she'd never done that before but wanted to with him?

He could either move in and let her get some practice, or he could do the gentlemanly thing, knowing that there had to be someone better and more deserving of her out there than him, and back off.

Even if backing off to make sure she saved herself for someone who actually deserved her nearly killed him.

At the riding stables on the other side of the camp, Gabriel and Alice Book walked around the ring on either side of a wide-eyed Sasha, holding him atop a small, gray pony.

"He's wrong, Alice, I know it."

"Who, Jeth?"

He nodded.

"Not to Allyn." She pursed her lips thoughtfully. "But I do think she's lying to us about something—or anyway, not quite telling us the truth."

"I don't like him," Gabriel said flatly. "If she wasn't married to him, I'd tell him to get the hell away from her."

Alice touched her husband's hand lightly, motioned her head at Sasha. "Little pitchers," she suggested. Then, "Allyn is a big girl, dear. Not much we can do about her choices anymore—if there was ever anything I could do about them."

"Well, I don't get it. Why'd she get married so fast? Why didn't she at least call and tell us? What happened with school and career and all the stuff she's been working for from the day I met her? This is not like her. She doesn't make decisions this fast. Why did she suddenly show up here after I called out the law? Do we know what this guy does for a living? Did she—"

"Gabriel." Alice shushed him with a finger to his lips. "For one thing, it's exactly like her to make decisions this fast. How many times did we hear from someone or other that if it hadn't been for her quick thinking a classmate would have drowned on a botched dive, a research ship might have sunk in a squall, a beached whale or dolphin wouldn't have made it. She has a gift, love. She uses it. You taught her to use it.''

She smiled softly at her husband, a promise, a thank-you. ''And that's not to mention that she comes by the ability to fall in love at the drop of a hat honestly, too. I hadn't known you a week before I knew I loved you. And she does love him, Gabriel, make no mistake. *She* might not be sure how much she loves him yet, but I can see it in her face. It's the forever kind. Lock, stock and bring on the kids. Including this little bit of baggage—'' she ruffled Sasha's hair lovingly ''—that I'm not sure even belongs to him. But he'd lay down his life for Sasha, I'm sure of that, Gabriel, and for Allyn, too. Maybe especially for Allyn.''

''Oh, good,'' said Gabriel darkly. ''We need another guy in this family who'd lay down his life for his wife—not to mention another woman who'd bust him upside the head rather than let him do it. That's a hell—heck of a reference, suggesting, as it does, that there might actually be some *reason* for Jeth to need to think about dying to protect Allyn or Sasha. And just because you think he's willing to die for them doesn't make him a right guy.''

''Yes, dear,'' Alice murmured, not quite laughing at her fuming husband.

''Stand-up, maybe,'' Gabriel muttered, glaring at her. ''But not *right*.''

''Anything you say, dear,'' Alice agreed, eyes gleaming.

Predicting that his wife would sing quite another tune later when they were alone, Gabriel lifted Sasha out of the saddle and stalked out of the pony enclosure, telling the little boy that his new grandma was bonkers and that if Sasha knew anything about anything he'd listen to Grandpa first, foremost and always, because *this* grandpa would never steer him wrong.

Grinning, Alice followed man and child at a discreet distance, greatly looking forward to Gabriel's predictions about "later when they were alone."

Chapter 10

As though some demon of chance had placed them there for this very bit of irony to take place, Allyn spotted the crushed box of condoms on the table beside the bed the moment she opened her eyes.

Guilt set in immediately—guilt, that is, complicated by regret, chagrin and the gut-sinking realization that, once again, she would be the one to call a halt to a moment that had not quite arrived.

A moment, that, because she'd had too much time to think about it, she couldn't think of any responsible reason to allow.

Eyes on that accusing container resting too near her pillow, she slid upright in the bed and pushed her hair out of her face, rearranged and pulled up the cotton knit camisole that had stretched down to fully expose one breast at the neckline.

"Don't cover up on my account."

From the depths of the shadows near the windows, Jeth's voice was thick and gravelly, raw with hunger and restraint.

Heat climbed from her belly upward through her chest, her neck, her face at the sound; Allyn shrank into the pillows and yanked up the sheet, fisted it in front of her. "Geez, Jeth, you startled me. I didn't know you were there."

His chuckle was harsh and uncomfortable. "I'm here." He indicated the nearby table. "Your aunts stopped by. They brought more strawberries and champagne, and enough romantic dinner to feed an army. Which one was it—Helen, the Colonel?—said honeymooning was hungry work. She wanted to make sure we kept our strength up in order to enjoy it to the fullest without having to interrupt what we were doing. I personally think they were just doing recon so they could give some sort of report to your mother and Gabriel. He doesn't like me much, in case you didn't know."

Allyn moistened her mouth, let the taste of indignation relieve some of her embarrassment. "Of course he likes you," she assured him firmly. "You're with me. He has to like you. Whatever gave you the idea he doesn't?"

"He did." Jeth shrugged, rose to stalk the room. "In so many words. And if he hadn't, one of your aunts took me aside when I stopped to see Sasha while I was out jogging. She said, and I quote, 'He doesn't like you, but don't pay any attention to him, he'll come around eventually, it's not like he was exactly the whole-truth-and-nothing-but kind of guy when he met Alice, after all,' unquote." He looked at her hard. "What the hell does that mean?"

"I'm not sure," Allyn said—not quite truthfully. She didn't know for certain, but she could guess. And her guess would be that her mother's family's tendency toward Irish feyness coupled with an uncanny ability to read between the lines had led them all straight down the garden path to a point just shy of the facts. "They say things like that a lot. It's—really, it's best not to pay any attention to them."

Her turn to twist her lips and shrug. "They always say what they mean, they just hardly ever explain what that *is*."

"Ah, well," Jeth said dryly. "I guess that clears that up, then, doesn't it? It also shows me where you come by the tendency to speak your mind as though I could possibly have any idea what you're talking about."

"You do *not* have to be sarcastic about my family," Allyn snapped, preferring to take offense rather than return to remembering she was bottom-half naked and in bed with a box of condoms and the man who lit her up from the inside out close at hand. "They've been perfectly nice to you. I mean, they have their doubts about you, but they relieved you of your *son* anyway and sent you to shack up with me, so what more could you ask?"

Jeth eyed her, lips twitching. "To shack up with you? In a real shack like this one?" He shook his head, only slightly skeptical. "Yeah, well, I suppose there's something sort of poetically cockeyed enough about it that would appeal to what I've seen of your family."

"You...oh!" Allyn tilted her nose and turned her back on him, giving him huffy. "You...*man*."

Jeth paused beside the bed where she either had to look at him or twist away again and swept her a sardonic bow. "I am that." He bent, retrieved her panties from the floor where she'd left them. "And I'd take you calling me a man as a compliment except I don't think you meant it as one." He showed her the teal cotton, hip-cresting, French-cut briefs. "Are these yours?"

Reddening, Allyn made a grab for them. "Give them to me."

Ignoring her, Jeth held them up and looked at them. "Practical but very sexy," he told her. He tucked them into the pocket of his T-shirt. "Definite souvenir material."

Allyn was almost off the bed before she remembered her state of undress. "You bastard."

Jeth gave her mock-serious and thoughtful. "Not according to the man my mother's married to. No, he's pretty certain I'm legitimate—especially since I didn't come along until five years after he married Mom.''

"Fine." Furious, she wrapped the top sheet around herself like a sari, crawled awkwardly off the bed and headed, with as much dignity as possible, for the armoire. "Just fine. Keep 'em. I'll get another pair.''

"From where?" Jeth viewed her innocently, enjoying himself to the hilt. He undoubtedly would pay for teasing her in the long run, but damn, while it lasted it was fun. "The van's half a mile from here, and I don't believe we brought much of your luggage in.''

Caught in mid hobble, Allyn paused. Her hands jerked into fists at her sides, and a small, frustrated, "Ergh" escaped her. Jeth was fairly certain the look she sent him would have scalped him if it was any sharper.

"Fine," she said grimly. She spun and waddled around the bed. Used her toes to pick up her discarded shorts and hike them into her hand. "I'll go commando." She eyed him ominously when he would have said something smart to that announcement. "Wait," she advised him with steely gentleness. "You will not get the better of me, Jeth Levoie.''

Then she turned and headed for the bathroom.

Jeth grinned. "Should I cringe now or save it for later?" he asked.

She slanted him a killing glance but shut the door without a word. A moment later she opened it again and came out, wadding up the sheet and looking a little uncomfortable as she strode-sidestepped across the room to dump the linen on the bed. Jeth choked back laughter. She was not, he guessed, used to going without her underwear.

Out of the blue he wondered what she'd think of wearing thong undies, decided the very idea, especially coming from him, would leave her both scarlet and appalled—not to mention ready to commit mayhem upon his person.

He splayed his arms wide from his sides. "If you want them, come and get them," he urged.

"Fiend," she muttered, crossed to him, snatched her panties out of his pocket and swung away.

He playfully snagged her wrist to haul her around; something vulnerable yet unreadable flashed in her eyes, and Jeth would have sworn that the air around her crackled with tension and then she growled, "Don't."

"Touchy," he suggested gently, but let her go.

Warily.

She relaxed only slightly and sighed, offered him a lop-sided smile. "Lousy nap and stolen panties," she mumbled by way of apology, and awkwardly minced-sidestepped to the bathroom and shut the door.

It was, at best, an uncomfortable evening.

Something had changed between them. Expectation, desire, their private decisions to back off, all created a situation edgy with doubt and mistake.

Confinement brought upon them by their own subterfuge generated a tension no amount of effort could break. The atmosphere was pensive with unspoken lies and half-truths, thick with vigilance and wistfulness. The ice in the pickle bucket melted around the unopened bottles of champagne, and the conversation ebbed more often than it flowed.

Not sure how to tell Jeth that the winds of her whims had changed yet again, Allyn ate her romantic cabin dinner in silence, eyes shifting back and forth between her food and nothing, and nothing and Jeth.

Sleep hadn't dulled her appetite for looking at him in the slightest. Time to think left her awash in uncertainty over...

Everything.

Every movement of his hands, his fingers, recalled to mind pictures of how else, where else he might use them, the sensations they had roused before thought and slumber had interrupted them. He plucked a peach slice off the tray of fruit between them, sucked the juice out of it, and her nipples puckered in sudden and unwanted reaction, budding tight against her shirtfront. She caught her breath and flicked her tongue nervously between her teeth; she crossed her arms and looked away. She had too much bustline to ever need or want to wear a padded bra, but sudden insight showed her one good reason to laud their existence. If she had one on right now, at least she wouldn't feel embarrassed over him being able to witness her body's reaction to his antics.

Only Jeth knew his antics were unintentional. If Allyn had told him what she experienced, he might have explained.

He enjoyed peaches from way back, sank his teeth into them with the relish of one who'd grown up with happy memories of summers spent with an aunt who owned an orchard and turned him loose in it. Peaches meant song and dance, pies and preserves—hot, sweet-scented evenings skinny-dipping in the placid lake beside which he'd lost his virginity. He only vaguely remembered the girl anymore, but the taste of peaches filled him with nostalgia for joys past, moments gone....

Of a time long before his first—and only other—blown undercover had gotten Marcy killed.

He blinked and looked at Allyn, hating himself for wanting her, despising himself for beginning to need her beyond reasons he could name.

Reviling his body for its sudden and entirely primitive response to her quickened breathing and the sight of her nipples going taut beneath that damnably seductive camisole she hadn't changed out of.

If she hadn't picked up the strawberry to nibble on, he'd have been fine, but the sight of her luscious, juice-stained lips parting to take the fruit between them undid the last vestige of civilized man in his control. He captured the hand holding the strawberry, overcame her wide-eyed tug of resistance and guided her fingers to his mouth. Eyes locked on hers, his breathing none too steady, he hooked his tongue around what was left of the strawberry and sucked it out of her fingers and into his mouth.

She made a small sound, part dismay, part wariness, part encouragement, and watched his tongue while he licked the juice off her fingers, the palm of her hand, her wrist.

Whatever Allyn had decided not to do with Jeth was forgotten, reservations fled. The only thing she knew was the feel of his lips sampling the sensitive inside of her wrist, the lash of his tongue along her pulse, dabbing lightly at the nerve points in the center of her palm.

The tightening spiral of excitement and urgency threading upward and outward from that single point, spreading slowly throughout her body, becoming lightning, smoke and flame.

She swallowed and tried to say his name, ''Jeth,'' but wasn't sure the word that left her throat was anything more than guttural sound.

Whichever, sound or name, he took it as request, incentive, invitation and—gaze still on her face, lips still creating havoc among the nerves along her arm—rose, kicked his chair out of his way and rounded the table to haul her chair out and switch it around so he could kneel in front of her.

His tongue lingered, moistening the inside of her elbow, teeth nipped the soft skin over the pulse that beat there. The hand not holding her wrist slipped between her knees, coaxed them open. She instinctively squeezed them closed, resisting him for less than half a heartbeat before she parted her legs and let him slide between them.

He groaned something unintelligible but approving against the spot he worshiped on her arm and slid his hand over her thigh and up her hip to her waist, fitted it into the small of her back to pull her forward to the edge of the chair. Her knees trembled, but she came willingly; her breath was short and raspy, her eyes on his wide and fathomless.

He dropped her left hand, lifted her right to lavish upon it the same attention he'd given her other arm. His gaze locked with hers, communication without words, seduction at its most intense. He breathed into her palm and she sighed, touched his tongue to its center and she stiffened and whimpered. When he brushed his lips over the pulse at her wrist, she puddled.

Once again he worked his way up the soft inside of her arm to find the pulse inside her elbow; at the same time he grazed feathery patterns over her thigh with his free hand, then urgently massaged it, kneaded his way under her shorts hem, tugging her against him. When she moistened her lips, let her head loll back and moaned, then flexed and twisted her body to bring herself in closer contact with him, he dropped her hand to his shoulder and dragged his down her back to her hip and brought her tight to his belly, held her there while she sought a rhythm she didn't yet know.

Her head fell forward, forehead touched his.

"Jeth."

The single word was harsh, breathless; she wasn't aware she'd said anything, but he heard, understood the half-frantic plea and dipped his head to find her collarbone with lips and tongue and teeth, licking, sucking, nibbling from one shoulder to the other. Stopping between to take a quick and less than satisfactory foray down the center of her chest to the rise of each breast, dragged his mouth over the spot behind which her heart pounded.

Let his tongue mimic other actions, sliding it in and out within the sheath created by the valley of her breasts and her camisole.

The teasing was almost more than she could bear. Her hands tightened on his shoulders, her thighs tensed hard on either side of his hips, her body arched and twisted violently, seeking respite from the sensations coiling inside her.

"Please," she begged. "Please."

Jeth might have said, "Easy, love, slow down," but he was in no mood to soothe her; he was only in the mood to give her what she asked. Craved pleasing her, pleasuring her, sinking into her. So he slipped one hand inside the loose leg of her shorts, under the elastic of her panties and over her rump, anchoring her tight against him. Then he bent his head and opened his mouth over one breast, one cloth-covered nipple, and simply breathed a single, hot, humid breath over it while at the same time he glided his free hand inside the other leg of her shorts, traced his fingers lightly up the inside of her thigh to slip them under the front elastic of her panties.

Threaded his thumb through the wiry curls hidden there and settled it gently into the dampness, seeking until he found the delicate pearl at the heart of her need and touched it.

Allyn gasped and went rigid for a moment at the unaccustomed sensations, the invasion. Then Jeth flicked his tongue across her cotton-covered nipple and she cried out and surged forward, lacing her fingers in his hair, pressing her breast into his mouth, riding his thumb. Suddenly everything inside her seemed to flame, boil, liquefy and she was calling out, shuddering apart, being lifted out of the chair and straddled across Jeth's lap so he could shift his grip on her and press a finger inside her, then two.

Then she was shouting, sobbing, hostage to the tension, the pleasure that built higher and stronger than before— exploded again before her body had a chance to recover from its first release, and once more when he touched a spot near the entrance of her channel that seemed to be made of fire and light and stars—

And the most absurdly blissful oblivion.

Awareness returned in stages: sensation and boneless giddiness first; euphoria in the taste of wine and strawberries, the tang of Jeth kissing her both senseless and vitally alert in every pore; desire and unabated passion in the scent of musk that enshrouded them; urgency and wildness in the roughness of their breathing, the sounds that were not words but that communicated all; in the touch of fingers gone clumsy with need, the feel of the rag rug against her back; in the sight of Jeth's dark visage rising above her drenched with hunger, with greed....

With the intent to claim what was his and give back all he had to give in return.

Then he bent his head and poured himself into a purely savage kiss and she got lost inside it, drowned in the overwhelming power, the strength that was Jeth.

Gloried in the reciprocal strength and power she discovered were hers to command when she laid her palms along the sides of his head and kissed him back, thrust her tongue deep into his mouth, sucked his hard and evocatively into hers, made him groan.

Eager to explore the power, the rawness of his passions, the newness of her own, she skimmed her hands down his face, his neck, the sides of his chest until she reached the hem of his shirt. Pulled it high enough to slide her hands underneath and knew it had to go; she wanted his skin, craved the feel of hard, lean muscle and flesh-covered bone with nothing between her and it.

She dragged the shirt higher, tried to yank it off him but was waylaid by his reluctance to leave any part of her untouched and untasted even for an instant. He nibbled at her breast, teased it, laved and abraded the cotton over it, and she thought she would go mad. When he finally bit down, rolled her nipple with his tongue then suckled her hard, her mouth opened on a silent cry, and she arched upward nearly double; his shirt shredded in her hands, and she had his skin.

Undone.

If Jeth had thought anything at all before when he'd forgotten himself and let his baser appetites rule, he'd thought her fearless, headlong flight into her first, her second and her third climaxes by his hand had undone him. He'd been wrong.

Oh, he'd been demolished, pulverized, shattered by the initial shock, then the fierce abandonment, the unguarded ecstasy he'd seen written on her face, but that had been little compared to this: the fire in her touch; the ferocious and uncompromised joy in her exploration of him; the potent and wholly erotic knowledge that she sought to give back to him everything he could teach her—and anything she could make up in her turn.

He tasted her breasts, and she offered them fully, straining to feed him, nourish him, sustain him; he slid his ring hand inside the already stretched neckline of her camisole and jerked it down to free the flesh he'd been torturing both of them with by leaving it covered, and like his shirt, the straps of her camisole tore, then the three-button center broke open, the top ripped. She laughed breathlessly at the sound the rended cloth made, caught her breath and stiffened, trembled in his arms when his tongue at last made contact with the puckered flesh tipping her breasts.

When he nosed aside the remnants of her shirt and trailed his tongue down the center of her belly, dipped and swirled it in the pouting flesh above her waistband, then dragged the waistband lower with his teeth, her body bucked in reaction, and she whimpered and reached for him. He held her hands away and continued his openmouthed exploration, finally using his hands to haul her shorts that last bit off her belly and away from the dark curls below.

Lips and teeth explored her mound; his tongue sank between her thighs.

She whimpered again and tried to open her legs to him, to close them against him, but her shorts hampered her.

Jeth smiled ferociously against her thigh. "Patience, love," he advised tersely, though he felt no patience himself. "All in good time."

"Please, Jeth." A sharp gasp followed by a ragged moan when his tongue darted into her crease and found its silken core. "Don't make me beg. You're killing me."

"Why d'you think you're the one on your back right now?" Jeth's murmur was muffled; he planted a lingering kiss in her most secret of places and, when she frantically but involuntarily pushed herself off the floor into it, he tore her shorts the rest of the way down her legs and off, settled himself between her suddenly open thighs and drove his tongue deep inside her.

She shrieked and coiled upward, hips jerking, body tightening without warning, pulsing and spasming in sudden release. He kissed her until the tremors lessened, then hauled himself up her body to kiss her mouth, bite gently at her lips. His fingers wandered into the dampness his mouth had created in points south, stroked and fondled and caressed until her insides were a molten mass, a shivery starburst waiting for a single meteor brush to send it spiraling out of control.

"Tell me again why I'm the one on my back?" Allyn's voice was thin, taut with the excitement his fingers, his breath, his nearness generated.

He brought his lips to her ear, teased the lobe. "Because if you were doing this to me, you wouldn't just be killing me, I'd be dead by now."

She moaned and shivered, twisted against his fingers. "So instead you're torturing me to death."

He ran his tongue down her neck and around both breasts until he'd corkscrewed up and around each tip. "Tell me you're not enjoying this. Slap my face. Tell me to stop."

"No." She inhaled sharply, struggled to keep her train of thought. "I can't. It feels—it feels…. Oh, heavens, Jeth-Jeth-Jeth! Please-please! It's not fair, I want to make you—oh, yes, there, Jeth, there—make you crazy, too!"

The word ended on a squeak when he suddenly rolled onto his back and sat her astride him, right over the bulge behind his zipper. Still stroking her with one thumb, he tucked the first two fingers of his other hand into his watch pocket, withdrew a single foil-wrapped package.

"Please," he said simply. "Touch me. I'll either let you know when I can't stand it anymore, or you'll put this on me when you're ready. I want to be inside you, Lynnie. I want to come inside—"

She shut him up with her mouth on his, while her hands fumbled the button and zipper of his jeans open, spread his pants wide.

He went commando, sans shorts, butt bare within the soft denim.

She bit back surprise by biting Jeth's lower lip, suddenly intimidated to find herself handling the flesh that sprang to attention within her palm. She'd thought she'd have boxers yet to slide off him; she wasn't sure she was as ready as she'd thought to find him positioned *there,* manhood already prodding her belly, boldly seeking entrance to that hot, wet place inside her.

Jeth moved his thumb, and her body wept to hold him there.

"Take your time," he whispered, "Get used to it—to me. There's no rush."

But the tension written across his face and the slurred strain in his voice told another story, made her belly hot with its own need.

Still, just as he had done, she could wait, could make him wait....

Or maybe not.

She touched the tip of his sex with her thumb, ran the edge of it around him, taking in the shape and texture of him, while her fingers sidled down his length. His body jerked, convulsed upward, spearing him into her palm, sliding the base of his sex through the slickness at the mouth of hers. Moisture beaded beneath her thumb; perspiration glistened on his face, slickened his chest. He stiffened and tried to hold himself still, groaning with pleasure, with pain.

"Judas, you're killing me," he gasped. "I'm sorry, Lyn, I want to make this last, but I don't know if I can. Put that thing on me before something happens that I can't control."

Heavy-lidded, smiling like the proverbial cat teasing the mouse, she undulated against him. "Who said you get to call me Lyn?"

The question was as close to a purr as he'd ever heard in a human.

He closed his eyes and shuddered; his body bowed violently off the floor, involuntarily rubbing against her. Sweet baby Jane, she learned fast.

"Lynnie, quit. I want you too badly right now. I can't—I can't—ah, damn that feels good!"

He opened his eyes, watched her run a fingernail through the beaded moisture at the tip of his sex, drag it gently down his length, then cup him. He saw what she did through a haze of understanding, yet his body still flexed and jerked instinctively, frantically seeking entrance to hers.

"Oh, woman, do you know what you're doing to me? You can't know what you're doing to me...."

"You said I could touch." She bent forward, and her hair draped around him, tickling, tantalizing, torturing and rousing nerve endings he'd never realized he had. "I'm touching." She planted an openmouthed kiss on one of his nipples, then the other, laved each of them thoroughly. Her nipples brushed his belly, breasts cradled his burgeoning manhood between them. "I may be inexperienced but I'm not unread."

"Allyn, please." Need was unrefined, breath as serrated as the edge of a steak knife. He shut his eyes again, braced his hands on her shoulders and thrust into that heavenly, sweat-glistened passage knowing that in a moment or two the ability to stop would be beyond him; the ability to think was already fading. "No amount of reading can have made you understand where I am right now, or how close I am to it. If you don't put that damned condom on me, this is going to happen here, now, just like this."

The bewitching but audacious bit of baggage astride him kissed his belly and rubbed against him, raised her head high enough to smile naughtily into his eyes. Her tongue flicked between her teeth. "Bring it on. You got to watch me, it's my turn to see it happen to you—"

"Not this time, lady," he said harshly. "Maybe later, but not now."

Too fast for her to see it coming, Jeth flipped her onto her back, snatched the condom out of her hand, ripped it open and rolled it on. Then he was between her knees, lifting them, nudging as gently as exigency would allow at the entrance to her womb.

"Jeth!" Surprise, dismay, delight, breathless laughter.

"I warned you, little girl." He withdrew, pressed into her again, deeper this time. Her eyes closed, throat arched, lips parted, features took on a hold-your-breath concentration. The tiny but constant accommodations her body made to fit his, her tightness were exquisite torture. "If you play with fire you're going to get burned."

She opened her eyes halfway. The blue of his eyes was fierce and brilliant, avid. She pressed her hips upward, breathing hard with the heightened sensation of fullness, the delicious pressure, her sudden sense of personal vulnerability to the physical power he visibly struggled to hold in check.

For her. Because he didn't want to hurt her. Because no matter what his body craved at the moment, he would not simply take his own pleasure and leave her behind just because she'd tortured him practically beyond bearing.

The realization came to her that she was not the only

one experiencing vulnerability or who held physical power in this situation.

That Jeth was, as she'd known all along, the right man, the only man, the only first she would ever have or would ever want to have.

Not to mention the only second, third, fourth…to infinity and beyond she ever hoped to have.

Warmth engulfed her, flushed from her head to the soles of her feet, washed through like silt when the floodgates open. It was too soon to name this secret, this catastrophic understanding. She buried it deep where it could do no harm to either of them at the moment.

Closed her eyes so he wouldn't see the evidence she was sure must lie plainly in them.

Cradled his head in her hands and arched into the touch of his fingers, his mouth worshiping her breasts.

"Are you going to burn with me this time?" she whispered.

"Definitely," he muttered. "Yeah." He bent and kissed her deeply, tongue plunging quickly in then out as he withdrew from her. Then he hooked her knees over his shoulders and reached down to fork two fingers gently inside her, spread them open slowly as he guided himself into her. "This might hurt," he warned her.

"I know," she gasped. "It doesn't matter. I want you, Jeth, I *need* you inside me, please, please—ooh!"

He stroked the pearled nubbin above her channel with honey-wet fingers, and she opened to him fully. What was left of any barriers collapsed rather than tore, and he plunged heavily home.

And paused.

"Are you all right?"

Sweat slicked his body, made hers slippery beneath him. Her legs trembled, the muscles in her thighs shook with reaction, her belly flexed and contracted trying to roll her hips around him, embed him deeper. His fingers continued to pet her, cherish and fondle, wanting to please, to comfort, to relieve.

"Allyn, please, look at me." Desperate. Jeth had to hear her say it before he went further.

Before he went mad.

"Are you all right?"

She smiled, features drugged, intent on what he was doing. "Yes," she murmured. "Are you?"

He closed his eyes and sighed. He should have known she wouldn't say what he'd thought she might. "No." The truth. "But I will be."

"Good." Another small, absorbed and intoxicated smile. "Now come home, Jeth. Bring me home...."

That was the last he heard before she undulated her hips again, cried out over the stroke of his fingers, and the ripple of earthquakes inside her tore sense from him. He could only pump and buck and flow with the lava, with the heat that forged and molded him, milked him, held him, drank from him. And at the last, he went shouting into one shattering, hugely drawn out volcanic eruption that finally became the unearthly glow of unbelievable satiation. Then he sank—for the first time in his life—into utter, complete, uncomplicated and peaceful darkness.

Chapter 11

After that Jeth couldn't seem to keep his mind, his eyes or his hands off of her.

His mouth didn't particularly want to keep to itself, either.

He'd come to himself collapsed on top of her, his pulse still pounding in his ears, cognizant only of the fact that something irreversible had happened to him both before but especially within that moment of little death.

Primitive as it sounded, this woman was his; his body both recognized and clamored for the awesome responsibility, the commitment to her even as his mind fought the recognition. There would not be another woman in his bed, on his floor or anywhere else who was not Allyn. Gut deep, soul deep, he knew it.

He'd never blacked out in climax before, never had a woman faint with him. And, good grief, he'd never even gotten all the way out of his jeans.

Too sluggish to lift himself off her, Jeth simply slid sideways in their mutual sweat and flung an arm across his eyes. Damn, he hadn't known. He hadn't. If he'd known how he would feel after, what this would do to him, he would never have...

He felt her stir, felt her hand rove lovingly, dilatorily across his chest and turned his head to look at her. Her eyes were barely open, she was hardly returned from that place that had made her one with him, but already she was aware of him, already reaching for him, soothing him, being with him.

He shut his eyes and knew that Judas be damned or not, he'd have made love to her tonight because making love with her was as inevitable as breathing, as loving her might also be. And even though he didn't want to love her, not now, not in the middle of this, not because of it, not when he couldn't trust his emotions, he would not have stopped himself if he'd tried. Hell, he *had* tried and look where it had gotten him.

"Hey."

Allyn brushed a butterfly kiss across the hollow of his shoulder; he dipped his head to plant a circumspect reciprocal kiss on her mouth, pulled back a little and smiled at her.

"Hey, yourself. You all right?"

"Mmm." A delicious murmur that tickled his chest when she snuggled her cheek against it. "That was...I didn't know."

He huffed wry laughter. "Trust me, neither did I." The understatement of the century if ever he'd made one. "I've never...that never happened before."

She was suddenly alert, rolling over to prop herself up with her arms braced across his chest and her chin resting on the backs of her hands.

"What do you mean, that never happened before?" she asked, interested. "I thought you weren't a virgin. You mean you've never had an orgas—"

Laughter roared out of him, drawn from the tips of his

toes through the pit of his belly. He caught her arms and hauled her up, stopped her mouth by slanting his across it

"More," she muttered, reaching for him when he pressed her away. "More."

"Glutton," he chuckled, but drew her back, caught his hands in her hair and gave her what she asked for—what he wanted beyond reason.

"Mmm," she sighed when they came up for air at last. "I liked that. That was very nice. Now…" Her voice was brisk, businesslike, no longer sighing.

Jeth choked, understanding too late that sidetracking Allyn was only temporary at best and, at worst, he'd been had.

By a master.

"As I was saying," she continued, "you mean to tell me that in all the times you've made love or had sex or whatever you called it—and how many times was that, by the way, and what *did* you call it because you seem pretty damned talented at it to me, although I'm no judge, of course, but still—you mean to say you've *never,* not even once, um, what is the term? Oh, yes—" she blinked innocently at him "—come?"

Torn between astonishment and outraged laughter, he could only ask in return, "Do you ever not say what's on your mind?"

She batted her eyes, all outlandish something or other with the accent to match. "My momma done taught me the onliest way ta learn anythin' was ta ask th' questions you wanted answers to."

Jeth snorted. "Yeah, well, my momma taught me it's polite to keep a civil tongue in your head and keep it there without wagging it on occasion—especially if you're questioning somebody's manhood."

"I'm not questioning your manhood," Allyn told him blithely, draping herself more comfortably across him. "I'm asking whether or not you've ever actually sown any wild oats before since you just said, and I quote, 'that never happened before,' end quote.''

He stared at her. "You are unbelievable."

"I know," she agreed immodestly. "Now answer the question."

He gave her a devilish grin. "How crude shall I be?"

She pursed her lips and blinked beguiling, schoolmarmish eyes at him.

He sighed, chuckled ruefully. "You'd charm the devil out of his socks if you had reason, wouldn't you?"

Allyn shrugged, offered him solemn. "I'd do it for you, I'd do it for Sasha, I'd do it for my family. Whatever it took, yeah."

His heart clenched; he traced a few strands of hair out of her face, humbled by an admission he wasn't entirely certain he was ready to hear, an honor he wasn't sure he deserved.

It was an awesome burden: frightening, challenging, gut-wrenching, gladdening. He held it inside himself, half wishing he didn't believe her, that he could ignore what she'd said, toss it away.

That it would be forever true.

He puffed his cheeks and blew out the breath. "Okay," he said. "You want serious, here it is. I don't sow wild oats, I wear a condom or sometimes two if I don't know who I'm sleeping with. I've been the 'don't know who I'm sleeping with' route exactly twice and didn't like myself much afterward. It was right after my baby sister was killed by some guys who were looking for me and I was drunk on my ass both times." He cupped her face, traced her brow, her jaw, her lips. "The thing that's only happened with you that never happened with any other woman is…" He stopped, blew out another breath, made an inadequate gesture. "Geez, how to put it. I guess… I dunno. Maybe it's the difference between having sex and making love.

Suffice it to say it's never been like *that*. I've never been so…high, so… Damn.''

His lips twisted; he dropped his head and made the confession to the ceiling. ''It's never been so intense that I've blacked out before, okay?''

He should have known that simple revelation, however difficult for him, would never be enough to satisfy her heretofore virginal curiosity.

''Is that good?''

He lifted his head, grinned and shrugged. ''As far as it ranking among the most incredible experiences in my life? Yeah. Very.'' Then more honestly than he intended, ''And no, because it scares me to think what it might mean.''

She leaned forward to kiss his chest, the hollow of his throat. ''For what it's worth, if it helps any, it scares me that I wanted to make love with you at all. The fact that it's so soon after we met…'' A butterfly's caress of her lips in the center of his sternum. ''Well. But I'm not backing away from this, Jeth. Whatever it is, for however long it does or doesn't last. You should know this about me. I only back up to go around or to get a running start in order to jump over or go through. Wherever this leads, I'm going through, Jeth. All the way.''

Something in the way she said it chilled him to the bone.

''Not if I tell you to stop, you're not.'' His eyes glittered; the hand cupping her chin went suddenly hard. ''Not if it means—''

She peeled his fingers off her chin, gentled them by kissing his knuckles, turning his hand palm up and kissing its center. ''*Whatever* it means, Jeth,'' she assured him calmly. ''Whatever. But not tonight, hey? Just be with me tonight—''

Before the invitation was completed, Jeth pulled her up across his body and took her mouth. Roughly. Savagely.

Gently.

His mouth slid through the hair at the side of her face,

left moist, unearthly shivers running her spine, knotting in her belly.

"Mine," he whispered darkly, passionately. "Just for tonight I'm going to pretend you're mine."

Then he settled her in his arms and took her mouth again before she could think to protest that she'd be his for a lot longer than now.

They lost the night to each other, to everything but the darkness, lightness, newness, rightness of this thing between them.

He took her into the shower, wanting to bathe her with warm water, to be sure her muscles wouldn't be sore with unaccustomed stretching in the morning—then wound up teaching her things he wasn't aware he knew.

She showed him the benefits keeping fit by bicycling, horseback riding, spinning wool and straddling surfboards for long hours during her studies provided them both now, taught him things he'd never thought to learn.

The night lengthened, straining toward dawn, and still they couldn't get enough of each other.

Each coupling made the next more inevitable, more powerful, toppled whatever barriers existed between them.

Trust developed, softened, then betrayed him.

He told her things he thought he'd never tell anyone: about his family—three brothers and one remaining sister; about the case he'd been working on before Marcy died— a case that bore a marked resemblance to this one in its war over drug territory and the way he'd been sent undercover by his then lieutenant and now supervisor Jeri Fishburne. About how he hadn't been home in three years since losing Marcy when she opened the door to someone she thought was a friend of his, someone who'd called him and threatened to kill her if Jeth didn't do what they wanted. About how he hadn't believed the threat because he'd been young, stupid and invincible and afterward, when he'd called home to check on her, Marcy was there and fine.

About getting the message from his oldest brother less than a week later that Marcy was missing.

About the madness that had claimed him when he knew he was to blame. About searching for her and catching the men who'd done the kidnapping, but not capturing the person who'd ordered it.

About finding her too late.

He told her about himself, about his need to see Sasha safe whatever the cost. He told her about growing up on the reservation in Arizona, about growing up Indian at his mother's and his grandparents' insistence even though his heritage was only one-quarter Supai.

He spooned himself into her back and told her about his parents, still together after nearly thirty-five years; about the fact that regardless of what tonight felt like he could not guarantee anything even remotely similar to Allyn. Then he kissed the knuckles of her ring finger, laved its pad and sucked it into his mouth, matched his ring to hers, dipped his mouth into the hollow between her neck and shoulder, drew her hips tight against him and made love to her again as if the world might stop or end before he was through.

The night lasted a minute and it lasted forever.

At dawn they breakfasted on the remains of their supper, then made slow, peaceful love and fell asleep, pillowed together, legs entangled, exhausted but secure, holding only to the moment.

They were both uncomfortable when they awakened in late morning: Allyn more physically than emotionally, and Jeth more emotionally than physically—although even he experienced twinges in places he hadn't realized could twinge. But such, he decided, was the price that better than a year of celibacy exacted on a man.

Then he looked at Allyn, smiling sleepily at him, and didn't regret either the year or the twinges in the least.

Found he was actually profoundly glad of both.

Which scared him badly, but not badly enough to allow him to stay away from her even now that daylight had come.

It took a while full of wincing, husky laughter, and making sure they each kissed away the other's pains in all the parts that ached, but they finally managed to shower and dress, bring the newness of their discovery of each other to hand enough to leave the cabin.

Even then, though, Jeth found he could not stop himself from touching, could not keep himself from spooning behind her, could not prevent his mouth from finding the spot below her ear and just left of the nape of her neck that made her catch her breath, sigh and sink into him as though no one else could possibly exist in her world at the moment.

Could not inhibit himself from dragging her into convenient shadows and getting drugged all over again on her kisses, her response to his sly though only marginally indecent touches—nor his response to hers.

It was as though they shared a secret, imperfectly kept, visible to anyone who looked at them but unique, as well, solely their own. They didn't quite forget Sasha, but they didn't concentrate on him entirely, either; he was part of the bargain they'd made and kept; he was part of them, this thing between them, this lie, this relationship—the reason for it.

Knowing this, they tickled him and cuddled him and thanked him for it whenever they saw him, which wasn't often that morning. Sasha was far too busy playing with his new cousins to have time for his equally new parents, and that was fine for the moment.

Although in some dark and deliberately tamped-down part of himself, Jeth worried about the growing affection he saw developing between Allyn and the little boy—and

heck, between himself and Sasha, as well. That tenebrou
and cynical place in him understood the disadvantages o
personal involvement, niggled him with doubts that sai
*Come on, boy, admit it, you've got to cut this out, you'r
screwing up.*

Because it felt too good just to be Allyn's lover, Sasha
makeshift papa for this little while, though, he ignored th
nagging of his conscience and threw himself with will int
the role he portrayed but no longer had to pretend to pla

The barely contained desire sizzling hot and hotter be
tween him and Allyn worked to his advantage with he
family, making him look like what he assured himself h
was not: a man gone heels over head over his new bride

For one thing, he reminded himself, Allyn wasn't hi
bride.

For another, being thoroughly wrapped up in her wa
bad for Sasha's protection.

He found himself wrapped up in her anyway an
couldn't bring himself to let go even when he realized h
might be drowning.

Even upon discovering and rediscovering that if he coul
barely maintain decency with her in public, in private h
was lost, wrapped as tightly in her web as she was in his–
in this thing they created together.

He forgot everything.

He became wholly himself for the first time in his life.

He maintained the lie, but threw caution to the wind
and made himself temporarily comfortable in Allyn's fam
ily's world.

He just had to keep reminding himself it must be tem
porary, is all.

Sasha was returned to Jeth and Allyn over a lunch fille
with knowing glances and grins, a tight-lipped stepfathe
and head-shaking mother.

The toddler's English vocabulary had grown in leaps and bounds overnight.

Though moderately pleased to see Jeth and Allyn, Sasha was in no hurry to leave his newfound aunts and cousins behind when it came time for him to have a nap. Jeth, on the other hand, found himself most anxious to take both the little guy and Allyn to the cabin for a nap—although he very much doubted he and Allyn would get any sleep.

The very thought of not getting any sleep with Allyn made his groin tighten with anticipation. The smoldering look she sent him when she plucked Sasha up and headed toward the woods where their cabin lay made him want to pluck *her* up and head for the nearest private bower and have his way with her.

And vice versa.

It was insane, it was merciless, it was the hunger of a lifetime of starvation, a belly that had to be fed and fatted while the harvest was plentiful to live off when the time was lean.

And it was not to be.

The tensions that had been idling between Becky and Michael since Becky's seven-year itch had set in about the same time as Allyn's graduation erupted in the middle of their path to the cabin, putting paid to all manner of sensual feast Allyn and Jeth might have shared after Sasha went to sleep.

As a law officer, Jeth knew better than to interfere in the petty bickerings between a man and his wife; he would have ignored the situation completely unless violence threatened—which it didn't. Far from it, in fact, Michael was attempting to console and cajole his agitated wife, who clutched their two-year-old to her chest and sobbed into the little man's T-shirt, muttering incoherent something-or-others at her distressed husband while their four-year-old clung to her leg. Which meant that other than to reluctantly wonder whether or not he and Allyn ought to collect Becky and Michael's youngsters and leave the adults to sort things out, he planned to walk on by—or actually, give the couple a wide berth for the sake of privacy.

That is, he would have if Allyn hadn't suddenly stopped short in the path before she even saw her sister and brother-in-law, clasped Sasha tight to her chest, covered his ears, then blistered Jeth's with an impolite version of, "Men are pigs!", before bursting into tears and tearing off up the path to collide with Michael.

To make matters worse—or at least more confusing—when she saw Becky crying and clutching her youngest, Allyn sobbed an under her breath oath of, "Oh, for the love of Silly Putty," swung about and handed Sasha to Jeth with a teary, "Don't ask, I'll explain later," snatched Becky's kids into Michael's waiting arms and dragged her sister off in the direction of peace, quiet and temporary childlessness.

Taken aback, Jeth and Michael eyed each other.

"Well," Michael said uncertainly, "I guess that's that."

"And that would be?" Jeth asked warily.

"A twin thing?"

"Okay," Jeth said. "If you say so." Then, "What twin thing?"

Michael shrugged. "They experience the same things at the same times once in a while. Allyn always seemed to be more in tune with Becky than the other way around, but lately, I dunno. Something's going on. Last night…" Still looking worriedly after his wife, Michael nonetheless grinned suddenly. "Last night was interesting. I have a feeling I owe you thanks, man. But today…" He shook his head. "Whoa."

Jeth nodded, ignoring what he had no intention of dignifying with reference to last night. He didn't want to know. And if he needed to know, Allyn would, he was certain, for better or worse, fill him in later.

"Let's get these guys down for their naps," he suggested

neutrally. "Let Allyn handle it. Sounds like she knows what she's doing."

"I hope somebody does," Michael said softly. "I have the feeling Beck's getting ready to leave me, and I don't know why. I don't want to lose my wife."

And that was how, against his better judgment and his druthers, and silently calling himself seventeen kinds of fool, Jeth wound up in the Catton cabin watching Michael pace and listening to him talk while Sasha and the two youngest Cattons napped.

"I thought we made a pact," Allyn sniffled to her sister without preamble when they were sufficiently beyond earshot of men and children. "You stay out of my psyche, I'll stay out of yours."

"I don't want to be in your psyche," Becky lamented, dabbing away tears with the edge of a forefinger. "It was an accident. Besides, you've been leaking all over me for months with your, 'I don't think I want to really do this, be this,' rubbish. I just didn't know it until last night. I mean really, Lyn, if you don't want to be who you are, who're you going to be?"

"I'm sure as heck not going to be you!" Allyn said flatly.

"Then why'd you find the first hot stud who came along and marry him and his kid three minutes after getting your doctorate?" Becky asked. "If that's not being me, I don't know what is."

"That was circumstances beyond my control," Allyn told her twin loftily. "Not to mention you didn't get your doctorate before you got married."

"No," Becky shot back, "I got it afterward. Only mine's in mom and marriage, not marine biology."

"And now you want the one in marine biology, too?"

"Heck, no." Becky looked appalled. "I'm not that big on water sports, if you'll recall. No." She huffed a sad sigh, pulled a tissue out of her hip pocket and blew her nose. "I just want..." She gestured ineffectually. "More. I don't know what yet, but I want to find out. Lately, it seems like there's no way to compensate. I talk to babies all day. They're challenging, sure, but I want to talk to adults. I want to know life isn't passing me by, that it's more than diapers and don't-do-thats. You always knew you wanted something more. Me, it's like I've been married to Michael since I was fourteen."

"You wanted to be married to Michael since you were fourteen," Allyn pointed out, not unkindly.

"I still *want* to be married to Michael," Becky responded ruefully. "I just don't know if I *can* be anymore."

Allyn stared at her sister. "Crumb, Beck, you don't—I mean he's not..."

Startled, Becky laughed, a weak, humorless sound that ended on a sob. "Oh, God, no. Michael? I don't think he's ever even *looked* at another woman, let alone *thought* about one. No." She looked away, dabbed a damning knuckle into the corner of each eye where fresh tears gathered. "No, it's me. It's just me. I just don't want to be who I am anymore. I don't like me."

"Why?" Allyn was instantly curious, infinitely interested.

"I yell." Becky's entire body, her face included, shrugged. "I lay down the law. I screw up the budget. I say no a lot. Some days I wish I didn't have so many kids. Some days I wish I could run away. Mostly I wish I could trade lives with somebody else for like a day and a half, fall in love for the first time all over again and know what it's like to actually have a life."

"You have a life," Allyn said. "You have more life and more diversity in your life than any other six women I know—well, outside Ma, Grandma, Great-grandma and the aunts, that is."

"Exactly." Becky nodded morosely. "Most of the

women we know have more life than me, and they've got kids.''

"Not Aunt Helen. Uncle John got custody of Libby. Aunt Helen's too married to the Army."

"Oh, well." Becky rolled her eyes. "The major or the colonel or whoever she's been promoted to this year doesn't count."

"And Aunt Grace is sort of tied up with her kids, like you."

Becky nodded, thoughtful. "True."

"And—" Allyn warmed to her topic. "Aunt Edith's kids are old enough to baby-sit themselves. Aunt Meg's separated at the moment, but she uses a nanny so that doesn't count. Aunt Sam and Uncle Charlie work different shifts. Aunt Twink only works part-time, and her in-laws baby-sit when she needs them to. And Mom's got Gabriel, and he takes Rachel to school with him half the time when she doesn't take Rachel to the store with her."

"So you're saying there's a solution to this if I just look for it," Becky said dryly.

"Yes."

"Even if part of the reason I don't like me much is because I feel like I wasted my potential by not going to college like you."

"Whoa." Allyn gaped at her sister. "Back up. You don't like you why?"

Becky nodded. "You heard me. No college degree. Must mean I'm just some dumb old hausfrau, right? I mean—" she spread her hands at the trees "—Michael's always taking training courses, updating his schooling. I almost never understand what he's talking about. How can he keep finding me interesting if I don't do something to better myself? What if I can't keep up with him, Lyn? What if—"

"Don't be a dolt," Allyn snapped, loyal to the ground. "You're one of the most intelligent people I know. You just have this self-esteem problem."

"Yeah, but—"

"And besides, *I* like you." Allyn hugged her sister's arm. "Not everyone can say that about their sisters."

Becky grimaced. "Thanks, but you don't count."

Allyn snorted. "Swell. Boost my ego to kingdom come, why don't you."

A grin this time. "I will."

"Brat." The name was affectionate and huffy all in one, then the grin that twinned Becky's kicked in. "Okay." Allyn linked her arm through her sister's and started them off down the trail toward the cabins. "We've established that you want what I've got and I want what you've got. Now what?"

"Now that you've turned up with Jeth and Sasha, you've got what I've got, too," Becky pointed out. "And the one's pretty blessed hot and the other's awfully cute. So it looks to me like you hit the career-marriage jackpot all in one week."

"True, but I don't know what I'm going to do with my doctorate now that I've got them," Allyn pointed out. *Or how long I'll have them,* she finished silently, miserably. She drew breath and shook away thought, brought herself back on track. "I mean, we did go into this pretty fast. I don't even know where we're going to live or—" She hesitated. Lord, she hated lying to Becky. "Or anything—"

"Mom, Mom!"

There was a sudden flurry of activity through the brush and wood beside the trail, and three puffing six- and seven-year-olds materialized in front of the twins.

"Mom!" Becky's Andy bent over, trying to catch his breath.

"Allyn, Becky—" Rachel collapsed in a heap atop some leaves that Allyn hoped would not turn out to be poison ivy.

"There were these men." Libby, hardly panting, eyes gleaming with excitement, looked at her cousins.

"And they were asking us—"

"About Sasha and Jeremy." Becky's two-year-old.

"And they tried to get us to show them—"

"No, you dunce, to come with them—"

"No, they wanted to take us—"

"One of us—"

"And we yelled no, then we ran to tell—"

"But they didn't offer us candy—"

"And they didn't have a car—"

"And they didn't 'xactly try to grab us—"

"So we didn't know—"

"But they were strangers and we're not supposed to talk—"

"Even if there are a lot of strangers around here—"

"But they looked different," Libby finished. "An' we decided we didn't like them so we came to tell an' you were the first family we saw."

"Wait a minute." Allyn laughed. "Slow down, back up, try that again. What?"

So they repeated it. And Becky and Allyn stopped laughing and looked at each other in dawning horror. Before the children could finish the story, the twins had caught their hands and headed toward the cabins at a run.

Chapter 12

The news made Jeth's gut knot and clench; he schooled his face to keep the appearance of overreaction out of his features.

To no avail. Whether Becky and Michael saw it or not, Allyn took one look at him and read fear as clearly as if he'd printed it upon a page in one of her textbooks; he understood this in a heartbeat, comprehended, as well, that she'd interpreted his intention to take Sasha and run at the first available opportunity that wouldn't arouse suspicion.

And leave her behind.

Concluded from the thing that hardened behind those fascinating eyes of hers that he hadn't a chance of leaving her anywhere but with him while she was conscious—unless he could convince her that the only way to throw the bad guys off Sasha's trail would be for her to stay behind.

We're in this together.

The echo of her less-than-a-week-old affirmation slithered unbidden out of the depths of his mind, lurked unwelcome amid the gathering debris of his fears for Sasha, for Allyn, for her family, raised a haunting mist that seemed to cloud everything but instinct.

Jeth heard himself ask the questions as from a distance, heard the answers as something disconnected from him. There were three of them. The men had asked if the children knew the names of the two little blond boys. They hadn't asked about any of the bigger kids, only the babies. They'd said they were camp counselors, but they weren't wearing uniforms. They were sort of old, like Aunt Edith, but not as old as Dad or Uncle Gabriel.

Which meant somewhere between thirty-five and forty-five, Jeth translated, swallowing a grim smile.

They didn't have beards. One had curly hair—brown, with that funny yellow color on top like he'd dyed it. One had straight hair, sort of white like Sasha's. The last one had long, black hair and something wrong with his lip. It looked puffy.

Jeth nodded and tried to collect scattering thoughts. The descriptions didn't quite fit any of the men he was familiar with in any of the pieces of the undercover, but they didn't quite *not* fit, either. His mouth thinned. Judas damn, he hated this. He needed to choose a direction, had to. Now.

Carefully.

Because whatever he did, good, bad or stand-your-ground, one way or another, it meant life.

Having one, or not.

Damn, maybe Allyn was right. Maybe he should talk to Gabriel.

It was hell not knowing who to trust.

He eyed the children, Allyn, Becky, Michael, and tried to convince himself all would be well.

"Did the men follow you when you ran away?" he heard Michael ask.

"Uh-uh." Andy shook his head. "We're littler than them. We went places they couldn't go."

Rachel nodded emphatically. "If they were from here, they didn't know things very well."

"Yup." Libby pursed her lips sagely. "We were good. We got away clean."

In spite of himself and the tenseness of the moment, Jeth choked on disbelieving laughter. Got away clean? Who were these children and where did they get their language from? He didn't remember Marcy talking like this when she was ten. But then, she hadn't known—would never know—Allyn or her family, and he'd been fifteen years older than his little sister. He hadn't lived at home long enough after she was born to have known her much at all.

In that moment of memory, of discovery, everything and nothing changed. What had happened was exactly what was happening now. Marcy had died because he screwed up, called the wrong shots, mistook true threat for mere warning.

He'd reacted, in short, much as he had when he'd stolen Sasha out of hell six days ago: he'd done it on a wing and a prayer—only he'd probably used a lot more wing and only a third as much prayer as might have been useful.

In through his nose, hold it, out through his mouth; three times he breathed, cleansing, steadying, purposeful. No, he would not turn on himself, weaken Sasha's, Allyn's, his own chances by thinking like that right now. Such thoughts were killers: crippling, exhausting, debilitating. He had no time for them. *They*—Sasha, Allyn, her family—had no time for him to court such recollections, dwell selfishly on either the things that certainly were, but especially those things that may not have been, his fault in Marcy's death. *God grant me the serenity,* he thought. No matter what guilt he pursued, however justified, he could not bring Marcy back. But Sasha was here. Sasha was alive and growing healthier by the minute. Jeth wouldn't give that up easily, if at all.

He glanced at Allyn, who raised her chin in recognition

of what he was thinking, in challenge and a dare to leave her out of it—and who eyed him with expectation, surety and hope. And he was pretty certain he wouldn't give her up at any price.

Partly because, he understood at once and with awful clarity, giving her up would be the biggest mistake he'd ever make in his life. And partly because—and this was far worse—giving her up would not be a choice she'd allow him to make for her. If a choice had to be made, she would make it herself.

With sudden knowledge came power and definition, the icy coolness of decision. He looked at Michael, Becky and Allyn.

"We've got to round up the kids and the families," he said tersely. "Warn the camp office, let them call the local police—" He ignored Allyn's start of surprise at that, turned to Rachel, Libby and Andy. "If you don't think the men followed you, did you see which way they went, and would you recognize them again?"

"Oh sure," Libby said, unperturbed, competent and, as her mother's daughter, a front-lines general and Nate the Great series mystery detective at the enthusiastic yet unflappable, slyly self-important age of seven. "After we ran and hid, we watched them. Then we followed them."

Evening slanted multihued across the sky, scattered rays of tangerine and vermilion amid deepening shades of purple and blue, painted the ground in a chiaroscuro of grays and golds, in a twilight that insinuated itself sooner and murkier among the trees.

Above the hills and horse pastures where it could be seen, the moon rose, bloodred and full.

"Trouble," Allyn and Becky whispered to each other, shivering when they parted company as the exhausting day drew to a close. Neither remembered where the notion came from that dissonance attended a full red moon, only that it dated from somewhere early in their childhood, was tangled together with nights they'd shared similar—and occasionally identical—dreams and nightmares. As adults and women with periodically romantic inclinations, each appreciated the beauty of the crimson moon. Still, neither could help but regard it warily even as they told themselves they were too old to fear it.

Especially after the day's events.

Libby's afternoon announcement had been both heartstopping and galvanizing, Jeth's reaction to it swift.

The local sheriffs arrived, descriptions were issued, the search began—and ended two hours later with the apprehension of two of the three men the children had not only described but could also identify. The third man, with the long black hair, was absent, and the two in custody refused to identify him.

They also protested their innocence and refused to talk, but they were definitely not camp staff. When the sheriff's office put their names and fingerprints through the computer, they both came up with records that were varied and long. Among the busts listed were several for alleged babysnatching and black-market baby trafficking. Nothing had been proven in any of these instances, so there'd been no time served. But it certainly gave everyone—especially Jeth and Allyn—pause.

When they came together that night after Sasha went to sleep it was urgently, desperately, with none of the playfulness of the previous night.

Mouths fused, hands frantic, they pushed and tugged each other into the bathroom and shut the door, shed clothing without regard to how it came off as long as it did. Then they had just enough presence of mind to roll a condom onto him before he hoisted her against the sink, pulled her legs around him and drove into her.

Hard. Deep. Fast. Sweaty. Powerful. Thoughtless. Thought-consuming.

Violent.

Primal.

Their joining was not pretty, not tender, but it brought them closer, linked them, bound them, separated them—and made them more in tune with each other than anything else.

Together they affirmed life, deposed mutual fear—bore witness to their shared desire to escape what lay beyond the moment. Together they strained and gasped, grunted and scrabbled for purchase, caught each other's cries in their own throats when climax caught them unaware, crested suddenly and sharply and sent them tumbling to the floor, hips working in tandem, slamming them together until the first peak blended into a second, a third, then finally exploded in a shattering rain of lava and an endless trail of falling stars.

Afterward they lay where they'd fallen: Jeth flat on his back, one hand on his chest, the other arm flung wide; Allyn beside him, not quite on her side, neck pillowed in the crook of his elbow. Their hearts thundered, their breath was harsh, their bodies were as slick and wet as though they'd been swimming.

"What was that?" Allyn gasped, struggling to control her breathing.

"Sex." Jeth rolled sideways, mouth twisted. "Sweaty, mind-numbing sex."

Allyn studied his face, the hooded darkness of his eyes, the deliberate callousness of his expression. "Really." It might have been a question but it wasn't. "I thought it felt more like goodbye."

He tightened his arm around her neck, leaned in and kissed her savagely. "Sex, Allyn, that's all it was. Are you listening to me? Nothing more. I am not here to fall in love with you. I *will* not fall in love with you."

"No one asked you to," Allyn said bitingly, while inside her something shriveled and sank. "No one said you had to.'' She pushed away from him and scrambled to her feet, turned on the low-wattage, bare-bulb overhead light to be sure he could see her and looked at him. ''Still, be that as it may, you're not leaving here without me.''

He jacked himself upright, elbow first, surging to his feet in one fluid, catlike move to eye her squarely before sinking onto the stool—both literally and figuratively getting away from the all-too-painful recognition in her blue and green eyes. His jaw tightened; a muscle ticked in his cheek. Damn, she'd gotten good at reading him. How had that happened? He'd changed his mind again about taking her with him the minute he'd heard about the black-market guys and brought the local law into it. Because if they'd had law tailing them here, there would be law again once they left, no matter how likely it was that Gabriel had called off his dogs because he'd had a chance to see Allyn was all right. The very nature of that call would also inform somebody else of where they were. Where Sasha was. But now... ''Allyn—''

Her mouth thinned; she shook her head. ''Not a chance, Jeth. I'm in this. You brought me into it. Don't even think about leaving me out now.''

''It'll be safer—''

''For whom? Not for me. Not for my family if I stay with them. Sure as hell not for you and Sasha. Because I know you now, Jeth. I know where you'll go. I know where you'll hide him.'' She stooped to be eye to eye with him. ''I *know,* damn you, do you hear me? And that means if I stay here whoever's looking for you and Sasha, whoever saw us together that first day, saw my car, probably ran the plates and knows who I am. Whoever followed us here knows I'm with you or have been and'll come looking for you by starting with me. Which means they go through my family, and you've got to know that's not going to happen. I won't let it.

''No.'' She shook her head. ''Way I read it is we've got

three choices. One, we talk to Gabriel and see if there's something he can do to help that doesn't jeopardize the family. Two, you leave with Sasha and I take off on my own and we split our defenses in half—not to mention you've got no one to stay with Sasha while you figure out how to go play macho protector."

"Or three," Jeth said sardonically, half-angry, half-amused by Allyn's reasoning, "I take you with me, and two out of three of us are happy."

"Two out of three?"

"Yeah. You and Sasha. Me, I gotta figure out how to keep three of us alive, instead of just two."

"Oh, well, that." She smiled suddenly; relief etched her features. "No problem—and it's better than having me furious with you for going off and getting yourself killed without me. As for the part about you having to figure out how to protect three of us instead of only two... Not to worry. Libby may be good at following people, but like you, part of what I do in my work is figure out how to keep things alive."

Chapter 13

They packed up and pulled out in the humid prelight of just before dawn, ghosts fading into the heavy morning fog, the van pitifully masked only by license plates borrowed from a vehicle in the main parking lot.

Worn out from a day full of playmates, Sasha protested once in his sleep when Jeth moved him into the van and buckled him into his safety seat. Then he subsided into the deep, lightly snoring slumber he'd been rousted from.

They drove, trading off, going straight through except to pick up gas and food, to stretch briefly and move on. At one stop, Jeth considered changing vehicles, but instead only appropriated a different set of license plates, again under cover of darkness and behind Allyn's back. It was little enough, but it was what he could do while keeping them moving.

States blurred together, individual landscapes lost to sleep and darkness and dull concentration on the road ahead. The green hills of Kentucky bled into first the urban then the rockier parts of Indiana, to Missouri, to the I-44 west and through the dust of Oklahoma and Texas, into New Mexico and finally, after a little more than thirty hours of driving, into northern Arizona around mid-morning of the second day.

Jeth drove from there, picking up Route 66 into Flagstaff. There he parked Allyn and Sasha to lunch at the back of a small, quiet diner that was off the beaten tourist path while he went to rid them of the van.

Aside from the trip she'd begun the day after she'd graduated from high school, this was Allyn's first trip west. Everything was a far cry from what she was used to. She couldn't get over the view of the San Francisco Peaks that backdropped the city, nor the dryness of the air—nor the sensation of shortness of breath that immediately plagued her when all she did was cart Sasha and most of his belongings into the restaurant with her. At seven thousand feet above sea level, Jeth assured her the condition was both natural and temporary, but his confidence didn't lessen her feeling that she was seriously out of shape when she knew she wasn't.

While Sasha lunched on his favorite macaroni and cheese sandwich—also known as grilled cheese on white bread— Allyn feasted on tamales such as she hadn't tasted since her grandmother had taken her and Becky into the migrant camps to teach religion classes to the youngsters during cherry picking season when they were very young. The memory startled her; cherry picking and migrant workers, churros, tamales and being a child were things she hadn't thought about in years—didn't even know she'd forgotten about until she remembered by accident. Still, once the dam opened the flood didn't hold back. Nostalgia waged a war with her senses and won, sharpened taste buds she didn't know had gone stale, reminded her nose of scents and aromas she'd forgotten how to recognize, fitted her mental ears with the music of Spanish.

Her physical ears, however, were treated to the accents

of Southwest twang, of Native American inflections, of native pipes mixed with country-and-western music mixed with country rock mixed with rock. Her eyes found colors and images that were different from those in the migrant camps, softer, tonier, as though filtered through sand. She felt oddly at ease in this place, this city, in a way she'd never experienced before.

Her pulse quickened. She blamed it on the thin air making her slightly giddy, but a tiny ball of excited recognition stirred in her belly. Home. She'd be of no use as a marine biologist here, but it didn't matter. Some part of her felt strangely tied to this soil. She'd never been here before but she knew this place, understood…something, even if she couldn't be sure what.

She shook her head, dismissing the thought. It was nothing, less, strictly fancy. For seven years she'd been tied to her studies, too, at home with them, then felt cut strangely adrift the moment she held her doctorate. It was the way she'd felt after high school, starting the cross-country trek that had ended within a week with her heading home.

With her having chosen the course of her life to date.

And now here she was after another eventful week knowing she was ready to choose another course, change one she hadn't doubted.

Until graduation.

Until Jeth.

Knowing, too, that he could have little or nothing to do with her choice, that they were only a temporary measure— he'd said as much, what was it, three, four nights ago.

He hadn't said much of anything else to her since.

Something stirred the fine hairs at the nape of her neck and shimmied down her spine, lifted the light fuzz on her arms. Allyn stiffened without moving, let her gaze drift from the dim interior of the diner in Flagstaff toward the front door. A man stood there, obviously searching for something or someone, dark, muscular arms showing against light shirtsleeves, long black hair pulled into a ponytail. His top lip might have been puffy.

Allyn breathed. Lots of dark men with long black ponytails here, she reminded herself. It was the place for them. No reason to suspect—

Sasha made a strangled noise, and Allyn turned to him instantly, afraid he was choking. He was spitting out a mouthful of sandwich, but not because he was choking. Eyes wide with terror, he was staring at the man in the doorway and getting ready to scream.

Quickly Allyn wiped his lunch from his mouth and clapped her hand over it, hauled him as quietly as possible into her lap and shielded the man from sight with her body, hugged and rocked Sasha, murmuring as calmly as she could, "Don't, baby, don't, don't, don't. It'll be all right, I've got you, I won't let him hurt you, just please be quiet, love, shh, I need you to be quiet. Maybe he won't see us, maybe he'll go away, maybe it's not him."

Not whom? she wondered nonsensically. But whoever he was, it didn't matter. He frightened Sasha, and Allyn had known far too many little kids in her life to dismiss this one's obvious distress. Why had Jeth left them on their own, indefensible? Where was he, anyway? Aw, heck, this was stupid. Jeth wasn't here, and she'd have to come up with a plan on her own. She was good at coming up with plans on her own, at thinking on her feet. She'd disarmed Jeth the day she'd met him, hadn't she? She could handle this guy, too.

Of course, she could manage this guy. She bucked up her courage and gave herself a firm mental nod. Absolutely, she could manage him. But since this guy was probably a lot more dangerous, she just wouldn't deal with him as directly as she'd dealt with Jeth, that's all.

Yeah, right. *That's all* was more than plenty. Because when she'd dealt with Jeth she hadn't known about Sasha.

And not knowing had made her a great deal more willing to take incautious risks than she was now.

Plus she now knew Jeth hadn't been out to hurt her, only to look after Sasha the best way he could without a getaway vehicle. That made a difference.

Particularly since she currently had no getaway vehicle. Damn it.

Patting Sasha's back to quiet him, she tried to melt deeper into dimness that couldn't possibly hide them for long if this man was looking for them. Strained to move Sasha's diaper bag and gear into a nearby corner, out of sight. Strived to observe the man while she tried not to move and attract his attention, attempted not to appear like she was looking for an employees-only exit out the back if she did attract it. It was damn certain he'd be able to move faster unfettered than she'd be able to move carrying Sasha.

None of it was easy; Sasha's terror had the better of him, made him well nigh hysterical. Subduing a two-year-old in the full throes of hysteria of any sort was often a process where the best you could do was prevent him from throwing himself around and hurting himself until the hysteria passed. Calming one whose hysteria was born of fear and panic brought on by situations he'd lived through was an exercise in futility. The only thing Allyn knew to do was to try to reassure him she would not let harm come to him by getting him far out of sight of the thing—the person—frightening him.

Before that person took real notice of him.

There were few other patrons in the diner. Three men and a couple of women. For a breath Allyn considered options. Then she drew air gently in and stopped thinking altogether, calmly covered Sasha's hair with one of Jeremy's baseball caps, bundled the sobbing toddler into her shoulder, collected his diaper bag and headed for the sign labeled Restrooms—hoping even as the man's face shifted in her direction that if she went naturally, in plain view, without hiding, she'd remained largely unnoticed. In her experience most lone adults tried to ignore women carrying toddlers in tantrum.

Experience seemed to be on her side this time. A surreptitious glance in the man's direction confirmed that his gaze slunk right by her and Sasha. Relieved, Allyn took Sasha into the bathroom and sat him on the sink, pulled a washcloth out of his diaper bag and wet it, used it to wipe his face, soothe the back of his neck and generally cool him down. He clung to her, shuddering, for a while, but she talked and sang softly to him. He gradually relaxed enough for her to check his diaper. He protested when she set him down briefly to glance out the door, to see if the man who'd scared him was still around, but quieted readily enough when she picked him up again.

Which is, of course, when she realized she had no idea what to do next. Because the man was no longer where she could see him out front, but that didn't mean he wasn't there somewhere, occupying one of the back tables the way she had. And she suddenly decided that to slip out the back, Jack, was such a movie cliché that anyone professional enough to track Sasha cross-country despite the weaving route she and Jeth had driven was also probably professional enough to have covered the diner's employees-only entrance.

Not to mention that, unlike most suspense-movie and television restaurant restrooms, this one didn't have a convenient window.

She worried the inside of her lower lip. Nope, nothing for it but to brazen her way out the diner's front door where she was more likely to find people and hope for the best. That or sit until Jeth came back—blast him, where *was* he?—and hope that the guy who scared Sasha wouldn't do anything in front of the other patrons—and that the other patrons would stick around as long as she needed them to unwittingly guard her back.

Oh, heck, she decided. As long as she was hoping, why not simply hope he was gone, period?

And why not hope she and Jeth could keep Sasha, keep the family they'd formed, keep each other?

Even though there wouldn't be anything for a doctor of marine biology to do in Arizona except sling hash or maybe hunt fossils in the canyons.

She drew a shaky breath with the admission. Dear Lord, she wanted to keep Jeth.

Her mouth twisted and firmed as she calculated. Right after she crowned him for taking so long about doing whatever he was doing, that is.

Sasha snuggled into the hollow of her shoulder, snuffling a bit, his body growing heavier and more slack with each passing moment. Allyn smiled tightly. Panic was an exhausting business. He'd be asleep soon, she knew. She looked around the small restroom, felt the box-like atmosphere and claustrophobia set in. One thing was sure, she couldn't keep him in here. Her driver's ed instructor had taught her never to let herself get boxed in by traffic, to always leave herself an escape route when she was driving. The same principle applied to fires and when you had bad guys chasing you: if you didn't leave yourself an out, you could die trying to stay safe by hiding from the smoke, the flames or the bullets in the broom closet.

Not that there'd been any bullets, of course, thank goodness, but still. It was, all in all, a nauseatingly bad idea as far as Allyn was concerned.

Breathing deep a few times as though preparing for a plunge into deep waters, Allyn gathered Sasha and his equipment tight to her chest and set her back against the door. No way was this baby going out of here first. Dangerous to back out or not, she couldn't very well lead with Sasha, could she. Nope. Not a chance.

She grabbed one last breath of disinfectant-cleansed air and slid sideways to open the door quickly and duck out.

The moment she did, a man's hand clamped over her mouth, his other arm slid around her waist, glued her to him.

Instinct took over on the spot, and she'd stamped down hard on Jeth's instep, kicked him forcefully in the side of the knee before she comprehended what he said.

"For cripe's sake, Lynnie, it's me. Give over. We're out of here."

"Where what how—"

"Later." He let her go and grabbed her arm to drag her toward the employees-only entrance she'd discarded as an escape route not fifteen minutes earlier. "Right now we got trouble."

"But—"

He shook his head and paused at the door. For the first time, Allyn saw he had his gun in his hand. The safety was off.

"Keep behind me, but stay close." An order.

The rebel in Allyn made her grind her teeth and mutter, "Yassuh, boss," under her breath, but the smart woman with the toddler in her arms did what she was told because sometimes commands were given for a reason. And from the way Jeth looked, this was definitely one of those times.

He glanced at her, jaw taut, eyes hard, weapon pointed ceilingward, available. "Ready?"

There was nothing to say. She nodded, one sharp jerk of her chin downward. Then Jeth pressed the door open and took a fast look in all directions. Satisfied, he pushed the door wider, motioned his head to urge Allyn out. He followed, herding her into the alley, both hands wrapped around his weapon, raising it, lowering it as he made a continuous circle within a circle around her, marking every crack in the building's walls, every pebble in their path and each nook and cranny in between.

"Jeth, what's—"

Again he shook his head. "Not now. Keep moving. Get in the jeep."

"Jeep? Where—"

A stab of his chin in the direction of a Dumpster butted up to the wall of the building across the alley. A worse-for-wear-looking former Army jeep with top sat just beyond it, facing the alley's far end.

"Jeth, we can't. There's no place for Sasha—"

"Trust me," Jeth snapped. "There's a place. I made sure."

Keeping an eye on their surroundings, he relieved Allyn of the diaper bag and tossed it into the back of the jeep, guided her around the other side and stood guard while she put Sasha in his car seat. It was only when she turned in preparation to climb into the front that she noticed the body angled half upright in the space between the Dumpster and the wall.

If it wasn't for the blood still spreading across the front of his shirt, she might have allowed herself to assume the body was a wino catching some sleep while he waited for a handout. Not only was the blood seeping and staining, but the body belonged to the man who'd scared Sasha in the diner, long black hair, muscular arms, graying dark skin and all.

Air choked in Allyn's throat. "Jeth?"

"He's dead." His jaw clicked audibly. "I found him back here. He tried to kill me. He didn't succeed. Now let's get the hell out of here so I can find some place it'll be safe to throw up."

The world flashed by in unreal pictures, scenery blurred and forgotten—caught like Allyn's ability to breathe between one moment and the next.

While Sasha slept, Jeth pushed the jeep's speed to its limit, grinding up and down through the gears until they exited Flagstaff, then throttling it into high gear and flooring it.

Space-shuttle speed wouldn't have been enough to escape what was done.

He'd never before had to put down a man. Wanted to, perhaps, wished he could destroy whoever had killed Marcy, but always there'd been another way, channels that didn't carve irreparable ridges in his psyche or leave his conscience wanting to disown him. And the worst of it was, he was pretty sure that even though he felt a bit like throwing up, he didn't feel a whole lot of remorse. The guy who'd exited the rear of the diner—and who was now lying dead in that alley—and his partner had tried to take him down. He'd had no choice but to fire back. And the worst of it was he wasn't sure in his own mind if he'd fired the killing shot or the guy's partner had—or where the partner had gotten to. Either way, there were shell casings from his weapon back there, and that was bad for Allyn and Sasha.

Allyn touched his arm. He stiffened and shrank from the contact.

"What happened?" She had to shout to be heard over the rush of the wind and the whine of the motor.

"You tell me."

"That—that man back there. Behind the diner. He came inside. Sasha recognized him and got scared. I didn't know what to do." Pleading for forgiveness, for understanding, and she didn't know why. This wasn't her normal life, after all, it was his. "I wanted to go out the back, but then I thought he might have figured on that so I decided maybe to brazen it out the front where there were people or wait till you came, but you didn't and I had to do something. But I didn't. Then you came. That's all. If you shot him, why didn't I hear anything?"

"Silencer." Grim and clipped. "His—or his partner's."

Horror dawned. She put a hand to her throat, unable to wrap her mind around the implications, her breath stolen again when she thought it couldn't be. "Jeth. He came to kill you. Maybe us."

"Us. Or so he said."

"But you—how did you—did you know him?"

His mouth twisted; he nodded. "Colombian. I knew him in Baltimore. He was muscle. I've seen his work before."

She swallowed, nauseated by the thought of what he'd had to do because of her and Sasha. "Are you hurt? Are you all right?"

"Dandy."

"Jeth—"

"Drop it, Allyn." Hard and unforgiving. "It's my fault. I screwed up. Now let me drive."

And for the next hundred miles that was all he would say. His focus was fierce, intense, and Allyn could only eye him warily and worry, do her best to behave as though she understood the incomprehensible—otherwise known as Jeth.

Despite the jeep's stiff suspension and the thud and rush of the highway around and underneath them, Sasha slept for most of the trip, innocent of the emotional havoc and physical peril his existence wrought for the adults in the front seat. Allyn checked on him constantly, craning to look over her shoulder at him, touching his leg—anything to feel she was contributing something when it was clear to her she had nothing to contribute.

Except silence, caring and support—for whatever they might be worth under the circumstances.

The farther west they went, the more ferocious Jeth's concentration became. If Allyn hadn't been so intent on making sure Sasha didn't bounce around too much in his seat, she might have paid more attention to the fine gray pallor that edged his features, the sweat that sheened his skin. The desert wind was hot, but this was something more than reaction caused by the air. It wasn't until they jounced unexpectedly off the route that marked a prohibited trailhead into one of the canyons and Allyn reached over to steady herself against Jeth that she realized what appeared to be simple perspiration was more the kind of clamminess related to shock than to heat. Her hand tightened on his arm; she glanced sharply at him. Sight confirmed what instinct told her: he held on to himself by will alone.

"Jeth, damn it, stop here. Let me drive."

He didn't take his eyes off the road, merely blinked sweat out of them and swallowed.

"Jeth, can you hear me? I said stop, damn it, you're sick, you need help before you kill us."

Another dogged swallow, this time accompanied by a tiny negative movement of his head. As though if the movement were any bigger either his head would shatter or his attention would. "I'm okay. Not much farther unless the damned rancher's blocked the way. Road's bad, you don't know it. I do. Get in back and buckle up. Pad Sasha so his neck and head are braced and hang on."

He wasn't kidding about the road. Unmaintained, it appeared to be rarely if ever utilized—hence the Prohibited sign. She couldn't tell how long they'd been descending before she found herself trying to brace Sasha into his seat more securely by covering and cushioning him with her body. She also had the distinct impression that by the time they reached wherever they were going, she was going to wish her tailbone was more padded. Her arms, stretched hard across Sasha's car seat, already felt as battered and bruised as the thigh she'd crammed against it to help keep the seat more stable.

Jeth seemed oblivious to everything but the road, but by the time the narrow switchbacks through limestone, sandstone and shale that shut off even occasional views of the distant rimrock leveled out, he looked far rockier than the canyon around them. Appeared a good deal less stable than the occasional *scrush* of detritus that clattered out beneath their tires.

With each decrease in elevation, heat collected more heavily under the jeep's metal roof, stifling. The first sight Allyn got of the blue-green waters that flowed through Jeth's birthplace would have been startling in any case, but through heat-limned eyes they were surreal, too bright—beautiful. She wanted to be in them, to dunk the sweaty Sasha and cool him down—to explore them at her leisure, to...

She straightened with the road, put a hand on Jeth's shoulder to grasp his attention, started to say something about the verdancy of the land they entered, the spectacular beauty of what she assumed must be the creek he'd told her about.

And froze at the wet and pulpy texture beneath her fingers, jerked her hand quickly at Jeth's agonized gasp of surprise. Shocked, she looked at her palm, damp with his blood.

"You're hurt." It was an idiot thing to say, but it was the first thing that came out of her mouth.

"I'm fine." His voice was weak, and he sounded anything but.

She unbuckled and grabbed a towel and a liter of bottled water out of Sasha's bag, angled herself so she could see around the back of Jeth's seat to assess as much of the damage to his shoulder as possible.

And discovered with a gut-wrenching sense of fear that the damage was not so much to his shoulder as it was to the upper left quadrant of his chest below his collarbone. The pulpiness was actually a makeshift pressure bandage he'd fixed to give them all time.

"You have to stop now." Her voice shook. She was terrified for him and for Sasha, afraid for herself. It was too soon, too insane, there hadn't been enough time to know anything for certain, but she didn't want to lose Jeth.

She couldn't.

"Please, Jeth. For me. For Sasha. So we don't have an accident."

"Not yet." Faint but ferocious, determined.

"You have to, Jeth. You're bleeding. You need help. Let's get you help."

"No." Guttural and harsh. With effort he removed his left hand from the steering wheel, raised it to clasp her wrist where she tried awkwardly to apply pressure to the wound she couldn't see. "No. Gunshot. Too much paperwork. They'll find you. They'll find Sasha. I promised him, Lyn. Nobody hurts him anymore. Nobody gets near you without going through me. Nobody."

The struggle to speak, to make her understand, cost him dearly. For an instant his right hand wavered on the wheel and he started to slump. Then they jolted over a rock and hit a rut on the other side. Allyn's chin banged hard on the back of his seat and hit his shoulder, causing her to nearly bite through her lip. He snapped to; both hands clutched the steering wheel, fought the jeep for control.

Something viscous that smelled faintly of salt and iron soaked into the collar of his T-shirt.

"Lynnie?" The query was faint but worried. He struggled to keep the world from blurring, while she once more reached over his shoulder and tried to put pressure on his bleeding wound.

"We're all right. I bit my lip, don't worry about it."

Her mouth was close to his ear. It felt *right* there, Jeth thought absurdly, and he felt fuzzy. If only he could close his eyes and feel her breath there for a long time, he could die happy.

"Jeth."

Her voice was sharp and insistent, furious. He tried to shake the fury away by nuzzling the side of his face close to her mouth. Something about her bottom lip didn't feel quite right, but he couldn't think what.

He couldn't think.

"Jeth!"

He felt her angle between the seats to get in beside him, try to take the steering wheel from him. He wanted to curl in toward her, to hold on to her to keep himself from slipping into the darkness that lapped around his vision, knew he couldn't. He had a mission to complete before he could take any more comfort in her. If she got too close to him before then he might not be able to protect her.

His mind couldn't quite put the word on why, but he knew the reason was paramount. He had to protect her.

Had to.

The future of the earth, sun, wind, moon and stars depended upon her safety. His life depended on it.

"Jeth, damn it! Don't do this to me and Sasha. I won't let you."

He recognized the panic, understood something must be terribly wrong or she wouldn't sound that way. She wasn't a woman made of panic; she was forged of steel and iron, as easily controlled as flames in dry grass. Whatever made her frantic, he wanted to do something about it.

Another deep rut jolted him, knocked his knee against the gearshift and put them into a sudden stall. Something thunked against the dashboard, and as from a great distance he heard Allyn swear. Then the jeep bounced perilously sideways a foot or two and went still at a slight slant. Somewhere behind him, Sasha loosed a thin wail and subsided. He tried to straighten, to gain control of the situation, but he kept slipping against the seat, sliding through a substance that seemed familiar though he couldn't remember why. His body felt like lead, his entire left side numb and unresponsive. His pulse thumped inside him, but it didn't feel like life flowing through; it felt like the tide ebbing out.

Allyn's mouth found his ear again. "Sit still," she told him tersely. "You're making it worse."

"Lyn..." His tongue felt thick, his mouth drier than it had ever been. He swallowed, tried again. "Lynnie..."

"Not now, blast you." Her hands on him were anything but gentle. "Save your strength. Don't you dare die on me." She pressed a wad of something to his left chest, planted his left hand over it. "Hold this."

He heard something tear, then she was wrapping something around him, strapping his hand tightly into place on his chest, tying his arm to his side. The sensation of the life pumping slowly out of him subsided to a dull, indifferent thrum. She drew his right arm across her shoulders, wrapped her arms about his waist and hoisted him slightly forward in his seat.

"I want you to help me move you over here," she said tautly. "On the count of three. Ready? One...two...*three*."

The word and her yanking him toward her came at the same time. He struggled to use his feet to push himself in the direction she wanted him to go. The undertaking was more costly than he could have imagined, left darkness tightening the edges of his vision.

"One more time," he heard Allyn plead. "Don't pass out on me yet. Just help me get your legs...ah. There you go, you did it. Jeth, can you hear me?"

He nodded—or thought he did.

"Good."

He felt her relax a degree even as she leaned over to buckle him into the seat. Why did her body always feel so good against his, even now when most of him was so numb and out of it he shouldn't be able to notice?

But he did notice. His belly, his loins noticed and recognized her at once. He was pretty darn certain they always would. *He* always would.

Laughing ruefully, Allyn made sure the shoulder harness clicked shut and kissed Jeth's temple as she drew away from him.

"Thanks," she whispered. "I guess if that can happen, you can't be too far gone, can you?"

Jeth tried to wink at her, failed. The moment he shut one eye, the other wanted to follow it. Neither could be forced to reopen.

Striving to stay with her, he thought he heard Allyn say something else, ask a direction. He only hoped she understood whatever answer he attempted to make before he finally lost consciousness completely.

Chapter 14

Allyn put her ear close to Jeth's mouth and hoped she understood him correctly as he tried to tell her which direction to take when they reached the bottom of the track into the canyon. He needed water and medical attention, but she knew he was right about the kind of paperwork gunshot wounds required. Probably almost as much as killing someone in the line of duty mandated. And since God alone knew who they could trust, she didn't dare second-guess Jeth again.

Yet.

She glanced sideways at the center of her thoughts. She only hoped she'd be able to find where he planned to hide them, then be capable of taking care of his wound. It had been a while since she'd done the kind of dissection removing a lodged bullet might require. And even if she managed, there was always the threat of infection. Sea botany she knew. Land botany...those classes had been a while, and she wasn't familiar with anything in Arizona's indigenous plant life that might be used in place of antibiotics in any case.

Oh, God, oh, God. Her fists white-knuckled the steering wheel. How stupid she'd been to think that side trip to allay her family's concerns about her was the right thing to do. Because sure as shooting all she'd done was make matters worse for all of them. Especially Jeth and Sasha.

But she didn't have time to consider past mistakes, nor anything other than the *now*. Sasha was wakening in the back seat and crabbily trying to unstuff all the things she'd stuffed around him to keep him from flopping about and getting hurt during their journey down the canyon. Beside her Jeth looked a whole lot grayer around the gills than she liked, and the heat was griddle-caking her brain into muddled eggs so the only thing she could think was that when she *did* get them to where she thought they were going there would probably be rattlesnakes waiting in the corners to terrify her. She'd never met one personally, but she really didn't think she'd like rattlesnakes any more than she liked the men who'd tried to kill Jeth.

It also occurred to her in passing that she was glad at least one of the guys was dead because if he wasn't she'd have to do something quite serious about him—them. No one went around hurting her man—whether he was exactly *her* man yet or not.

See, brain-fried.

The track ended at last on the verge of lush farmland and an open, dusty road that ran along the river. Allyn downshifted and pulled to a stop, looked to the right, the left, trying to choose between what she thought she'd understood Jeth to say and what he might have said.

Cottonwoods and willows edged the river, leaves fluttering lazily, inviting. A lone truck with an open bed approached from the east, dust billowing behind it. It slowed as it neared the jeep; a pair of dark copper faces looked Allyn over, then disappeared into the cab, apparently conferencing. Wondering what she'd say if they decided to talk to her, Allyn started to bite her lip, hissed and winced when her teeth found the cut she'd acquired earlier. The truck moved on without stopping, however, and she breathed a sigh of relief. One less lie to manufacture. But sitting here wasn't getting Jeth help. It also wasn't getting Sasha out of his car seat and sweaty clothes or getting fluids into him.

So much to think about, to do. Damn Jeth, anyway. He was supposed to be awake to help out, not slumped half-dead in the seat next to her, scaring her to bits. She hadn't been born to be a packhorse, the overseer of three lives hanging in the balance.

She hadn't been born to be Becky.

Which, she suddenly understood by experiencing the situation out of context, was exactly what Becky'd been saying. Becky hadn't been born to simply be Becky, either. But you did what the moments required of you, made your choices, your compromises, then took your chances and—

Allyn whipped the steering wheel to the right and jammed the jeep into gear.

Made her choice without a sense of compromise and took her chances, because she realized with unexpected clarity there wasn't a risk in the world she wouldn't take for Jeth and Sasha.

Allyn hadn't driven far before a white SUV appeared in her rearview mirror. A red light, cocked at a jaunty angle on the driver's side roof, whirled madly in the sunlight. Allyn glanced at Jeth who muttered something unintelligible and fumbled weakly at his left arm in his stupor. Stop, don't stop; both options bore stunning implications, risks she wasn't prepared to take with either of her charges.

As it happened, she needn't have worried about making the choice herself; in another minute a dilapidated tan truck, also wearing a flashing light, came toward her at a break-neck clip, then suddenly slewed sideways in front of her, blocking the road. When she stopped and considered backing up, the SUV behind her did the same thing.

For an instant her heart stopped, and she looked at the floor between the seats where Jeth's weapon sat. Despite the fact that she'd learned how to handle a handgun, she'd never fired one. But hey, the guys with the flashing lights didn't have to know that.

All too aware of Sasha fussing in the back seat, of the unconscious Jeth beside her, Allyn reached down to close her hand around the Browning's grip.

And waited.

Copper-skinned men she hoped were Jeth's tribal brethren climbed out of the vehicles and sauntered toward her. Something about the looseness of their movements, their physical structure seemed unnervingly familiar, but Allyn couldn't quite place why. She was far too intent on remaining calm and gauging her options if push came to shove. After all, Jeth might have killed for her. The least she could do was contemplate doing the same if it became necessary in order to protect him.

The idea made her shudder, but it didn't put a dent in her resolve.

Quite.

The man approaching from the front stuck his hand in his back pocket, pulled out a small folder and flipped it open, held it up as he came forward. The one behind the jeep also pulled something out of a pocket and clipped it to the pocket of his T-shirt. It took Allyn but a moment to realize it was some sort of police badge.

"Hey," the one in front called. "Supai collection agent. You want to cross the rez you gotta pay the fee."

"I'm sorry, Officer—is it officer?" Allyn called, and saw both men start and stare. "We—I didn't know there was a fee. Can I pay it and go? I've got…" She hesitated, choosing her words carefully. "My husband is sick and there's my son…I need to get them to…to my husband's home—"

The men were on either side of the jeep before she even realized they were coming.

"Wife?" the one who bent to peer at her asked. "Jeth got married?"

"Sick?" queried the other, who'd opened the passenger door and stooped beside Jeth. "He looks a damn sight more than sick to me."

He reached in as though to unbuckle Jeth and fiddle with the bandages, and Allyn brought the Browning up and leveled it at him.

"Back off." A warning, flat and unequivocal.

Surprised, the man raised his hands wide, jerked his chin toward his badge. "Easy there, sis," he said. "I don't know what's going on here, but you're holding that thing on a tribal cop, you oughtta know that."

"And?" Allyn eyed him, then marked the location of the man who'd proclaimed himself a collection agent. Their features were similar, reminded her of someone. "Doesn't necessarily make you the good guys. Far as I know you helped set him up to be killed. Uh-uh. Drop your badges in here and back off. Now."

"Aw, now, honey," the one on her side of the jeep objected. "We don't need to do this, do we? It's pretty simple far as we're concerned. If you're married to Jeth, that makes us your brothers-in-law and you our new sister. I'm Guy Levoie, that's Russ." He showed her the wallet ID that named him a member of the Bureau of Indian Affairs law enforcement division. "All right? You got our baby brother in there next to you. Let us help you get him home where we can get your own baby outa that seat and into somethin' to drink and figure out what kind of help Jeth needs."

Things moved quickly after that.

Almost before Allyn knew what was happening, Guy and Russ had returned to their vehicles and escorted her to an unpainted and weathered wooden structure with an east-facing porch set not far from the river among the cotton-woods and willows, and somewhere behind and out of sight of the village. There, while Allyn fretted about them re-opening his wound and played packhorse to Sasha, they gently transferred Jeth inside and into an airy back bed-room. Then, when Russ left—over Allyn's heated objec-tions—to get his brother medical help, Guy started to strip Jeth's bandages away. At that point, she dropped Sasha's bags, hefted her makeshift son securely onto her left hip and grabbed Guy's arm to haul him bodily away from Jeth.

"Don't," she snapped. "You'll have him bleeding again."

Guy looked at her. She jammed her tongue into her bot-tom teeth and stiffened her jaw to keep her mouth from trembling. Her lip was sore and tasted crusty, and her knees were starting to feel spongy.

"What happened?"

Allyn shook her head. "I—I can't. Just…get my bags out of the jeep and find me some alcohol, hot water and towels."

Guy measured her for a beat, came to a decision. "We double as a lot of things here on the rez. How 'bout I get my equipment from the truck instead?"

"Thanks," she said, and he went.

When he was gone, she breathed deep and folded onto the bed, laid the back of her hand along the side of Jeth's face, checking his temperature before finding someplace safe to temporarily corral Sasha. Whatever happened, she could not give in to the urge to fall prey to a case of screaming-meemie hysteria. There was too much to do, to take care of.

She squinched her eyes shut and rocked back and forth, no longer sure whether she was trying to comfort Sasha or herself. *God, let him be all right, let him be all right—*

Beside her Jeth's eyelids wavered with her touch; his free hand made a slow motion effort to snag hers.

"Lyn…" Dry-throated and barely audible. He moistened his mouth and tried again. "Lynnie." He attempted to touch her mouth with his fingertips. "You look…bad. You…Sasha?"

Allyn squeezed his hand, brought it to where he could touch Sasha's leg. "We're okay, Jeth, both of us, I promise. We're here. We're fine. Guy and Russ found us. It's you we need to take care of now."

"Guy…Russ." The names came out with an effort that looked almost more emotional than physical. "Judas. Don't…" Something spasmed through him, and squeezed shut his eyes for a moment, clenched his teeth, tightened his jaw until it clicked. "Don't…" A breath. "Tell them…" Another breath. "I mucked it up…again. Don't…let them tell Ma."

Heart clutching, Allyn kissed his fingers. "You didn't muck anything up," she promised gently. "And they won't say anything to anyone about anything, trust me." She glanced at Guy, who'd entered the room, a box of medical supplies dangling from either hand. "Will you."

Not a question, a statement. The sort that any man worth his salt knew better than to ignore.

Guy, who was also, Allyn learned later, known as Guy-api, or *Candiu,* and who stood a good six foot two and was almost frighteningly handsome despite—or perhaps because of—the line of blue war paint painted above and below his right eye and the rattlesnake art that spiraled up his left arm, was often worth the salt of two or three men. Which meant he simply nodded at Allyn, stepped to the bed and set down his boxes, touched his brother's hand, then relieved Allyn of Sasha and helped her get down to the business of caring for Jeth.

The wound was bad enough, but it was not worse. The bullet didn't seem to have struck anything vital. *How* not was anybody's guess, although Allyn laid it down with a prayerful thank-you to the divine intervention of heaven's grace and Sasha's, Jeth's and her own guardian angels.

The doctor Russ brought with him wanted X rays to be certain of the damage, but Jeth, who'd roused sufficiently to be aware of what was going on, put up such violent opposition that the tiny young woman, named Kaze, changed her mind. Any man who could, she said, be so pigheaded in regard to his own health deserved what happened to him. Then she turned her back on her cousin and gave Allyn two handfuls of antibiotics to administer on a regular schedule with instructions for keeping Jeth's wound clean and admonitions to keep him still. After that she inspected Sasha before Allyn had a chance to ask, suggested a course of vitamins for the toddler and turned her attention to the lip Allyn had forgotten biting. Three tiny stitches closed the wound, then Kaze was gone as briskly as she'd arrived.

It was only after she'd left that Allyn realized the young doctor hadn't asked a single question regarding the hows or whys of Jeth's injury.

After assuring themselves of Jeth's well-being, Russ and Guy unloaded the jeep. Along with the family's luggage, it contained boxes of non-perishable groceries and other household supplies that could last them quite some time. In between checking on Jeth and playing with Sasha, Allyn stocked the cupboards and debated how many of Jeth's brothers' questions she could answer, how many to leave blank.

On the whole she was as inclined to trust them as she had been Jeth; they were solid and apparently imperturbable when it came to filling her in on a few of their younger brother's exploits. Still…

She looked at them, and the urge to protect them the way Jeth had chosen to protect her family—by leaving them in the dark—was strong. Of course, Jeth hadn't been gunshot when they'd been with her family, and both his brothers seemed not only big but good-natured, intelligent and capable—not to mention they both wore badges.

Blast, what was the rule when you had three big guys hanging around willing to do what had to be done, but one of them was lying hurt and macho trying to protect the other two by leaving them out of what he considered his business? Allyn didn't have any brothers. She didn't know what you did with them—although she was seriously inclined to start busting chops the moment Jeth was well enough to take the hit. Because between him and Sasha both requiring her attention she sure as shooting didn't know if she could handle this entire keeping people safe gig on her own. The one thing of which she was fairly certain, however, was that a huge amount of activity at a dwelling that had apparently been vacant for a while was likely to arouse notice within the immediate community and the sparse summer tourist population.

"They won't talk, you know."

Allyn started and turned. Russ's voice was very like Jeth's and Guy's in tone and timbre. But where Jeth's had an undercurrent of intensity and passion toward things unresolved and Guy's was as open and unruffled and filled with laughter as the rest of him, Russ's voice was like the rest of him, too: quieter, gentler, milder and more circumspect.

More…forgiving.

"What?"

"The village. We pretty much steer clear of outsiders. This is our home. We're farmers, the people of the river. You can't keep your values if you let everyone who passes through have a piece of you."

"I don't—how did you—"

Russ shrugged. "He hasn't been home for three years. Now he shows up with a wife and a blond baby who looks like he's been undernourished until recently and who doesn't look like either of you. Someone basically put a gun to his chest and squeezed the trigger. You're all in trouble or he wouldn't have brought you here. Especially not stocked to the gills with groceries for a long stay.''

''And nothing fresh because we can get that here.''

''Just so,'' Russ agreed.

Allyn looked away, at Guy who stood in the kitchen doorway, a small box in his hand, at Sasha happily ensconced at the kitchen table with a bowl of dry cereal and a juice box.

''I can't tell you what you want to know,'' she said softly. ''It's not mine to say. I think he got shot partly because I screwed up taking us to the last place we were. This time I don't know if it's better to tell you or leave you in the dark.'' She lifted her chin and eyed both men squarely. ''I'll understand if you think we ought to pull out of here as soon as Jeth's well enough to travel, though. He will, too. That's all I can say.''

''Pull out?'' Guy looked at Russ, who snorted. ''Before Ma has a chance to meet her new daughter-in-law?''

''I don't think so,'' Russ agreed. ''Nah. We just want to know if we need to beef up tribal firepower to keep this blood from getting you all killed.''

''Yeah.'' Guy held out his hand, offered her the box of nonpermanent black hair dye he'd brought with him. ''Kaze figures you can use this and maybe a little sunless tanning lotion on the short man there. You…'' He reached for her chin, tilted her face to the right, the left and back. ''Eh. Braid your hair so it doesn't look too wildly Irish, and you've got enough color you can probably pass from a distance, as long as you don't go about topless.''

Outraged, Allyn knocked Guy's hand away. ''As long as I *what?*''

''Well, fine, then.'' Eyes dancing, Guy backed up.

''Maybe I misspoke. Maybe you've got an all-over tan and *can* go about topless, what do I know?''

''Not a blessed thing, from the sound of it.'' Disgusted, Allyn turned her back on Guy. ''I mean, really, is this the way you treat all your sisters-in-law?''

''Sadly?'' Russ asked on his brother's behalf. ''Yes, since you're the only sister-in-law we have. None of the rest of us are married. But if it's any comfort, he's always said things like that to Mabel and Kaze and our female cousins, so...welcome to the family, sis.''

The day eased gently but exhaustingly toward the early canyon sunset.

Kaze and Jeth's sister, Mabel—a small, quiet woman who bore more resemblance to her mother than her brothers—turned up shortly after Russ and Guy departed, to help Allyn color Sasha's hair. It was a process easier talked about than accomplished until Jeth's mother showed up, too, and, after glancing at her prodigal son, took hold of the situation at the kitchen sink. Sasha responded to yet another new grandmother like a dry house afire. Whatever Sada did, she apparently had the touch in capitals, because he almost instantly settled down to the game of coloring his hair and eyebrows the way he might use crayons in a coloring book.

Unsure what to do with her make-believe husband's real-life mother, and feeling awkwardly underfoot, Allyn retreated to the bedroom to check on Jeth, who was propped on his right side with pillows stuffed behind his back, muttering and moaning in restless sleep. A basin of cool water sat on a stand near the bed; she dampened a cloth and squeezed it out, pressed it along the side of his face and neck. Squeezed his hand, stroked his face, side, hip, trying to calm his thrashing.

''Jeth, lie still. You'll hurt yourself.''

His right hand snaked out to grip her shirtfront and jerk

her down, eyes opened wide, face turned in her direction, but it wasn't her he saw. "Tell me where she is, you bastard, or I swear to God I'll put you down now." He shook her violently. "Tell me, damn you, tell me—"

"Jeth." Sharp and insistent while she grabbed his wrist to hold him still and attempted to gently pry his hand loose. "It's me, Allyn. Let go."

"She's hurt, I'll do to you whatever you did to her, you hear me, scumbag? I'll freaking kill you—"

"Jeth." A frightened gasp. He was choking her and didn't know it. There was nothing else for it. Allyn tucked her middle finger under her thumb, loosed it hard to snap the bridge of his nose to get his attention. "Jeth, stop it!"

He blinked; his grip on her relaxed, fury subsided. "Lynnie?"

She ran her palm up the side of his jaw. "I'm here, Jeth."

"Good." He slid his fingers along her arm, searching for her hand. "They didn't take my ring, did they?"

"Ring?" Puzzled, she stared at him, then realized he was fumbling with the rings on her left hand. A fist of something achy wedged in her throat. She swallowed it, raised his hand to her mouth and kissed it. "No, they didn't take it. It's right here in the drawer."

"No." He licked his lips. "Not…there. I want it…on. Show them you…me…together…rings…on."

She couldn't help it. Tears stung the backs of her eyes, and her throat closed. They weren't married but even now when he was mostly out of it he remembered the masquerade, the cover, and insisted on using it. "Oh, Jeth."

"Please." A request, a plea.

"You're hand's swollen. And I'm wearing my rings. They see."

"But you don't." Soft, intense—filled with much the same passion as the night he'd assured her he didn't plan to fall in love with her over her virginity, shared dangers and a fake marriage. The fingertips she held close to her face brushed weakly at her jaw. "I want...you, need you...to see it on. Please. Do you...understand?"

She wanted to and was afraid to. "I...I'm not sure. Maybe."

He sighed. "Close enough. For now." He tried wiggling the ring finger on his left hand. "Please."

How could she resist when he'd used the magic word more times in the last five minutes than in the entire ten days or whatever that she'd known him? She drew his ring out of the drawer and slid it onto his finger. It was tight, but not too badly so.

"Okay?" she asked.

He nodded, smiling slightly, eyes drifting closed. "For now," he repeated. Then when she made to move away, he squeezed her hand, tried to haul her back. "Stay?" he asked. "I...need you to..."

What he needed of her was lost in the sough of deep, regular breathing and sleep.

Looking at him, Allyn understood clearly and irrevocably for the first time that the word she'd been trying to ignore for the last many days when it came to how she felt about Jeth Levoie was *love*.

Chapter 15

The four-letter mental revelation threw her for a loop.

Feeling suddenly shaky, Allyn hooked a foot around the leg of the rough rocking chair nearby, drew it to the bed where she could sit without letting go of Jeth's hand and tried hard not to think about anything. His color was better, she decided; she would concentrate on that.

Yeah, right, her mental demon teased. *I'm going to let you study his flush or lack thereof when you left open a word like* love. *Dream on, sucker! Love, love, love, love, love. See? You can't stop thinking about it, so dance to the beat. Love, baby, love.*

"Shut up," she muttered to the demon. "Of course I love him. He's a human being. I'm supposed to, so go arrest yourself. It doesn't mean squat."

Sure, honey. Anything you say, the demon agreed cheekily and skipped to the back of her mind.

Allyn thought she heard it laughing itself silly as it thunked around in there creating havoc until it made its way into her pulse, slam-dunking a basketball all the way to her heart.

Good grief, she thought. *Can one little word really do all that to me?*

Fortunately she didn't sit alone with her thoughts long enough to find out. In a rush of giggles and short legs outdistancing longer and older ones, Sasha and Jeth's sister blew into the room, his mother close behind. Shushing him, Mabel whisked the toddler into her arms and departed before Allyn had a chance to get a look at anything beyond the fact that his head appeared to be covered with... something. Then Jeth groaned and struggled to shift in his sleep, and Allyn switched her attention to quieting him again. His mother leaned in to tuck the pillows more securely beneath him, then rounded the bed to look into his face, pursed her lips in sad bemusement and turned to Allyn. Uncomfortable under her scrutiny, Allyn kept her eyes on Jeth and wished for better circumstances and no need to lie.

Sada Levoie's lips twitched as she watched Allyn. "He goes from home for three years, no word, and comes back like this." She spoke with a native cadence, a thick lilt that said though she spoke English well, she didn't use it often. "I would have him home for Peach Festival, not to hide because he is shot."

Allyn nodded, her mouth worked, tasting guilt. "I know."

"So." Sada touched the ring on Jeth's finger. "You married my son. You know him long?"

Allyn glanced up, down, at the dark copper hand cupped in hers. "No." She shook her head. Against her will, her mouth twitched with humor and she shrugged. "Really I've just known him long enough."

"There was a ceremony? Your family was there?"

"No. No one. It was very..." She searched for the truth amidst the lie. "Private."

"And your son. Where is his father?"

"His father is scum," Allyn said flatly. "His father will never lay a hand on him again if I can help it."

"Ah." Sada nodded as though that explained a great deal. Then, "Who hurt my son?"

Allyn raised her chin, looked Sada in the eye. "Someone who will never hurt Jeth or Sasha or anyone else again."

Sada smiled. "Good." Another pause. "Do more come?"

Allyn didn't hesitate. She couldn't. "I don't know. Maybe."

"For your son?"

"Yes. I think so."

Sada's eyes and mouth firmed. "Then we will not let them find him."

Relief and fear flooded Allyn. "Thank you," she whispered. "But I can't let anyone else—"

"You take care of my son," Sada told her gently but firmly. "We hide yours. Don't be a mule like Jeth. My husband is up top working, but we will be fine. Mabel will take Sasha where he won't be noticed, and that will make you less noticed." She held out a hand. "Hey, we make this pact now, woman to woman, before he wakes. Men don't know how to do this. Grandmothers know how to protect the children. The mother leaves the wife to mend the man."

It was wisdom Allyn found difficult to argue with—especially since it was largely the same as that passed down within her own family. Of course, there being so many women in her family, they might have been slightly prejudiced as to which gender knew how to do what better, but hey, you learned what you learned, filtered the rest and hoped for the best.

"Okay." She put her hand in Sada's. "But I want to see him every day."

Eyes somewhere just this side of sober and that side of

innocence, but features revealing nothing, Sada nodded, and Allyn knew instantly where Jeth came by his ability to shave the truth without telling a lie. "You will see him. And we will all keep watch for men who don't belong in our canyon."

Night wore on, seeming darker than Allyn was used to.

Familiar evening songs blended with regional noises she couldn't readily identify. She ate because Kaze came by to hang a new IV for Jeth and made her. She braided her hair because Guy stopped in and teased and goaded her into doing so.

By darkness she packed up the supplies of diapers, toddler snacks and the individually packaged macaroni and cheese meals that were Sasha's favorites and sent them to wherever with Russ when he poked his head in the door to make sure things were all right. They weren't, of course, not with Sasha gone and Jeth in the shape he was in, but since there was nothing life-threatening immediately in the works, all right was relative.

Two days passed in which Jeth drifted in and out of consciousness. Each waking found him a little more lucid and aware of his surroundings, made Allyn relax further. He also left her somewhat breathless when, each time he opened his eyes, his first waking act was to find and reach for her, inspect her mouth with weak but gentle fingers and find her ring hand to kiss before he asked about Sasha, let her help him take care of necessities and rode sleep out again. And with each waking Allyn found loving him harder to resist, ridiculous to deny.

The third morning she woke to him stroking her hair where she slept sitting in the rocking chair and slumped over the bed beside him. She raised her head to look at him; his eyes were clear and aware, blue as midnight.

"Hi," she said.

He touched her cheek. "Hi." His voice was rich with sleep, rough from disuse.

She turned her face to kiss his searching fingertips. "You going to stay with me for a while?"

"Long as you'll let me." He felt her bottom lip. "Stitches are out."

She nodded. "Yesterday."

"Sasha?"

"Black-haired and black-browed. He'd look like a negative of himself if Kaze hadn't found that sunless tanning stuff that almost looks natural. 'Course he sort of looks more orange than copper, but she thinks a heavy sunscreen and slow exposure to real sun should help that."

Jeth's mouth twisted with wry humor. "Shoulda known I couldn't bring you here without them finding some way to get involved."

"Can't say hello to people without affecting them or involving them in your life to some degree, Jeth."

"Or law in the family and tons of questions, depending who you are," Jeth muttered sotto voce.

Allyn cleared a laugh from her throat. "Or that," she agreed straight-faced.

Jeth made an attempt to grab her that she dodged easily, sank weakly into the pillows on a hiss of pain when his injured shoulder protested the movement. "You dissin' a wounded man, woman?"

Allyn patted his cheek. "Only when he deserves it." She batted her eyes at him and backed out of the room laughing freely for the first time in days, leaving Jeth to his own devices.

A week went by.

Kaze discontinued the IV and recommended Jeth take it slow. Allyn might have told her to save her breath. Jeth's agenda didn't allow for stealthy healing.

He wanted to be operational, needed to be, to get back

into the role he'd created for himself and away from the family who didn't ask for or require explanations for the past three years of his life, but to whom he was strongly inclined to give them. Seeing his parents, brothers, sister, cousins again reminded him that not only had his family lost Marcy a little over thirty-six months ago, they'd lost him, too. But unlike his baby sister, he'd chosen to remove himself from the picture, to add ache to pain and broken heart because he'd convinced himself he couldn't face them when the person he really couldn't face was himself.

And the thing that was almost worse than anything else was the way they took him back, offering wordless forgiveness for his uncommunicative absence and joyful welcome and no resentment whatever.

If it hadn't been for Allyn, Jeth wasn't sure how he'd have coped with himself. But she made him forget what he blamed himself for, busted him when his knitting shoulder made him a thoroughly rotten patient, dealt with his night sweats and nightmares, his self-directed curses and one-handed ineptitude. And when he was healed enough that he could no longer stand having her near but not near enough, she pressed him back into the pillows and took him inside her and made love to him until there was nothing left of him alone; until he looked at the demon in the abyss and banished it with her name on his lips; until he knew who he was because she held his reflection in her eyes.

Until he wrapped his good arm tightly around her and held her to his chest while his body pumped and pulsed and spilled deep inside her and the awesome, terrifying and extraordinary need for her was written indelibly on his soul.

Until he slept, deep and contented and wondrously exhausted; slumbered peacefully for the first time in years without dreaming.

Another week went by.

It was enough time for them to slip naturally into village life, tranquil enough to make Jeth uneasy but unwilling to rock the status quo. He'd begun to want to make promises to Allyn, elicit some from her, but was afraid of making vows before he could keep them. So he took the time with her he had and endured his brothers' gibes about feigning injury in order to bar the cabin door and keep Allyn to himself instead of getting out of bed to do an honest day's work with them.

Somewhere in plain sight but just out of reach, safe from contact that might jeopardize him, Sasha continued to flourish. Jeth and Allyn went out of their way to spot him as often as possible, to assure themselves of his well-being without appearing overeager about it.

Though easily tired and often weak, Jeth continued to recover. To regain his strength, he walked as much as possible, early in the morning and later in the evening when the waning sun cooled the canyon. Allyn went with him, at first simply to be with him and make sure he didn't overdo, and then because the beauty of the place rocked her and struck her dumb. The more she learned of it, the more rooted but contrarily restless she felt.

She also walked because she understood Jeth well enough by now to recognize what his frequent jaunts were really about. Every move he made he scanned the canyon's rim, watched for anything or anyone out of place. When he began to carry a rifle with him even before he could properly hold it with two hands, then handed her his Browning to keep with her, she protested—to deaf ears. In this more primitive country, he told her, a weapon was a tool and occasionally a necessity.

Not to mention that what had happened in Flagstaff made him want to be sure Allyn knew how to do more than point a gun convincingly. Sort of like being prepared by carrying a speargun when she went diving.

She didn't use a speargun, she snapped, still adamantly

opposed to the idea. Study, not killing, was the point when she went diving.

Then she sighed and amended the statement for the sake of honesty. Well, at least she didn't carry a speargun often.

And Jeth smiled crookedly and kissed her hotly behind the ear, then pulled reluctantly away and went to solicit his younger brother's help to set up some targets for practice.

Allyn hated it. She didn't like the Browning's kick, she abhorred the noise in this place she'd mistakenly come to think of as some private Eden, and she loathed even the idea of firing at pieces of paper with silhouettes of men on them. Still, after a few false starts and some grim getting used to simply squeezing the trigger, then learning—with some hands-on guidance from Jeth—how to compensate for the weapon's kick, she proved to be the natural she'd looked the first time she'd held Jeth's gun on him.

When she'd managed to shred the kill zone a couple of dozen times she gave him a tight-lipped, jaw-working glare of *okay?*

"Shooting targets isn't the same as shooting at people," Jeth said to the wordless question.

"I should hope not," Allyn told him tartly. "I hope it's a hell of a lot harder and that I'd think five or six times at least before I'd do it."

Jeth cupped her face with one hand, stooped to peer into it. "If things don't work out you might not have time to even think once. Will you shoot if you have to, to protect yourself or Sasha?"

"Or you."

His hand tightened along the side of her neck; a muscle ticked in his cheek. "I don't want you anywhere near a line of fire for me."

"Too late," she said softly.

Jeth nodded grimly. "I suppose it is. Will you? Can you?"

She looked at his mouth, his eyes, his shoulder, his eyes.

"I don't know," she told him honestly. "But I didn't know I could really drive like I did the day you picked me up, either. I imagine if I have to I'll muddle through somehow."

"Don't joke, Lyn." Savage. "I have to know you'll do what you have to, do you understand? I *have* to know."

She studied him in silence for a moment, then leaned forward into his intensity and kissed him long and hard, melting him. "I don't know what I'm capable of, Jeth. But Becky would kill to protect her kids or husband in a heartbeat, and the rest of the women in my family would do the same for theirs. I'd say it's pretty safe to assume I'll do whatever needs to be done to defend what's mine, too."

Then she ejected the empty clip, slid a fresh one home, snapped on the safety and handed the gun to Jeth. Turned and picked her way along the turquoise creek and disappeared into the trees that screened Jeth's place from the village.

He didn't take his eyes off the set of her back, the length of her legs or sway of her hips until the last glimpse of her denim-covered derriere was lost to view. Then he sucked in his cheeks, looked at the gun and let himself be rocked by the implication she'd left of exactly who she considered hers.

Grinning, and whistling something jaunty, he followed her home.

Another two days went by. Jeth's shoulder ached and itched like crazy, and his restlessness grew.

He was not a man used to sitting still and waiting for trouble to come to him. If there was going to be trouble, he generally preferred to go out, find and eliminate it. But this wasn't one of those times when he could simply go look for trouble then try to force his opponent's hand. No, this was one time when sitting tight and waiting it out was the only way to win. And win he must.

Knowing that didn't make things easier, however. The holding pattern that appeared to have developed around them seemed to go on forever—it felt unreal, a vacation that couldn't possibly last and that would somehow only make matters worse when real life returned because they'd taken the time off when and where they couldn't afford it.

The longer the idyll lasted, the more impatient Allyn grew about wanting to call her family to reassure them she was fine and the more careless she became about visiting Sasha. Jeth understood her impatience, her need to see the little boy who'd brought them together, but it also made him afraid that when the day arrived that he could least afford to, he would let down his guard and lose his edge.

So he did what he could to make himself fit and keep himself busy—and make amends to his family for his absence without also making explanations he knew were only excuses.

Allyn turned brown and more beautiful in the sun, continued to amaze him at every turn. But even she couldn't tame his encroaching disquietude, the gut instinct that raised the hairs on the back of his neck and told him that the thing whose arrival he awaited was already here, watching them. That he would see it plainly if only he turned quickly enough to catch it when it passed the periphery of his vision.

Try as he might to guard against it, it snuck up and took him unaware.

It was Russ who brought him the news that the body had been found and identified in Flagstaff. He stepped onto the porch where Allyn sat shucking peas into a bowl and stopped in front of Jeth, who was doing a frustrated job of trying to help her.

"Talk to you, little brother?"

Warned by the tone in his voice, Jeth glanced at him. "Talk."

Russ looked meaningly at Allyn. She gazed calmly back

and didn't move. Russ sighed, said to Jeth, "You might want to hear this alone."

"No," Allyn said before Jeth could respond and in a voice that advised them both she meant it. "He doesn't."

Jeth swallowed a grin. Never had to wonder what the woman thought in any given situation, no, sirree, Bob. "I guess not," he told his brother.

Russ's mouth thinned. "Seriously, bro."

Jeth gave him a clipped nod. "Seriously. It involves me, it involves her. I haven't done anything recently she doesn't know about. Talk."

Russ sucked in a breath, blew it out on an oath. "Fine. Here it is. Bureau of Indian Affairs office just got this in from D.C. via Tucson. You're wanted for the abduction of a two-year-old in Baltimore and the murder of a federal witness in Flagstaff." He looked at Allyn. "Jeth's also wanted for questioning in the possible car jacking of a woman in Baltimore. I'm guessing that would be you and that the child is our Sasha."

He swung to Jeth. "BIA asked Guy if we knew where you were. Said we'd heard from you once in the last three years. They figured if you were in Flagstaff you might come here. If we see you we're to bring you in as peacefully as possible or they'll find someone to bring you in any way possible." His mouth thinned, features hardened. "That sounds like a threat to me, so I'm here. You were in a jam once before and didn't come to us about it, it didn't work out for Marcy. Doesn't matter none of us could have done anything more than you to stop it. Benefit of the doubt runs out soon, baby bro, so don't tank it by lying to me now."

Jeth mouthed his single favorite curse and turned to Allyn, who looked the way he felt: gut shot. They hadn't figured it to go quite this way, either of them.

He hadn't really stopped long enough to figure it at all, and that was the problem.

Numbed to the bone, Allyn whispered his word out loud.
'Judas.''

Russ nodded. ''Yeah.''

''But he didn't—I mean we didn't—I mean— Ah, hell.''
Without thought she reached for Jeth.

Equally oblivious of the automatic action, he reached and
squeezed her hand. ''A federal witness?'' he asked guard-
edly. ''Since when and says who?''

''What do you mean, says who?'' Russ asked. ''The fact
you're wanted for something like this at all should stand
you on your ear. Why doesn't it?'' He eyed Allyn.
'Doesn't seem to've knocked the wind out of you as much
as it should, either. What the hell have you two done?''

Surprise of surprises, Allyn was for bringing Russ into
it, Jeth wasn't.

No matter how stinging his brother's comment about
Marcy had been.

When she thought about it later, she was astonished at
the amount, accuracy and clarity of the wordless communication they shared, second only to the levels of unspoken
exchanges she'd experienced with Becky. At the moment,
however, she was too intent on their silent battle of wills
and in foisting some sense onto Jeth in six words or less
to notice that they simply stared at each other and spoke
hardly at all. The contest was over in moments.

Jeth didn't win.

Of course, he didn't quite lose, either, but it was definitely no draw. Allyn used her six words to inform him
quite emphatically that his way hadn't exactly kept them
out of trouble so far—not to mention that he was in no
shape to handle protecting Sasha on his own at the moment—and since neither had hers, this time they were trying Russ's.

Sort of.

With limitations as to the amount of information he was given.

For instance, they didn't tell him that Allyn might be likened to the Patty Hearst of the piece, a woman who, for whatever reason, had wound up taking up her captor's cause. In fact, they didn't bother to tell him about the car-jacking at all. They let their sham marriage stand as real because they were both strangely loath to call it off. They *did* fill Russ in on a modified version of Jeth's assignment and Sasha's history, including where Jeth had found him, but left out the part where he wasn't really Allyn's son either. Russ knew they weren't telling him everything, but let them convince him that Sasha's safety was all that mattered.

Then it was his turn to convince Jeth to let him and Guy take their brother and Allyn into Kingman for questioning.

"No," Jeth told him flatly. "Allyn stays here, or I don't go anywhere."

"Your story'll go down easier if she's there," Russ argued.

"My *story?*" Jeth's jaw tightened. "You can't get the state prosecutor's office in Tucson to corroborate my cover?"

Russ laughed harshly. "Corroborate it? They're the ones gave you up on the alleged abduction and murder, babe. You're on your own with the feds and the DEA, and they want you bad."

"Because the guy in Flagstaff was supposedly a federal witness."

"That's what they say. My guess, there's more to it than that, but since they're not filling me in and neither are you..." Russ shrugged. "I got the fact you're my brother to make me believe you and the fact I haven't seen you in three years to make me doubt."

"Thanks," Jeth said tautly. "I haven't seen you in the same amount of time. Should I doubt you, too?"

"I'm not the one with the problem."

A muscle near Jeth's eye twitched. He looked away, across the hot afternoon haze and the lazy rustle of cotton-wood leaves.

"They tell you that federal witness was in that alley to execute a hit on an undercover investigator and his wife, then take Sasha back to Baltimore and dangle him between the Russian mob and some Colombian drug runners and see who bit first?"

Russ's turn to clench his jaw, anger alerted but contained. "No."

"They also forget to tell you there was another shooter in that alley, the *witness's* partner, and I think he killed him trying to shoot me?"

Another clipped negative from Russ, tied to an almost imperceptible thinning of his mouth.

Hand sliding over to cover Allyn's thigh, Jeth nodded. "Fact." He gestured his chin at his bandaged shoulder. "S'what happened here. They shot first. I fired, but don't know if I hit either of them. Casings from my gun were in the alley, but whether or not they took my rounds out of the guy's chest..." He shrugged. "I don't know."

Russ swore. "Who ordered the hit?"

"No idea. Weren't too many people knew I was under-cover. Couple people at the DEA, assistant director on the FBI end, my office. Colombians could have figured I was working with the Russians when I took Sasha. Unless somebody fed the info to the Colombians, only our guys could have figured my background and where I might go soon enough to find and follow us. We haven't seen any of the Russians, but Allyn's pretty sure we had law with us between Pennsylvania and Kentucky. Then I didn't no-tice anybody until Flagstaff."

Russ's mouth worked. The anger roiled, dark and hun-gry, behind his eyes. "You're tellin' me you think some-

body from the DEA, the feds or your office sent someone
to kill you?''

Jeth shrugged. ''I don't know what else to think. I do
know the idea of bringing Allyn or Sasha anywhere near
them doesn't sit.''

Allyn covered the hand he'd left on her thigh. ''You
can't go anywhere near them, either,'' she said fiercely.
''At least if I go with you they can't do anything as easily
because if they do, someone will find out.''

''No.''

''Especially if we call Gabriel first and—''

''No.''

''Gabriel?'' Russ asked.

''My stepfather used to be a fibbie,'' Allyn said. ''He
might be useful.''

''I don't care what he used to be,'' Jeth snapped. ''He's
got a five-year-old at home, and these guys don't stop be
cause it's a kid. Judas, think, Lyn. That's what happened
to Marcy. That's how we got here, because some mobster
wouldn't give ground and they got hold of his kid.''

''You think I don't realize that?'' Allyn snapped. ''Be
cause I do, maybe better than you.''

''Wait,'' Russ said, lost in the shorthand of their longer
term association. ''Your stepfather was with the FBI, but
you have a kid by a member of the Russian Mafia?''

''Only in a manner of speaking,'' Allyn managed to say
in a more or less truthful aside before Jeth interrupted.

''No other kid goes down for me, Lyn, none. Not Sasha
not Rachel, not any of your nieces or nephews or cousins
you got that?''

''Oh, I hear.'' Allyn flung herself off the bench, stalked
the porch. ''Now you listen to me, you big pigheaded, lunk
headed macho numbskull. Marcy did not go down for you
She was taken. She was used. Yeah, maybe you didn't han
dle things exactly right, but from what I gather you had
nowhere to go to handle 'em better and you did your best

to get her back. Maybe it wasn't enough, but it was all you had at the time, right? You got more now. You got me, and I'm not lettin' you *go down* for anybody without a plan and especially not without backup. You ask me, the reason you were sent into the situation in Baltimore was because somebody knew how you'd react to finding a kid in your undercover after what happened to Marcy and used *her* in order to use you again. So you can just stick that in your freaking pipe and suck on it!''

For the space of three heartbeats Jeth and Russ stared at her, stunned. Then they eyed each other, turned to Allyn.

"Say that again?" Russ asked.

"Judas stinking Priest," Jeth whispered, and slumped into the bench, all the fury going out of him. He'd gotten it the first time. "When did you figure that out?"

Allyn grimaced. "Just now, when I said it."

"But that would mean you were set up from the get," Russ began—and stopped, at a loss as to where to take it from there.

"Why?" Jeth asked, not them, but himself. "What earthly good could using me because they figured I'd take Sasha do anyone? Especially when... No." He shook his head, looked at Allyn. "It doesn't make sense."

"None of this ever made sense," Allyn reminded him. "It just started when it started for what appeared to be a reason but no real apparent end."

"Territory," Jeth murmured, rising to pace stiffly, unconsciously working the kinks out of his left side at the same time. "The Russians had it, the Colombians wanted it."

"Why pull a special investigator out of Tucson to work undercover in a territorial war in Baltimore?" Allyn asked. "Couldn't they find someone closer to home to set up an unknown exchange program with?"

"Uh-uh." Jeth shook his head. "Not someone as famil-

iar with the border-trafficking problems we've got dow
here as somebody from down here.''

"The Colombians aren't bringing their stuff into Balti
more through Miami or somewhere along the coast?'' Rus
asked.

"Not when it's safer to have mules and illegals pack i
across the Mexican border and any other place immigratio
will miss them.''

"How much quantity can they deal in that way?''

Jeth eyed his brother. ''You know the answer to that.''

Russ sighed. ''Yeah, I suppose. Plenty. The question re
mains, though. If Allyn's right, why set you up specifi
cally?''

"I don't know.'' The flash of near understanding tha
he'd reached in Kentucky became clearer. Marcy, h
thought. It always came back to Marcy. To the person o
persons he'd missed catching then. To the similarity be
tween the territorial wars and the way his assignmen
seemed to have him caught in the middle. To the way hi
cover had been blown, allowing his family, his baby sister
to be threatened and used against him in the first place
How many common links were there between the cases'
Not many. Only—'' His features hardened. ''But I thin
I'm beginning to guess.''

Allyn caught the unyielding determination of the loo
and seized his arm when he stopped near her. ''No,'' sh
said sharply. ''You can't. Not like this. You're in n
shape—''

He stopped her protests with a kiss that was deep anc
telling, uncompromising. ''It has to be done, Lynnie,'' h
told her quietly. ''You're the one said we couldn't do thi
forever. Well, it's time to stop running and see if we can'
figure out what tune the piper's playing and then make hin
pay.''

"Then I'm coming with you.''

"So I worry about you on top of everything else?" He shook his head. "I don't think so."

"Oh, good," Allyn said sarcastically. "Your shoulder's bandaged, your arm's in a sling, you don't have your strength back, but now you get noble."

Jeth grinned, roughed his hand across her cheek and through her hair. "Hey, a guy can't be a self-sacrificing chauvinistic pig when he's down, what good is he?"

She snorted, stuck her nose in the air and turned her back on him.

"Somebody mind filling me in?" Russ asked.

Allyn glared at him. "He wants you to broker a deal to take him in without saying anything about me or Sasha so he can figure out who's behind whatever this is that's been going on."

Chapter 16

In the end they came up with a plan that didn't really satisfy anybody.

Russ wanted Guy involved—three brothers was always better than two, he argued, especially when the extra two were also local law of one sort or another. Allyn still wanted to phone Gabriel, who'd had non-law enforcement friends in the right places to get her out of trouble in the past. Jeth and Russ both vetoed this—as did Guy when he arrived—but no longer just because of Rachel or the rest of Allyn's large family. None of the brothers was willing to trust the phone lines, or willing to trust that Russ hadn't been followed when he'd returned to the canyon. They were fairly certain that even the newest listening technology couldn't penetrate the canyon's walls without interference, but didn't want to chance phone lines into the village that might have been tapped or phone lines outside where they could be overheard.

As Allyn pointed out to all three of them, a little paranoia was a fascinating thing, but a lot was just damned annoying.

They turned three looks of similarly mild amusement in her direction and continued planning.

She had the last laugh on Jeth, however, when both Russ and Guy agreed that it would probably be in Sasha's best interests if Allyn was part of the deal the brothers brokered with the feds. Jeth didn't like it at all but caved when Allyn notified him as calm as you please that if he went and left her to her own devices, the consequences could just plain old be on his head because she was damned if she was going to sit and wait for word of his demise like some merchant seaman's wife, especially when she wasn't one. Not when Sasha was as well hidden in plain sight as they could possibly make him and leaving her behind would likely only convince The Powers That Be that Jeth had more to hide than they wanted those powers to think.

Jeth wasn't sure he tracked the logic behind Allyn's contention, but it really didn't matter; he couldn't change her mind and he knew her well enough by now to realize she would find some way to go with him no matter what.

The sun was a red glare behind the canyon walls when Jeth's brothers finally left to make arrangements for the morrow. The moment they were out of sight he spun stiffly on her.

"Damn it, Lyn," he started, "what the hell—"

But that was as far as he got before she was across the porch and in his arms, kissing him and knocking the breath out of him.

"Don't," she pleaded. "Not now. We knew it couldn't last. Tomorrow things change. Let's don't waste tonight."

Tomorrow things change. Looking into her face, Jeth shuddered at the thought, pressed some distance between them without letting her go.

"Tomorrow," he said, expression hooded. "We haven't talked about that, have we?"

She touched his jaw. "It doesn't matter, Jeth. If there's anything to talk about we can talk about it after. If there's not...I'll still always be glad it was you."

He bent his head, kissed her roughly. Rested his forehead on hers. "Damn, Lynnie," he muttered against her mouth. "If there was ever anyone I could promise things to it'd be you."

"I know." She traced his mouth, outlined his lips, ran her finger down his chest to hook it in the front of his jeans and pull him after her into the house. "Later, okay? Tonight let's just..." She smiled and let her voice trail off, leaving Jeth to fill in the blanks.

Which he did willingly.

She undressed him while he told her all the things he planned to do to her, starting from the top and nibbling his way down to her toes, licking his way up again.

"Later." She eased his shirt off him, gave him a simmering look. "Right now I'm in charge and this is what I'm going to do...."

And she told *him,* then suited action to words by tickling his nipples with her tongue, then planting openmouthed kisses over them before working her way down his belly while her hands worked his jeans open and drew them and his boxers down his hips, his legs. Her mouth followed, teasingly, agonizingly close to the root of instant desire but never quite close enough. When she'd tugged the jeans to his ankles, she pushed him into an armless chair and knelt to draw them off his feet before she rose, dangled them momentarily from a finger, then dropped them in a heap.

Jeth didn't know what she did to make the move seem so sexy, but his mouth felt suddenly dry, his pulse pounded, and his entire body flushed and went rigid with hunger.

"Sweet heaven." A rasp, a groan. "Now you."

"Soon." She moved behind him and kissed his ear, then disappeared into the bedroom, returned a moment later with a bottle of baby oil and set it on the floor in front of him. Rose again.

He looked at the bottle, at her standing before him reaching around underneath her shirt. "Judas, Allyn, you're making me crazy. What are you going to do with that?"

"Use your imagination." Her voice was smoky. Undulating her hips as she did so, Allyn slid a hand inside one sleeve of her shirt, then the other, drew her bra straps over her wrists, then reached in and pulled the scrap of cotton down the front of her shirt and tossed it to him.

He caught it and stared at her, torn between laughter and the inability to breathe, the increasing stiffness between his thighs.

"Damnation, woman, who taught you that? I know for a fact we've never done this before, and since there wasn't anyone before me…"

"True," she agreed, turned and spread her legs, bent to pick up the oil and give him a good look at her rearview. Straightened to pour oil into her palms. "But I've led a rich fantasy life."

He groaned when she sashayed toward him, warming the viscous fluid in her hands. "I can tell. Damn, you're going to kill me before you let me touch you, aren't you."

"No." She moved behind him again, began massaging his neck and right shoulder, bent to slide her hands down his chest, drag them up while she ran her teeth along the vulnerable area beneath his ear, over the pulse in his throat. "I'm just going to give you a night you won't forget."

He tipped his head back to meet her mouth, reached to spear his fingers into her hair, relishing the rapt attention of her kiss, the taste of her tongue exploring his mouth, coaxing his exploration of hers. If this was what drowning felt like, let him die here and now, locked with her forever like this.

"I will never forget any night I've had with you." The vow was fierce, soft, believable. "Ever."

"Good."

Her hands left him, her mouth didn't. Then her hands came back, followed the line of his jaw, neck, shoulder, throat as she moved in front of him, naked from the waist down.

And stood on tiptoes to straddle him and the chair without sitting down. She bent her head to look at him, and her hair spread around them, a wild cloud of brown velvet with auburn highlights burned into it by the Arizona sun.

His smile was slow and appreciative, seductive and welcoming. "It's about time." He wrapped his arm around her waist. "Come here."

"Not without you," she whispered, and dipped her head to kiss him while he pulled her into his lap and fitted himself inside her.

Their loving was slow and thoughtful and lasting, took them through the long night and into the dawn before Jeth finally put his back to the bed and let Allyn take him with her over that ultimate pinnacle where time seemed to stop and tomorrow existed only in afterthought.

The climax was long and molten, seemed to crest and rise, taper and recreate itself stronger than before until the last devastating explosion had them gasping and calling out, clinging wetly to each other for dear life, he her rock, she his life raft, while the world spun away from them and they were a new universe unto themselves.

Russ and Guy were on the porch almost too early, as was evidenced by the fact that Allyn found herself hiding behind Jeth and hastily buttoning the tangerine silk camisole she'd donned with a pair of lightweight cargo-pocket jeans after she'd helped Jeth with his shower.

The shower had gotten out of hand, then breakfast had gotten out hand, found them once again reaching for each other without inhibition, eager for one last joining, a final moment of staving off the inevitable.

One moment had turned into two, and two into…well, suffice it to say, Jeth's brothers were here and she was pretty thoroughly mussed again. Jeth was shirtless, his jeans mostly zipped but not buttoned, his attitude one of a man who'd been interrupted in the midst of something far more vital than answering the door to greet the end of the world. He crossed his good arm unselfconsciously across his naked chest and eyed his brothers.

"You ready?" Russ asked. "We're supposed to meet a guy from your office and a couple of feds in Seligman for a debriefing before they take you into Kingman." His eyes slid past Jeth at the movement of Allyn's shadow retreating toward the bedroom. "Sorry." He sounded like he meant it.

Jeth looked over his shoulder, gut full of regret. "Yeah," he agreed. His gaze raked his brothers. "Whatever happens today, you make sure she's out of it, you hear me?"

"Have faith, man," Guy said lightly. "Not that I think you have to worry about her, anyway. She seems like the kind of woman could handle an army easy. Now you comin' or what?"

Jeth's lip curled in sardonic amusement at Guy's assessment of Allyn. His second oldest brother was more right than he could possibly know. "Wait."

He shut the door and turned. Allyn stood behind him, hair once more braided, the glow of her skin heightened by the tangerine camisole and the matching strings of tiny beads that circled her throat and right wrist. A denim shirt for her and white T-shirt for him dangled from her left hand. Jeth stepped to her, cupped her face in his hands and kissed her.

"Have I had the good sense to mention how beautiful I think you are?"

Allyn smiled, nervous but trying not to show it. "I think you said that at least once or twice last night, yeah."

"Good. I meant it then, I mean it now."

"I know."

They looked at each other a moment, then gazes slid away, seeking someplace easier to rest. Sometimes just looking was the most painful thing in the world.

"Here," Allyn said at last, "I brought your shirt. Let me help you—"

"It's all right," Jeth returned quietly. "I can do it."

He took the piece of clothing from her, pulled it first over his wounded arm then, wincing, dragged it over his head and stuck his other arm through its sleeve. She reached to smooth the fabric down his torso, slipped her arms around him and hugged him tight.

"Whatever happens," she whispered.

Heart in his throat, he wrapped his good arm around her shoulders and pulled her into his chest. Bent his head to drop a kiss in her hair.

"Whatever happens," he agreed, and released her to open the door to his brothers once more.

The office where they met their contacts in Seligman was small and cramped, could have benefited from a coat of paint.

Allyn looked the place over, trying hard not to let fear get the better of her when Jeth was taken to a separate room for his debriefing. Her interrogation was cursory and curiously void of what she'd have deemed pertinent questions about Sasha, herself or anything else—almost as though the special agents and the Tucson assistant prosecutor weren't really looking for answers, but time.

Next door Jeth's questioning proceeded in similar fashion, although he was asked for his weapon so the lab could match it against shell casings found in the alley and bullets recovered from the body—a question that became moot when they discovered he wasn't carrying. When they asked where his gun was, he told them, truthfully, that his department issue was in his apartment in Tucson.

On the face of it, there was little to hold Jeth on, but both the fed and the state prosecutor's representative were adamant about moving Jeth to the larger facilities in Kingman where the agent in charge of the operation Jeth had been called in on awaited him. In exchange for his cooperation in this matter, they would release his wife. Jeth agreed to the trip with alacrity.

Knowing he'd finagled something to get her away from him just in case, Allyn was loath to leave Jeth behind—especially when they gave her a minute with him and she read the corded tension in the set of his muscles, the remoteness that hooded those beautiful eyes and strained his features. He shook his head slightly when she would have said something about it to him, and she realized then that he was afraid of being listened in on. So with great reluctance she kept her conversation light, talking about the mistake that had been made, her belief in him and things of that ilk. Then she kissed him lightly goodbye as though she were certain she'd see him later and turned to go. Jeth caught her ring hand and pulled her back, awkwardly maneuvered his left hand so he could lace his ring finger with hers and kissed her knuckle.

Then he hugged her and, with his lips close to her ear, warned her as softly as possible not to let anyone to follow her to Sasha.

She stiffened in his arms, suddenly terrified of the implications behind his warning. They planned to hold on to him, let her go, hoping she'd head straight for the baby they'd barely mentioned, then kill him. When reflex would have made her give them away, Jeth pressed her face into his shirt and kissed her hair, pretending to soothe away tears. With an effort Allyn brought reflex under control and, all brave newlywed stuck in a nuisance of a nightmare that must surely be about to go away, she straightened and dabbed at her eyes with the edge of a forefinger. Then she stood on tiptoes and brushed a kiss on her pretend hus-

band's cheek and preceded the waiting Guy out the door
and into the parking lot to his pickup. Climbed in and
looked at the man who wasn't really her brother-in-law.

"He told you to get me out of here, didn't he?" she
asked bluntly.

To his credit, Guy started but didn't choke at the question. He did study her for a minute weighing his answer,
however. Allyn nodded. His silence told her everything she
didn't need to hear. Her mouth drew a savage line.

"Damn him." She bit her bottom lip until the place
where the stitches had been ached, and stared through the
windshield at the office where Jeth remained. "*Damn*
him." She faced Guy. "He doesn't think he's going to
make it to Kingman, does he?"

"There's no reason to think that."

"Then why do I think it? Why am I sure he thinks it?
And don't mess with me, damn you, Guy. You haven't got
the face for telling good lies."

Guy studied her. "And you do?"

Allyn eyed him back. The muscle that created the dimple
in her left cheek twitched. "I've got a chunk of the Blarney
Stone at home to prove it."

For a moment he watched her. Then he gave her hard
and furious. "Are you telling me—"

"I'm not tellin' you anything," Allyn snapped, "except
that your brother doesn't think he's going to make it to
Kingman."

Guy's turn to hang his wrists over the steering wheel and
stare through the windshield. "We discussed the possibility. We're doin' what we can to prevent it."

"While you do what with me?"

"Get you to the nearest airport and put you on the first
flight out."

Allyn swore. Then said emphatically, "You know I'm
not going, don't you? I won't leave him, and I can't leave
Sasha."

Guy nodded. "Russ and I figured as much. That's why we didn't listen too hard when he told us to do it. I *am* getting you out of here, however."

"Where?"

"Same place we moved Sasha to last night."

"We can't go there, they'll follow us. They'll take him. Jeth thinks that's why they let me go."

Guy swore. "I thought it was too easy." A moment of silent study, then he looked at Allyn. "Trust me?"

"Will it help him and protect Sasha?"

"If it works."

Allyn viewed him with calculation. "We have a plan?"

Guy grinned tightly. "If you're game, we have a plan."

Over Russ's and the local sheriff's protests Jeth was handcuffed and locked into the back of a squad car for transport.

There was no reason for it, especially since he wasn't formally charged with anything, but that didn't prevent the fed from doing as much damage to Jeth's shoulder as possible when he yanked Jeth's wrists behind him, then snapped the cuffs into the safety locks in the back seat of the cruiser so he couldn't move.

When Russ had attempted to climb into the front seat to travel with his brother at the sheriff's invitation, the special agent waved him aside and said "back off, federal jurisdiction," and climbed in instead.

Jaw ticking, Russ waited until they were out of sight, then mounted his own vehicle to follow the cruiser at a distance.

Red dust and desert, saguaro and barrel cacti, sun and heat rising to a hundred and five and more. Battered windmills, poised to catch any wind, stood guard over land empty of anything except the hardiest desert scrub. A hundred miles from nowhere, it was the perfect place.

Doing his best to remain alert despite the throbbing pain in his still knitting chest, Jeth watched his surroundings trying to figure where, if anything was going to happen, it would most likely occur. The deputy sheriff talked aimlessly; too easily irritated, the federal agent told him to pipe down. Which meant, Jeth guessed, that if something was going to happen it would be soon.

Twisting as much as cuffs and shoulder would allow, he scoured the countryside for signs of life.

"Stop here," the fed said suddenly.

"What?" the deputy asked, puzzled. "This isn't—"

The agent pulled his weapon and leveled it at the deputy. "Stop."

The deputy did so.

The agent motioned with his gun. "Now get out."

Given little choice, the deputy complied. The agent slid into the driver's seat.

"What the hell am I supposed to do now?" the deputy asked. "It's too far to walk back without water and—"

"You're right," the fed agreed, and shot the deputy twice in the face and once in the chest, closed the door and pulled away. "Now," he told Jeth, "you and I can go someplace and talk private."

Three related things happened simultaneously after that.

In Arizona, Russ, who had been following the cruiser at a distance, came upon the deputy's body, still warm, at the side of the road. And two time zones away, in Michigan, Becky Meyers Catton doubled over with a gasp of surprise and pain and knew without question that Allyn was hurt and in serious trouble, while a city away her stepfather pulled the report he'd been waiting to get on Jeth Levoie out of the fax machine in his university office.

Russ immediately radioed for help and marshaled the forces he and his brother had arranged to have waiting in the wings in case, and stepped on the accelerator, following the distant billow of dust that had to be from the deputy's cruiser.

As soon as she could straighten, Becky called the one person she always called in case of trouble even when she wasn't sure she wanted to: her best friend and husband, Michael. Then she called Gabriel, who was on his way out of the office at speed after calling in a few favors that he hoped would help get Jeth out of the trouble he was headed into—if his supposed son-in-law wasn't already in it. Becky's call confirmed his worst fears. So he called his wife, apprised her of the situation and headed for the airport.

Allyn picked her head off the dashboard of Guy's pickup and looked blearily around. Her temples throbbed, and the taste of salt and iron flooded her mouth. Beside her, Guy slumped sideways against his half-open door, face, head and chest bloody.

Unlocking her seat belt, Allyn edged unsteadily toward him and put her fingers to his neck, looking for a pulse. Weak but steady. A good sign.

Carefully she checked him over, assessing the damage. He had a gash on his forehead from where he'd hit the steering wheel and a cut inside a nice-looking bruise on his temple where his head had bounced off the window. The blood on his chest was really from his arm, where a broken shovel handle had jammed through the window in the back of the cab and speared him. Ugly, but it didn't appear he'd sustained any permanent or life-threatening damage.

She hoped.

She shut her eyes and rested her forehead in a hand. God, her head hurt. What had happened? She couldn't seem to remember anything beyond… Puzzled, she canted her head and tried to think. A sound, she'd heard a sound, and then they'd gone banging all over creation and then…nothing. She couldn't remember. A blowout, maybe, at high speed, in the middle of Arizona nowhere between Kingman and the Canyon and—

Jeth.

That part of her memory came back in a rush. They'd been on their way to help him somehow. Guy's plan... She had to... Everything in her brain went muzzy for an instant. Had to what?

Rescue him if he needed it, that was what.

Relieved to remember what she was about, Allyn pulled her hand away from her face. Bloody. Not surprising, she supposed nonsensically. If she felt banged up, she must be banged up.

Focus, she commanded herself. *Guy needs help. Jeth needs help. Get help.*

Her gaze fell on the radio mike under the dashboard. She started to reach for it—and stopped at the sound of her door being opened.

"Thank goodness," she began, turning, "my brother-in-law needs help—"

"Too bad," the gal from the state prosecutor's office said. "I'm real sorry to hear that, he's kinda cute, but you're the one I'm here for."

Then she pointed Jeth's gun at Allyn and motioned her out of the truck.

The place where the fed took Jeth was a run-down shack in the middle of nowhere surrounded by a three-hundred-sixty degree view of nothing in particular. A good place, Jeth thought ironically, to see what was coming a long time before it reached you.

So much for the best-laid plans.

Grabbing Jeth's left elbow and jerking so it was all Jeth could do to keep from groaning, the fed hustled him into the hovel and shackled him to the only sturdy thing in the place: a solid metal shelving unit that was screwed to the floor. Then he grabbed a chair for himself and settled in, gun resting carelessly in his lap.

"Now what?" Jeth asked.

The other man shrugged. "Now we wait."

"For what?"

"For the person who's going to get you to tell us what we need to know."

"And that would be?"

The other man flashed a nasty smile. "Wait," he suggested, and said no more.

Not a man to waste time, especially when there was none to spare, Jeth took visual stock of his surroundings as best he could. Four rotting walls, a set of bunk beds, a junked cast-iron stove tipped on its side, a counter and cupboards either without doors or with the doors hanging off, a broken table and a couple of listing chairs. An iron skillet hung on the wall nearest the counter. A filthy sink in the counter. All in all, not much to look at.

"How long we got to wait?" he asked.

"However long it takes," his captor said comfortably. "You should look at it like no news is good news. The longer we wait, the longer you live."

"I appreciate that," Jeth said, then winced and groaned theatrically. "Look, man, my arm's killing me. You think I could sit before I pass out?"

"Stand still, you won't pass out," the man advised him, then sat back in his chair and closed his eyes.

Outside the windmill creaked. Beyond that was the sound of a small plane in the distance. It came closer then faded away. After that the silence lasted long enough for Jeth to count the boards in three walls, at which point the muffled roar of an engine approaching in four-wheel drive broke the stillness. The guy in the chair straightened, glanced at Jeth and rose.

"Time's up," he said, and went to the door.

The four-wheel drive thundered to a stop and shut down.

Jeth heard the engine tick for a minute, then doors opened. There came the sound of muted voices and doors slammed. Then came the crunch of approaching feet, the slough of something or someone dragged behind.

Nothing prepared him for the sight that got pushed through the door after the woman from the prosecutor's office entered and stepped aside. Swaying on her feet, Allyn viewed him through the blood dripping off her forehead and into her glassy-looking eyes. Recognizing him, she blinked and stumbled forward a step, only to be yanked back by Jeth's captor. She grinned weakly at him.

"Hi, honey," she murmured. "I'm home."

Then she crumpled to the floor unconscious.

In an agony to reach her, Jeth yanked at the metal shelves, trying to pull them out of the floor. Any thought he might have had of taking mercy on his opponents if— when, damn it—he got the upper hand fled.

"Lyn. Judas, Lynnie." He eyed the man and woman standing over Allyn. "What have you done to her? Damn it, Jeri, you don't want her. She's a civilian. Leave her the hell out of it."

"You brought her into it," the woman said. "You're the only one who can get her out."

"You're frigging cold, Jeri. I should have figured you for this somewhere."

Jeri shook her head. "Sticks and stones, youngster. You want to hurt someone you find out what matters to 'em— like your little sister. We found her, I knew you were the one'd help me get what I want eventually. You were such easy pickin's it couldn't't've been funnier."

Fury blinded Jeth momentarily. So he'd been right. Too late, but right. It had been *Jeri* who'd taken Marcy, not one of the criminals he'd been investigating. No wonder his sister had gone so easily. Jeth had introduced Jeri to her once when Marcy came to the office for a career day to learn a little about what he did. He looked at his supervisor's face and knew, *knew* that she was the one who'd given Marcy to the incompetents who'd buried her with the faulty air tank and unwittingly left her to die. Judas, *Judas...*

His jaw clenched; he bit down on the thing he might have named her—or himself—and got control of himself. There was no more fitting name for who Jeri was or what she'd done. And damn, if he lost control, he couldn't do Allyn any good. He needed time.

"You got the cards," he said tightly. "Deal."

"I want the baby," Jeri said simply.

Dumbfounded, Jeth stared at her. "For yourself?"

She hooted. "Don't be an ass. Of course not for myself—can you see me with a kid? Get real. No." She shook her head. "He goes to the highest bidder. I don't care if that's a couple who can pay to adopt him, if it's the Colombians or his KGB daddy. For whatever reason, the kid's a gold mine. Where is he?"

He looked at Allyn's face, turned toward him where she lay on the floor, wondering which answer would best buy time for her.

And nearly lost it when her eyes opened, she looked directly at him and winked. Was the blood an act, too? If they got out of this alive, he was going to throttle her, kiss her, then watch his step around her forever because she would damn sure keep him on his toes.

"I'm waiting," Jeri warned. She prodded Allyn with a foot. "You can't tell me, I'm sure your *wife* can. Where's the kid?"

Another glance at Allyn, who waggled her visible brow at him. Yep, he was definitely going to strangle her. "I don't know."

Jeri pointed her gun—no, *his* gun, Jeth realized with a start, wondering how she'd gotten hold of it—at Allyn.

"Fine," she said, "Don't tell me. I can make it look like you killed her here as well as anyplace."

Watching Jeth, she jacked a round into the chamber, drew back the hammer. On the floor Allyn slid her arm gently underneath her body, ready to use it for leverage.

Jeth swore—as much at Allyn as at Jeri. Blasted woman was going to get herself killed, and if she did, he was lost. "No, don't, damn it. I'll tell you where he was the last time I saw him."

Jeri didn't uncock the weapon, but she lifted it off Allyn. "Talk."

Jeth opened his mouth, but before he had a chance to say a word, the small plane engine he'd heard before came back. Only this time it didn't fade into the distance, but buzzed the shack twice and throttled to come in for a landing. From the anticipation on the fed's and Jeri's faces, the new arrival was expected.

"Just in time," the fed said.

"Pay dirt," Jeri agreed. She motioned him toward the door. "I'll handle things here. You bring 'em in. Tell him we're about to get the information."

The fed left. Jeri uncocked the Browning, pointed it in the air and unbalanced her stance enough to stick out her hip to rest her elbow there.

"Here's somebody'll want to hear—" she began, and turned, startled, unbalancing herself further at the sudden eruption of gunfire outside.

On the floor, Allyn rolled with the first shot, snaked out a hand and yanked Jeri's feet out from under her. Jeri's head cracked the counter, the Browning went flying, hit the wall and discharged a bullet into the doorframe, tumbled through the air and into Allyn's waiting hands.

"Softball," she told Jeth, who blistered her ears with nothing that remotely resembled a question that *softball* would be the answer to. Eyes on Jeri, she teetered to her feet, chambering a round just in case the way Jeth had taught her. "Center field."

"I don't care where you learned to catch a gun on the fly," Jeth snapped. "Either find a key or shoot these freaking things off me. In case you hadn't noticed, we've got a little more trouble."

"Trouble?" Russ asked, coming through the door. "Where?" He looked at Allyn. "Judas Priest, what happened to you? Where's Guy?"

Allyn viewed him with obvious distress. "You didn't see the truck when you flew over? We had a blowout—I think she might have shot out a tire, because that's where she picked me up. He's hurt."

"You don't look too healthy yourself."

"I'll live." She sagged suddenly. "Although some sleep might be nice."

"Would someone get these things off me and tell me what the *devil* is going on?" Jeth demanded.

Chapter 17

By the time Russ found a handcuff key and released Jeth, reinforcements were starting to arrive.

Jeth couldn't reach Allyn quickly enough, caught her on her way to the floor in the midst of another wave of dizziness. He smoothed loose wisps of hair from her face.

"What the hell were you thinking?" A demand, fierce and unrelenting—gentle as a kiss. "What would I do if you were killed?"

"Funny." Allyn offered him a fuzzy smile. "I thought the same thing about you."

Then there was no more time to talk because chaos broke out.

Guy had been located by one of the units in the area and had been taken to the hospital in Kingman for treatment. The muscles in his upper arm were damaged and would require a long healing process, but the doctors were hopeful. Allyn was treated for a concussion and kept in the hospital for two days of X rays and observation. Jeth received treatment for his arm, although it was only precautionary, in case anything had torn when he'd been banged around. As soon as he was released, he headed for Allyn's bedside and stayed there, letting Russ update him on Guy's condition.

Both his office in Tucson and the FBI offered him citations for exposing the corruption within; he turned the commendations down. The expense had been too high, he informed his superiors, and he hadn't been told enough to prevent much of what had happened. If he'd known his undercover operation was meant in part to expose internal corruption, had any idea how deep the corruption went or understood any sooner that it was Jeri's greed for power and money that drove her to manipulate her agents and underlings…

But he knew better than to head down that street again. He was young. He'd learned. He would learn—starting now—by leaving the prosecutor's team and seeking a position closer to home, with the BIA or tribal police or the local sheriff, if they would have him.

The Baltimore sting concluded with an unprecedented number of arrests—not only among the Colombians, but the Russian Mafia, as well, and most notably Sasha's genetic father—and the removal of an arsenal of weapons and several tons of heroin and cocaine from the streets.

Gabriel arrived on the scene too late to do anything but observe and assure himself that Allyn was all right. He also advised his stepdaughter in no uncertain terms to call her mother and her sister. Which Allyn did.

In fact, while Jeth cradled her in his arms in a comfy chair in her hospital room and kissed her hair and neck and fingers, she talked with Becky for a long time. The gist of their conversation revealed that Becky planned to stick with Michael because she loved him. Loving him didn't solve all the problems she saw with her life, but it helped. And the fact that he loved her to distraction and enough to help her explore new avenues and outlets for her energies went a long way toward taking care of things. Communication, she told Allyn complacently, that was the key. And Allyn agreed, watching Jeth's face as she said it, communication was paramount.

With a little help from Gabriel, Tucson, the BIA and a contrite Bureau, Sasha's existence somehow got lost in the shuffle, and a new birth certificate mysteriously appeared for a blond, blue-eyed foster member of Jeth's family. The child was to be left temporarily in the custody of Mabel Levoie while Jeth and Allyn recuperated, sorted out their relationship and answered questions and until such time as an in-tribe adoption could be arranged.

Which meant that all that was left to do was for Allyn and Jeth to dissolve a fake marriage and part company.

Yeah, right. As though it were that easy.

In the pink light of dawn they stood together on the balcony of the hotel room Jeth had rented in Kingman and studied each other, not knowing what to say. Down the hall in another room, Gabriel waited—despite Allyn's protests that he go away, she was fine—to take her home.

Home.

She looked at the man opposite her and knew that home was not in Michigan; it hadn't been for seven years. But home was also not Boston, nor Miami, nor any of the dozen posts she'd been offered in Hawaii, California, Maine, North Carolina and so on. Home had midnight blue eyes, bronze skin, black hair and a tush to die for.

Home's name was Jeth, with a dollop of Sasha.

Now if only the man in question would realize it.

But he only watched her without saying a word, until she looked at her hand and slowly took off her rings, offered them to him. When he didn't take them, she lifted his left hand and folded them into his palm, reached up to kiss his cheek and turned to go.

"Lyn."

Her name only, a single word filled with ache. She looked at him.

"I know you're afraid that what happened could happen again," she said quietly, "but I'm not. You're done with undercover, you said so. You won't let anyone use you again. I won't let anyone use me. Sasha's safe. So ask me to stay. See what happens."

He shook his head. "I can't do that. Even if everything else is true, keeping you here would be selfish. You just got your doctorate. You're a marine biologist. There's nothing here for you."

She faced him. "Let me make that choice. Ask me to stay."

"I don't know what I'm going to do. I'm not going back to Tucson, but I got no guarantees, no definite prospects, no way to even consider you, let alone Sasha—"

She moved toward him, steady, purposeful. "You drove by, you made me a part of *us* before there was an us, now you ask me to stay."

"Lyn—"

She stopped, drew herself up fiercely proud and tall. "Ask me, damn you. I want Sasha, too, but this is between you and me. I won't beg again."

He looked at the rings in his hand, the one that remained on his finger, and something tugged at the muscles around his mouth. He raised his head, looked her in the eye, held out the rings and said matter-of-factly, "Keep these. Wear them. Stay." Then he opened his arms and said it again, "God, Lynnie, save me from myself. Stay. Please. Help me figure it out."

And she took the two steps to him without looking back, wound her arms around his neck and grumbled, "What took you so long, you big dope? What did you want me to do, say I love you first? Don't you know that's against the rules?"

He nuzzled her cheek, feeling whole and at peace for the

first time in years. ''It might've helped. Now are you going to put my rings on and marry me for real or what?''

She put his rings on, married him for real *and* what.

*   *   *   *   *

Be sure to watch for Guy Levoie's
romance, coming only to Intimate Moments
later this year.

MONTANA MAVERICKS
Big Sky Brides

Legendary love comes to Whitehorn, Montana,
once more as beloved authors

Christine Rimmer, Jennifer Greene and Cheryl St.John

present three brand-new stories in this exciting anthology!

Meet the Brennan women:
SUZANNA, DIANA and ISABELLE

Strong-willed beauties who find unexpected
love in these irresistible marriage of
covnenience stories.

Don't miss
MONTANA MAVERICKS: BIG SKY BRIDES
On sale in February 2000,
only from Silhouette Books!

Available at your favorite retail outlet.

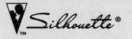

Silhouette®

Visit us at www.romance.net   PSMMBSB

Don't miss Silhouette's newest cross-line promotion,

Four royal sisters find their own Prince Charmings as they embark on separate journeys to find their missing brother, the Crown Prince!

The search begins in October 1999 and continues through February 2000:

On sale October 1999: **A ROYAL BABY ON THE WAY**
by award-winning author **Susan Mallery** (Special Edition)

On sale November 1999: **UNDERCOVER PRINCESS**
by bestselling author **Suzanne Brockmann** (Intimate Moments)

On sale December 1999: **THE PRINCESS'S WHITE KNIGHT**
by popular author **Carla Cassidy** (Romance)

On sale January 2000: **THE PREGNANT PRINCESS**
by rising star **Anne Marie Winston** (Desire)

On sale February 2000: **MAN…MERCENARY…MONARCH**
by top-notch talent **Joan Elliott Pickart** (Special Edition)

ROYALLY WED
Only in—
SILHOUETTE BOOKS

Available at your favorite retail outlet.

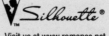

Visit us at www.romance.net

SSERW

Return to romance, Texas-style, with

ANNETTE BROADRICK

DAUGHTERS OF TEXAS

When three beautiful sisters round up some of the
Lone Star State's sexiest men, they discover the
passion they've always dreamed of in these compelling
stories of love and matrimony.

One of Silhouette's most popular authors,
Annette Broadrick proves that no matter
the odds, true love prevails.

Look for ***Daughters of Texas*** on sale in January 2000.

Available at your favorite retail outlet.

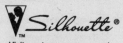

SILHOUETTE'S 20ᵀᴴ ANNIVERSARY CONTEST
OFFICIAL RULES
NO PURCHASE NECESSARY TO ENTER

1. To enter, follow directions published in the offer to which you are responding. Contest begins 1/1/00 and ends on 8/24/00 (the "Promotion Period"). Method of entry may vary. Mailed entries must be postmarked by 8/24/00, and received by 8/31/00.

2. During the Promotion Period, the Contest may be presented via the Internet. Entry via the Internet may be restricted to residents of certain geographic areas that are disclosed on the Web site. To enter via the Internet, if you are a resident of a geographic area in which Internet entry is permissible, follow the directions displayed on-line, including typing your essay of 100 words or fewer telling us "Where In The World Your Love Will Come Alive." On-line entries must be received by 11:59 p.m. Eastern Standard time on 8/24/00. Limit one e-mail entry per person, household and e-mail address per day, per presentation. If you are a resident of a geographic area in which entry via the Internet is permissible, you may, in lieu of submitting an entry on-line, enter by mail, by hand-printing your name, address, telephone number and contest number/name on an 8"x 11" plain piece of paper and telling us in 100 words or fewer "Where In The World Your Love Will Come Alive," and mailing via first-class mail to: Silhouette 20ᵗʰ Anniversary Contest, (in the U.S.) P.O. Box 9069, Buffalo, NY 14269-9069; (In Canada) P.O. Box 637, Fort Erie, Ontario, Canada L2A 5X3. Limit one 8"x 11" mailed entry per person, household and e-mail address per day. On-line and/or 8"x 11" mailed entries received from persons residing in geographic areas in which Internet entry is not permissible will be disqualified. No liability is assumed for lost, late, incomplete, inaccurate, nondelivered or misdirected mail, or misdirected e-mail, for technical, hardware or software failures of any kind, lost or unavailable network connection, or failed, incomplete, garbled or delayed computer transmission or any human error which may occur in the receipt or processing of the entries in the contest.

3. Essays will be judged by a panel of members of the Silhouette editorial and marketing staff based on the following criteria:

> Sincerity (believability, credibility)—50%
> Originality (freshness, creativity)—30%
> Aptness (appropriateness to contest ideas)—20%

Purchase or acceptance of a product offer does not improve your chances of winning. In the event of a tie, duplicate prizes will be awarded.

4. All entries become the property of Harlequin Enterprises Ltd., and will not be returned. Winner will be determined no later than 10/31/00 and will be notified by mail. Grand Prize winner will be required to sign and return Affidavit of Eligibility within 15 days of receipt of notification. Noncompliance within the time period may result in disqualification and an alternative winner may be selected. All municipal, provincial, federal, state and local laws and regulations apply. Contest open only to residents of the U.S. and Canada who are 18 years of age or older, and is void wherever prohibited by law. Internet entry is restricted solely to residents of those geographical areas in which Internet entry is permissible. Employees of Torstar Corp., their affiliates, agents and members of their immediate families are not eligible. Taxes on the prizes are the sole responsibility of winners. Entry and acceptance of any prize offered constitutes permission to use winner's name, photograph or other likeness for the purposes of advertising, trade and promotion on behalf of Torstar Corp. without further compensation to the winner, unless prohibited by law. Torstar Corp and D.L. Blair, Inc., their parents, affiliates and subsidiaries, are not responsible for errors in printing or electronic presentation of contest or entries. In the event of printing or other errors which may result in unintended prize values or duplication of prizes, all affected contest materials or entries shall be null and void. If for any reason the Internet portion of the contest is not capable of running as planned, including infection by computer virus, bugs, tampering, unauthorized intervention, fraud, technical failures, or any other causes beyond the control of Torstar Corp. which corrupt or affect the administration, secrecy, fairness, integrity or proper conduct of the contest, Torstar Corp. reserves the right, at its sole discretion, to disqualify any individual who tampers with the entry process and to cancel, terminate, modify or suspend the contest or the Internet portion thereof. In the event of a dispute regarding an on-line entry, the entry will be deemed submitted by the authorized holder of the e-mail account submitted at the time of entry. Authorized account holder is defined as the natural person who is assigned to an e-mail address by an Internet access provider, on-line service provider or other organization that is responsible for arranging e-mail address for the domain associated with the submitted e-mail address.

5. Prizes: Grand Prize—a $10,000 vacation to anywhere in the world. Travelers (at least one must be 18 years of age or older) or parent or guardian if one traveler is a minor, must sign and return a Release of Liability prior to departure. Travel must be completed by December 31, 2001, and is subject to space and accommodations availability. Two hundred (200) Second Prizes—a two-book limited edition autographed collector set from one of the Silhouette Anniversary authors: Nora Roberts, Diana Palmer, Linda Howard or Annette Broadrick (value $10.00 each set). All prizes are valued in U.S. dollars.

6. For a list of winners (available after 10/31/00), send a self-addressed, stamped envelope to: Harlequin Silhouette 20ᵗʰ Anniversary Winners, P.O. Box 4200, Blair, NE 68009-4200.

Contest sponsored by Torstar Corp., P.O. Box 9042, Buffalo, NY 14269-9042.

PS20RULES

ENTER FOR
A CHANCE TO WIN*

Silhouette's 20th Anniversary Contest

Tell Us Where in the World
You Would Like *Your* Love To Come Alive...
And We'll Send the Lucky Winner There!

Silhouette wants to take you wherever
your happy ending can come true.

Here's how to enter: Tell us, in 100 words or less,
where you want to go to make your love come alive!

In addition to the grand prize, there will be 200
runner-up prizes, collector's-edition book sets
autographed by one of the Silhouette anniversary
authors: **Nora Roberts, Diana Palmer,
Linda Howard** or **Annette Broadrick**.

DON'T MISS YOUR CHANCE TO WIN!
ENTER NOW! No Purchase Necessary

Silhouette®
Where love comes alive™

Name:

Address:

City: State/Province:

Zip/Postal Code:

Mail to ... in Books: **In the U.S.**: P.O. Box 9069, Buffalo, NY
14... **Canada**: P.O. Box 637, Fort Erie, Ontario, L4A 5X3

*No ... ary—for contest details send a self-addressed stamped envelope to:
Sil... versary Contest, P.O. Box 9069, Buffalo, NY, 14269-9069 (include
co... f-addressed envelope). Residents of Washington and Vermont may
omit p... to Cdn. (excluding Quebec) and U.S. residents who are 18 or over.
Void where prohibited. Contest ends August 31, 2000.

50¢

PS20CON_R